PRAISE FOR
JUAN JOSÉ SAER

"Brilliant. . . . With meticulous prose, rendered by Dolph's translation into propulsive English, Saer's *The Sixty-Five Years of Washington* captures the wildness of human experience in all its variety."
—*New York Times*

"While some of Saer's sentences are long enough to rival Proust's, they are infused with a palpitating sensuality, their breathing equally crafted."
—*The Nation*

"To say that Juan José Saer is the best Argentinian writer of today is to undervalue his work. It would be better to say that Saer is one of the best writers of today in any language."
—Ricardo Piglia

"Juan José Saer must be added to the list of the best South American writers."
—*Le Monde*

"The author's preoccupations are reminiscent of his fellow Argentinians Borges and Cortázar, but his vision is fresh and unique."
—*The Independent* (London)

JUAN JOSÉ SAER

SCARS

TRANSLATED FROM THE SPANISH BY STEVE DOLPH

OPEN LETTER
LITERARY TRANSLATIONS FROM THE UNIVERSITY OF ROCHESTER

Copyright © Juan José Saer, 1969
c/o Guillermo Schavelzon & Assoc. Agencia Literaria, info@schavelzon.com
Translation copyright © Steve Dolph, 2011
Originally published in Spanish as *Cicatrices*, 1969

First edition, 2011
All rights reserved

Library of Congress Cataloging-in-Publication Data: Available upon request.
ISBN-13: 978-1-934824-22-1 / ISBN-10: 1-934824-22-4

Printed on acid-free paper in the United States of America.

Text set in Bodoni, a serif typeface first designed by Giambattista
Bodoni (1740–1813) in 1798.

Design by N. J. Furl

Open Letter is the University of Rochester's nonprofit, literary translation press:
Lattimore Hall 411, Box 270082, Rochester, NY 14627

www.openletterbooks.org

for BIBY

Imaginary picture of a stationary fear
—Edwin Muir

FEBRUARY,
MARCH,
APRIL,
MAY,
JUNE

THERE'S THIS FILTHY, EVIL JUNE LIGHT COMING through the window. I'm leaning over the table, sliding the cue, ready to shoot. The red and the white balls are across the table, near the corner. I have the spot ball. I have to hit it softly so it hits the red ball first, then the white, then the back rail between the red ball and the white ball. The red ball should hit the side rail before mine hits the back rail, which it should make for at an angle after it's hit the white ball. Like so: mine will just kiss the red—which will then hit the side rail—and ricochet toward the white as the red comes back toward the white ball, in a straight line, from the side rail. My ball will trace an imaginary triangle. The red will travel the base of this triangle, from one point to the other. If the vector isn't perfect, the red won't have time to travel far enough toward the white. It will need to have crossed enough of the table—coming from the side rail—before mine hits the back rail and comes back again, slowly, at an angle.

That cold, filthy light coming through the window. It's colder than who knows what. And what we need is a sun that's like the people, not this watery light. All it's good for is showing how the cigarette he just threw on the tiles is still lit. A thin, disintegrating, blue smoke column that rises and disappears. And with everything so slow it always looks like the same thin column and always the same disintegrating trail, not a continuous trail of smoke rising and disintegrating into an imaginary block of light. No, not a block. That filthy light couldn't be a block. Who knows what rancid sun it came from. It shouldn't be here, there's no use for it. It should make for some other bar on some other planet, some godforsaken, misbegotten planet somewhere else. It shouldn't be here. We need something different, a hot, dry, blinding light. Because it's cold. It's fucking cold. Cold as the blessed mistress. The polar icecap is probably a sauna compared to this. It's nuts. In Antarctica you could be walking around butt naked, and here you hock up a ball of phlegm and an ice cube hits the sidewalk. Everyone goes around coughing up ice. Just the other day some guy walking down San Martín opened his mouth to say *Hi* to his friend on the opposite sidewalk and couldn't close it again because it filled up with frost. They had to take a soldering iron to his mouth because the cold was pouring in and freezing his blood. If this keeps up, the first chance I get I'm jumping in bed with like ninety blankets and not coming out till January.

Since flicking away that cigarette he hasn't done a thing. He's standing there, stock still, with the cue in his hand. Watching how I slide the cue, aiming, slowly. He doesn't seem to see. Thinking of something else, for sure. Who knows what. Maybe he's thinking about a pair of tits, because he's one of those guys whose brains are all at the back, pressed against their spine by a big pair of tits that takes up at least eighty percent of their skull. Some guys, all they have in there is a pair of tits—a pair of tits and nothing else. Some guys you can even see the nipples coming out through their eyes. Those are the guys with purple pupils. You

4

can tell right away by looking at the color of their pupils—they're purple. Maybe he's not thinking about that. Maybe he's thinking about the week ahead, one night, sitting down under the desk lamp and in one go writing something that changes the world. Tons of guys pass the time thinking one week to the next, *pow*, they'll rock the world with a single uppercut. All they have to do is raise their hand (condescend to raise their hand, as they see it) and like that they've covered the surface of the earth with the holy word. Maybe he's also thinking that the cigarette burned his mouth, that he should roll his tongue and collect some saliva to cool it off, then spit, or that now he'll take his right hand from the cue and put it in his right pants pocket. Or maybe nothing. Maybe even the tits are gone and now there's nothing in there, nothing but surface, not the pale cone of light or the dim field of sound echoing around the pool table, the cone of light that contains just the three balls, the cues, the table, and the two of us—and him just barely—nothing but the dry green-black walls, corroded by the built-up rust of old thoughts and memories, dark all throughout. Watching, motionless, hunched, as I slide the cue, slow, aiming. He looks, but I don't know if he sees. Who could swear he does? Not me. If someone wants to swear he sees, go ahead and swear. I won't. All I know is that after flicking the cigarette he turned his head toward where I'm bent over the table sliding the cue, that an exhausted, absolutely evil June light is coming in through the bar window, and that my task holds back every external thing that's flooding in toward the table. My task is to make my ball run slowly toward the red, hit it, then ricochet toward the white, connect again, then rebound off the back rail, returning at an angle, in the opposite direction, giving the red enough time—after it hits the side rail—to return in a straight line toward the white and reunite in a way that leaves my ball, which passed behind the red, in a good spot for the next carom.

—Six, I say. But it still wasn't the sixth: the ball was rolling close to the rail, after softly hitting the white ball, which belonged to Tomatis, on a straight line back toward the red. When they hit, I was moving toward the other end of the table and Tomatis was still standing there, leaning against his cue, which was pressed into the tile floor, his outline contrasting sharply against the yellow rectangle of light crashing through the bar window. The contrast covers his thick body with shadows, but a kind of luminous haze surrounds the outline. When the spot ball stopped, after hitting the red, I bent over it again and aimed the cue. Even though I was concentrating on my shot, I knew Tomatis wasn't paying any attention, standing there, holding the cue against the floor with both hands, looking at the tiles, or the tips of his shoes, surrounded by the haze, the sheen.

—Experience doesn't come with maturity, I don't think, he says. Or should I say maturity doesn't come with experience?

I aim and take a bank shot. After hitting the red ball and the rail, my ball makes for the white ball.

—Seven, I say.

—They're adding up, Tomatis says, not even looking at the table.

The spot ball hits the white and makes its peculiar sound in the large hall full of clatter, murmurs, shouts. The cone of light that falls on the green table isolates us like the walls of a tent. There are several cones of light across the hall. Each so isolated from the others, and hanging so perfectly apart, that they look like planets with a fixed place in a system, in orbit, each ignorant of the others' existence. Tomatis is standing at the very edge of that tent of light, with that amazing sheen behind him formed by the light coming in from the nearby window.

I get ready to shoot the eighth. I bend over the table, prop the side of my right hand on the felt, then three fingers, place the cue

6

on a kind of bridge I make with my thumb and index, and with my left hand slide the cue from the base. My gaze alternates from the spot on my ball that the tip of the cue has to hit to the spot on the red ball where my ball will hit, to where the white ball—or my opponent's, Tomatis, in this case—sits.

—Well aimed, Tomatis says, not even looking. He's not paying any attention at all to the game—I've made thirty-six caroms, and he's only made two. The two he made were completely by accident, and when he shoots it seems like he wants his turn to end as quickly as possible, so he can return to standing next to the table and running his mouth. The impression you get is that the more caroms his opponent makes the happier he is, since that will allow him more time to stretch out his speech. He's not clumsy, just careless. I would even say he handles the cue really well—you can tell by how he holds it—compared to lots of people who play straight rail. But, bearing in mind that he can handle the cue, that he's always the one suggesting a game, and that everyone he invites—Horacio Barco, for example—plays more than he does, I've decided that Tomatis uses the game of straight rail as an opportunity to be the only one to talk, and about whatever he wants.

Then he adds:

—Unless you're an exceptional specimen, but those don't count as people.

I raise my head before I shoot and say:

—There's a democrat among us.

—I've developed a reputation for wiping my ass with any shit-eating brat who tries to put the screws to me, says Tomatis, laughing.

And so on in that fashion. I started working at the newspaper on February seventh, thanks to him, and they gave me the courthouse section and the weather report. He did general reporting and edited the Sunday literary page. My relationship with Tomatis went back a year. I had just read one of his books, and one day I saw him on the street and followed him until I caught up. He was smoking a cigarette and didn't realize I was next to him until he stopped at a lottery kiosk and started examining the results.

—You're Carlos Tomatis, aren't you? I said.

—So they say, he said.

—I wanted to talk to you because I really enjoyed your book, I said.

—Which one? said Tomatis. Because I have more than three thousand.

—No, I said. One you wrote. The last one.

—Ah, said Tomatis. But it's not the last one. Only the second. I'm planning to write more.

Then he turned to the results, chewing his cigarette.

—Two forty-five, two forty-five, two forty-five, he muttered, looking at the list of numbers. Not once, two forty-five.

He said goodbye and left. But later we saw each other a few times, and even though we were never able to talk about his second book, I went to see if he could find work for me when my father died and I was left alone with my mother. I knew other people I could ask for work, much more connected than him, but I wanted to ask him. I wanted him to give me something. And he did, because somehow on February seventh at ten in the morning I was with Campo, the old man who had been in charge of the section for ages, and who was about to retire, going up and down the dark corridors between the courtrooms, up and down the polished marble stairs, in and out of desolate, high-ceilinged offices overflowing with filing cabinets.

—This, Campo was saying, wrinkling his old monkey nose, is the Second District Civil Court, that's the secretary. There's the law school. Go to the press office on the second floor if you have any questions and ask for the manager, a Mister Agustín Ramírez, he will help you with anything you need.

He labored over several words: "District," "legal holiday," "press," "Ramírez," waiting for me to write them down. I wasn't even listening. While Campo's old monkey face (a tame, sweet monkey, stranger to the civilized world) gestured with every one of its folds, I passed my distracted gaze along the dark corridors where the blurry outlines of litigators and staff came and went, the tall filing cabinets that easily called up the word Kafka, the marble staircases that ascended to the first floor with a wide, anachronistic curve, and the February sun penetrating the lobby through the large entrance.

With the weather report my role was pretty much God's. Every day around three I had to go to the terrace of the newspaper building and take notes from the meteorological equipment, which I never understood. And when I went to ask Tomatis, who had also started out doing the weather, he told me he hadn't ever understood them either and as far as he could tell the most rational choices were either duplication or fabrication. I used both methods. For twenty days, in the month of February, I sent the same information about the weather to the print shop, copied letter-for-letter from what had appeared the day before I started at the newspaper. For twenty days, according to the observational devices of the newspaper *La Región*, the meteorological conditions in the city were the following: at eight in the morning, atmospheric pressure 756.80, temperature 24.2 degrees Celsius, relative humidity 64 percent. With Tomatis's help I came up with a genius headline for the section: *No Change in Sight*. On the twenty-seventh of February, a piece of shit rain destroyed the project. Unfortunately I had already handed in the report, because I left early, so when I got to the publisher's office it had already

9

rained fifteen centimeters since noon the day before, and it was only eleven in the morning. The publisher had a stack of the February editions on his desk, and the weather report section on each copy was marked with a furious red circle.

—We're not going to fire you, said the publisher. We're going to suspend you for five days. Not out of charity. We don't want problems with the union. But the day I happen to feel like it's cooler than usual and a breeze is in the air, even if it's only because I woke up in a good mood and the sun is slightly farther from the earth, and that sensation isn't registered in detail in the weather report, you won't be walking out of here on your own legs.

So I switched to fabrication. At first I was guided by the opinions of the copywriters, and I guessed numbers based on their predictions. For the first week I took it to the publisher for him to look over, then I stopped after I had regained his trust, or maybe after I realized that he just glanced at them quickly and checked them off with the red pencil, completely satisfied. Eventually the copywriters' opinions on the weather weren't enough. It seemed like fabrication from scratch was better, and in accordance with the numbers printed in the columns of the paper, the city was oppressed, melted, felt more youthful with spring warmth, and suffered waves of blood in their eye sockets and furious, deafening popping in their eardrums from the atmospheric effects I had created. It was a real fever. I stopped and went back to fabricating prudently after realizing that Tomatis, who knew every detail of my work, was starting to offer increasingly exaggerated alternatives. It was March sixth, the night of the dinner party they threw for Campo because he had just retired. (After the dinner, old Campo went home and poisoned himself.) During the publisher's toast, Tomatis started suggesting I invent rainstorms that hadn't happened, for example storms that had supposedly happened at dawn, and which few people would be in the position to confirm or deny. I realized he wanted to get me fired. At the same time I understood that he hadn't gotten me the job at the paper out of sympathy or for any other humanitarian reason, but to have someone to talk to in the office, and to borrow money from once in a while. I told him that. And he started to laugh and recited:

> *I thought him half a lunatic, half knave,*
> *and told him so, but friendship never ends*

And he was right. But I held out and muttered:

—The weather report is mine. I decide if it rains or not.

—Still, said Tomatis, I am the author of the idea and I suppose I have a say in the matter.

He was smoking a cigarette, chewing it, and squinting his eyes while blowing smoke in my face.

—I'm getting to know you, I said. First I'm supposed to report a storm that never happened, and eventually I'll end up writing about a rain of fire.

—And why not? said Tomatis, chewing his words behind his cigarette. It wouldn't be bad. They'll feel burnt whether it happens or not. And in any case, Sodom was Disneyland compared to this shithole city.

Then he stood up, in the middle of the publisher's toast, and left the restaurant. He was always doing that—absentminded, I supposed. But people said Tomatis didn't do those kinds of things out of distraction, but because he was an asshole pure and simple. So the next day, at Campo's wake, I asked him.

—Tomatis, I said. Didn't you realize that the publisher was talking when you got up and left the restaurant?

—Yes, he said.

11

—Then why did you leave? I asked.

—He pays me a salary to write for the paper, not to hear him give toasts, he said.

So he wasn't doing it out of distraction. We left Campo's wake and went to a café.

—Are you writing? I asked.

—No, he says.

—Translating? I asked.

—No, he says.

He was looking at something behind me, above my head. I turned. There was only a blank wall, painted gray.

—What are you thinking about? I asked.

—Campo, he said. Didn't the old man seem to be laughing at us? I don't mean that figuratively. I'm not referring to the corpse. I mean last night, at the dinner. He shouldn't have gone to the party. He should have killed himself before. He made us all look ridiculous. He was always a piece of shit.

I told him he always seemed like more or less a good person to me.

But he wasn't listening anymore. He was looking over my head at the gray wall.

—I think he killed himself to spite us all, he said eventually.

During the five days of the suspension, I didn't leave the house once. Only on the fifth of March did I shave and walk out. I spent the five days lying in bed, reading, sitting in a wicker chair on the porch, in the afternoons, or in the mornings walking a hundred laps around the bitterwood in the courtyard. At night I would sit in the middle of the courtyard looking at the stars, in the dark, with a coil lit to keep off the mosquitos. At two or three in the morning sometimes, my mother came home. I would see her open the front door, her outline appearing for a moment against the doorway, and then disappear into the darkness and move quietly toward her bedroom. I would hear the slow, cautious creak of the door opening and closing and then nothing else. She thought I was sleeping. I wouldn't breathe normally again until I was sure that she was completely asleep. Then I would light a cigarette, fill a glass with ice and gin in the kitchen, take it to the courtyard, get naked, and sit down to smoke and drink the gin in slow sips. I would stay that way until I saw the first glow of the morning light. Sometimes I masturbated. The night of March fourth, when my mother hadn't gone out, I was out there with my gin in one hand and the cigarette in the other and suddenly the porch light came on, and I saw my mother looking at me from the door to the bedroom. She looked surprised. I had drank more than half a bottle. I jumped up.

—*Salud!* I said, lifting the glass in her direction and bringing it back for a drink.

She stood there blinking for a few seconds, stock still, look-ing me up and down. Then, without turning out the light, she went back in her bedroom and slammed the door. Only after she was gone did I realize that I was completely naked, and I had a hard-on.

At that point things started getting bad between us. It was nothing at first, but when we were together we soured. My mother was about thirty-six at that time, and kept herself up very nicely. She was tall and trim and dressed fashionably. Maybe she didn't have great taste, because she preferred tight clothes. A general idea of her look at that time: once I was with a guy I went to high school with and my mother passed us on the opposite sidewalk, called my name, and blew me a kiss, and when I turned back the guy said he knew that woman, that he had seen her do a strip tease in a cabaret in Córdoba the year before. I told him it was my mother and that he must have been confused because my mother hadn't been to Córdoba in at least seven years, I was

13

sure of it. Before I could finish the sentence, the guy had disappeared. I think my mother would have been much more attractive if she had left her hair dark instead of dyeing it the month after my father died. Blonde didn't suit her. My father, while he was bedridden with cancer, could talk to her about how much she went out, and I saw him outright angry when she told him she wanted to dye her hair. My father said he wouldn't allow it while he was alive. My mother replied that, in any case, the time when she could decide for herself wasn't far off.

So I was out of the house a lot, especially if there had been a fight for some reason. I was out mostly during the day, because at night was when she wasn't home. After leaving the paper I would walk around downtown or would go watch the river, and if I didn't have money to eat something, I would go back to the house around ten thirty—when my mother was sure not to be there—and make whatever I found in the fridge. Then I would take a shower and sit down to read. During the five-day suspension, when I didn't leave the house, I read *The Magic Mountain*, which I liked a lot; *Light in August*, excellent; this little green book called *Lolita*, a real piece of shit; *The Long Goodbye*, a seriously genius book; and two idiotic Ian Fleming novels. I read very quickly, and I think I remember pretty well. After my mother found me in the courtyard naked with a hard-on, it wasn't as easy to move freely around the house, and so at night, when she wasn't home, was better. Sometimes I would have a beer with Tomatis, until ten, and if I came close to the house and saw a light on, I would wait at a neighborhood bar until I was sure to find the house empty.

March and April were hell. My mother had turned into a panther. At first I decided not to let on, to face it only if it looked like things might get worse, but that wasn't always possible. And in the end she forced me into a corner. If, for example, I hung my shirt over her bathrobe—a bathrobe anyone with the slightest

14

hygienic tendency wouldn't touch with a cane—she would show up in my room, standing in the doorway with her legs wide, muttering furiously:

—I told you a thousand times not to put your filthy shirts on my things.

I would get up, walk to the bathroom, take my shirt from the hanger, and throw it in the hamper. She followed me the whole way. When I finished throwing the shirt in the hamper and was walking back to the room, she was blocking my way at the bathroom door, saying:

—Don't bunch up your clothes; I'm not your maid and don't need to be taking care of it. You're old enough to know how to treat your clothes.

I wouldn't say a thing and walked back to my room. She glared at me the whole way until I sat down, picked up the book, and started reading again. She went back to her room and less than half an hour later she was back.

—Are you going to sit in there all day? she would say. All that garbage you have in your head.

—Garbage? Head? I would ask, confused, looking up at her from the book, not understanding a thing.

She would look back furiously, the cigarette hanging from her lips.

—Do whatever you want, just don't play stupid with me, she would say.

Then she would disappear again. One afternoon she hit me for saying, as gently as possible, that I didn't like her answering for the milkman in her bra. She walked straight up and slapped me. I grabbed her arm so hard, to stop her from hitting me twice, that I cut her with a fingernail and she bled—it left a black mark for like a month. When I saw the blood stain on her round, white arm, I let go and let her hit me until she got tired. She went at it until

15

she had enough and then shut herself in her room crying and didn't come out until that night. All day I felt fine, and around ten she brought me a plate of bread and cheese and a glass of wine and then disappeared. She was dressed to go out, in a yellow dress that fit her like crazy. She didn't even look twice when she saw that I was using my white shirt as a towel to dry my sweat off.

Fall came at the end of March, though on the twenty-first I made a small comment in the weather report about the change in temperature, the odor of fluttering mothballs, the golden leaves falling from the trees and forming a crinkling carpet on the ground. When he read it, Tomatis cracked up laughing and asked if I had been reading the *modernistas* again. In the fall the nights under the stars and the glass of gin in the courtyard stopped, and instead I sat in my room, in an armchair, under a lamp, until the morning. My mother came in at dawn, clicking her high heel shoes on the tiles in the corridor. And it didn't matter if I heard her come in—she actually seemed to have some interest in me hearing her. Sometimes she even looked in my room and said, with some hostility: *Oh, you're still reading,* or, *It's obvious he's not the one who pays the electric bill,* and then disappeared. I knew when my mother was about to get home; first I would hear the sound of a car stop and then start up and drive off. Then the sound of the door to the street and then the high heels clicking. Only once did she come in my room after having been in the bathroom then gone to her room and even turned off the light. I was sure she was in bed, and I was completely absorbed in reading *The Long Goodbye,* which I was reading for the third time in a little over a month, when suddenly the door opened and my mother appeared, in a nightgown, barefoot. The expression on her face was a mix of resignation and distress. She looked at me a second, and just to say something she muttered, *Don't read so much, you'll get sick in the head.* Then she closed the door and left. I had jumped up, startled. Luckily, I was fully dressed.

On April twenty-third it broke out. It rained all day and neither of us went out that night. My mother, who was typically acting like a panther, that night seemed like that special kind of panther who has tasted human flesh and likes it. I always let her do whatever she wanted, but what I could never stand was her walking half-naked around the house, especially when strangers were around. A certain scruple had always existed between us, meanwhile, regarding the gin and cigarettes. The unspoken agreement, especially since my old man died, was that we each had our own bottle of gin and each our own pack of cigarettes, and whoever ran out simply went and bought some. And so around eleven, when it's raining like crazy, I go to the fridge looking for my gin, bought the day before and which I hadn't drank more than two fingers from, and realize she took it. I walk slowly down the hall (it was raining buckets), not annoyed at all, just the opposite, and I stop at her bedroom door and knock.

—Who is it? my mother asks, as if fifty people were living with us.

—Me, Ángel, I say.

She hesitates a second, then says to come in. She is laying in bed, reading a comic book, a cigarette hanging from her lips, a glass, the bottle of gin, and an ice bucket on the night table. I've seen a bunch of trash heaps, and every one has seemed cleaner than my mother's bedroom. If she had been naked, the impression would have been more seemly than the one you got from the underwear she had on. Less than three fingers were left in the bottle.

—Mamá, I say. Would it put you out if I poured myself a little glass of gin? That's the last bottle.

17

—I thought we agreed that if you need gin you go out and buy a bottle, my mother says.

—That's true, I say. But don't you think that with this weather and how late it is that it would be kind of problematic to go out and find a store where you can buy a bottle of gin?

—You should have thought of that earlier, my mother says. It's not my problem.

—That's fine, I say. I'm only asking you for a little glass of gin and to try to look away when you talk to me because I could faint any second.

—I hope you're not trying to say I'm drunk, my mother says.

—I'm not trying to say anything.

—Besides, my mother says, I never liked you drinking.

—Well I never liked my mother letting me see her practically naked, I say.

—I'm not the one walking around naked all night in the middle of the courtyard, my mother says.

—In the dark and when I'm alone, I can walk around however I like. It would be something else entirely if I knew people were watching, I say.

My mother pretends not to hear me and goes back to reading her comic book. Eventually she looks up and realizes I'm still there.

—Still raining? she asks.

—Yes, I say.

My mother looks at me a second, blinking. She puts out the cigarette, stretching her arm out to the night table, sitting up slightly, without taking her eyes off me.

—Besides, I say, staring back. It's my bottle. You drank my bottle.

I see her smooth, white face go suddenly red, but she doesn't move for a few more seconds. Then she leaves the comic book on

18

the bed and gets up, very slowly, without looking away. She walks toward me, not furious or hurrying, staring me in the eyes, and stops half a meter away. The flush that had stained her face gradually vanishes. My mother raises her hand and slaps me twice, once on each cheek, then stands there, staring, and probably the two red stains are now on my cheeks instead of hers, as though we traded them. After a few unblinking seconds I raise my hand and slap her twice, once on each cheek. The red stains, now disappearing on my cheeks, appear on hers. Tears gush out. She's not crying—they started gushing for some inexplicable physiological reason, because no one who is crying could have such a hard look on their face. A pale circle forms around her pressed lips.

—I should have died instead of your father so I wouldn't have to see this, my mother says.

—Not just this, I say. Any way you look at it, it would have been more convenient.

She slapped me again, and I went into a rage and started hitting and pushing her, threw her on the bed, took off my belt, and didn't stop hitting her until she started screaming. She didn't even try to defend herself. When I saw all she was doing was crying, I calmly put my belt back on and poured myself a glass of gin, careful to leave some for her, then dropped two ice cubes in the glass and went back to my room.

I couldn't concentrate on reading anymore because I had said one unfair thing to her, about the supposed convenience of her dying instead of my father. That was unfair any way you looked at it because my father was so insignificant a man that if the smallest ant in the world died instead of him it would have made more of an impact. He was a middle manager in a public office because ✓ he was too stupid to have a regular worker's responsibility and too weak a personality to be able to give anyone real orders. He didn't smoke or drink, never felt disillusioned or ever experienced any sort of happiness he might take pleasure in remembering. He had dodged military service through some defect in his sight (he told the story fifty times a day, in such detail and with such enthusiasm that you would have thought he was the general San Martín recalling the battle of San Lorenzo), but it wasn't such a bad defect that he was prescribed glasses. He was thin but not too thin; quiet but not too quiet; he had good handwriting but sometimes his hands shook. He didn't have a favorite dish, and if someone asked his opinion on anything at all, he invariably responded, *Some people understand those things—not me.* But there wasn't an ounce of humility in his response, rather an absolute conviction that it was the truth. And so when my father died, the only change in the house was that there was now air in the space he had occupied in the bed (for the last six months he hadn't gotten up). I think that was the most noteworthy change he ever produced: to make space. To open up 1.76 meters (because he was also average height) of vertical space and a certain width so that what he displaced with his body could be reconverted into a breathable substance for the benefit of humanity.

When I went to the paper the next day and found out that Tomatis had gone to Buenos Aires and wouldn't be back until the twenty-ninth, I felt bad. I had planned to tell him everything. I don't really know why, since Tomatis rarely seemed to be listening, but still he was the person I trusted the most, and he might understand me having hit my mother. She, meanwhile, stopped speaking to me, and when she had to she used the formal *usted.* We barely ever saw each other, and now that it was cooler out (it rained almost every day in April, which made it so I could copy the same weather information several times without anyone noticing) my mother didn't walk around half-naked anymore, like she often did in the summer. Truth is she would put on these loud sweaters that would have been too tight on a fakir, but that

20

was the way she liked to dress and I had to let her even though I didn't like it. She kept going out at night, and when she came back would go to bed without coming to my room. I would get up late and go to the paper at ten in the morning and wouldn't come back until ten at night, and sometimes not even then. I remember the fight over the gin happened on April twenty-third because ✓ the next day I turned eighteen. I asked for an advance from the management and went to eat a steak. I barely touched the food, but I drank a liter of wine. I wasn't angry or anything, just wanted to drink some wine, for the fun of drinking it and for the comfort of knowing that I could always have my cup full, to empty in one swallow, and if the bottle kicked I could call the waiter and ask for another from the long rows stacked up on the walls—all that made me feel amazingly good. Then I hesitated between the movies and a hooker and chose the hooker. I didn't have to wait or anything. They showed me through an entrance where there wasn't anything but a wooden bench and a standing coat rack, then down a corridor, and finally they put me in a kitchen with two women in it. Both were blonde. They were drinking *mate* and didn't even get up. One had a comic book in her hands. I picked the other one. They were so alike (both had on black pants and a white sweater) that now I'm not sure if in fact I went to bed with the one with the comic book or the other one because they might have passed the comic book from one to the other without me noticing, or the one with the comic could have left it on the table as I came in and the other one grabbed it before I noticed. In any case, my selection wasn't so precise, since I only made a gesture with my head in the direction of the one I thought didn't have the comic book, and I'm not even sure anymore which one of them got up first. The one who led me away—the one with the comic, or the other one, I'm not sure anymore—took me through a courtyard into a room filled with what I remember as the odor of

21

Creolin, and which was so clean and organized that immediately I thought of my mother's, by contrast. When she got naked I saw she had the mark of an operation on her belly, a half-moon scar, crisscrossed by the lines from the stitches. I went to bed with her and then went home to sleep.

Tomatis came back the morning of the thirtieth, euphoric, smoking North American cigarettes. He walked into the office with energetic steps and sat down in front of the typewriter. He looked freshly washed and shaved. I told him I had problems with my mother and wanted to talk to him.

—Come have dinner at my house tonight. Bring wine, he said, and started working.

Then I left for the courthouse. A light rain was falling, so that day I sent the same weather report to the print shop as the day before. The gray courthouse seemed more gray in the rain, but a shining gray. The wide, marble stairs in the lobby were dirty with wet mud. They had scattered sawdust on the floor of the entryway, which was full of people. I passed through the law school and then saw Chino Ramírez, from the press office. Ramírez poured me a coffee that looked like it was brewed from the mud in the lobby. Instead of teeth Ramírez had two tiny, brown sierras. I don't know what disease could have rotted them so badly. He stopped himself laughing to hide them.

—Your judge friend wants to see you, he said. He asked for you.

—I haven't killed anyone, I said.

—You never know, said Ramírez.

—I guess that's true, I said. I gestured toward the coffee and, standing up, said:

—Keep an eye on your staff, Ramírez. They're confused and are serving us the prisoners' coffee.

He would have laughed more, had his teeth allowed. He gave me the papers he had prepared, and I left the office. Ernesto was

22

working on his fucking Wilde translation. He took it everywhere. When he saw me come in, he closed the dictionary and marked a page in *The Picture of Dorian Gray* with his red pen.

—Lose my number? he asked.

Something in his face made him look like Stan Laurel, only slightly fatter.

—I haven't been able to call you because I've had a mess of problems with my family, I said. Then I pointed to the Wilde book.

—How's the translation coming?

—Good, he said, smiling. No one else would think to translate something that's been translated a million times already.

A report lay on his desk. I managed to read the word *homicide.*

—Have you sent many people to prison? I asked.

He squinted his eyes before responding and collapsed in his chair.

—Lots, he said.

—Have you ever been to prison? I asked.

—Visiting, a few times, he said.

He guessed what I was thinking.

—It's the same, he said, inside and outside. Everything is completely the same. Alive, dead, everything is exactly the same.

—I disagree, I said.

—Well it's a free country, he said, laughing.

—Ramírez said you were looking for me, I said.

—I wanted to see how you were and if you're free tomorrow night, he said.

—Tomorrow night? I asked. What's tomorrow?

—I can forgive the youth anything, he said, except coyness. Tomorrow is the first of May.

I must have blushed.

—Yes, I said. I'm free.

23

—Do you want to have dinner at my house? he asked, standing up.

I said yes, and so the next night I went to his house. It started raining about nine, after a bracing, cold day. I was walking from Tomatis's house, at the other end of the city, in the north, so I ended up walking through the whole city center to the southern end. The center was deserted, and it was exactly nine when I passed the Banco Provincial building, I could tell by the round clock mounted in the wall over the entrance. In the arcade I drank a cognac and then kept going. Now it was raining. Out on San Martín I walked, whistling, down a few dark blocks where the weak streetlights shone at the intersections. I passed the courthouse, crossed the Plaza de Mayo at a diagonal in front of the government buildings, then back onto San Martín, which at that point became a curved, dead-end street with a single sidewalk and the tree-lined edge of the Parque Sur bordering the opposite side in the darkness. After ringing the bell I turned and briefly saw the lake water glow between the trees. The door opened and I turned around suddenly.

—I was waiting, Ernesto said.

I shook my head.

—It's raining, I said.

We went upstairs and straight into his study. Ernesto opened the shades covering a large window and then poured two whiskies. On the desk were the Oscar Wilde book, the dictionary, and the composition notebook with the fucking translation manuscript. I leaned over the desk and examined the handwriting: it was so small and tight that it was impossible to tell the vowels apart. Ernesto handed me the glass.

—It's indecipherable, he said.

—So it seems, I muttered, looking again. Where are you?

Ernesto recited:

—Yes, Harry, I know what you are going to say. Something dreadful about marriage. Don't say it. Don't ever say things of that kind to me again. Two days ago I asked Sibyl to marry me. I'm not going to break my word to her. She is to be my wife. I've just gotten to *wife.*

I drank my whole glass at once, feeling Ernesto's eyes on my face. Then I went to the window. The lake shone over the trees in the park, their leaves glowing green in the darkness. It was crazy looking.

—I like your house, I said. It's comfortable.

—It is, yes, he said. It's comfortable.

He was staring at me.

—You should come more often, he said.

—I do what I can, I said, and crossed the room to pour myself more whiskey.

I felt just like one of those toys they sell on the street, which the barker controls with an invisible string, a dark string that he hides and no one else sees: *Sit down, Pedrito,* and Pedrito plops his cardboard ass on the pavement. His gaze was the string, and I felt cornered in his field of vision, in those square meters illuminated by the warm lamps of the study, and walking toward the bar or the window, it felt like the tension of his gaze would reach its limit any second and I would suddenly find myself stopped with my back to him, up against the end of it. But Ernesto spoke softly, and tried honestly not to hide what he was thinking. Or maybe that's just me, and it wasn't honest. We set up all these rules in advance to tell the good from the bad. Even if Ernesto knew he was capable of doing something I called bad didn't mean that he was honest, and he may have been hiding something even worse behind the thing they call bad. But I think this now and didn't then, the night of May first, because the night of May first I thought that Ernesto was honest because he was capable of recognizing the bad thing in him.

25

Then we went to the dining room, and just as we were sitting down (it was eleven), the telephone rang. Ernesto's servant told him the guard at the courthouse was on the phone. Ernesto put his whiskey down on the table (we were still standing, talking) and disappeared into the study, closing the door. I couldn't hear a thing. For several minutes it was perfectly silent in the house, so when Ernesto opened the door to his study, on his way back to the dining room, the sound rang out not only at the moment it was produced, but kept echoing the entire time it took Ernesto to cross the long, dark corridor that separates the study from the dining room. It dissipated when Ernesto's figure reappeared in the entrance to the dining room. He had a stony expression and looked pale. We sat down at the table and ate the first course in silence. Despite being more or less pudgy, Ernesto ate little, in almost insubstantial mouthfuls. I, on the other hand, devoured what the woman served me. During the second course—a chicken that was insanely good—Ernesto finally opened his mouth for something other than the tiny mouthfuls that would have starved a sparrow.

He had barely looked at me during the meal, and now he raised his eyes and whispered:

—A man shot his wife to death with a shotgun earlier today, in Barrio Roma, he said. They want me to take his statement tonight, because they don't have space for him at the station. I told them to wait until tomorrow afternoon.

—Why did he kill her?

—I don't know anything, said Ernesto. I know he shot her to death with a shotgun, outside a bar.

—Are you going to take his statement tomorrow? I asked.

—In the afternoon, probably. I have other appointments in the morning, said Ernesto.

—Can I come? I asked.

26

—We'll see, said Ernesto.

Then we went back to the study and Ernesto put on the record player. He poured whiskeys, and we sat down to listen to his favorite record, Shönberg's *Violin Concerto (Opus 36)*. We didn't say a word while the concerto was playing. I thought about a lot of things. I thought about a girl I was in love with for a full year two years ago. Her name was Perla Pampiglioni. The first time I saw her she was standing at the bus stop near the suspension bridge, on the train station side, to be exact. I went crazy the moment I saw her: we were two meters apart, both standing at the curb, looking sidelong at each other. She had on a yellow dress that showed her arms and neck and her suntanned legs. Her hair was like polished sheets of copper. We took the same bus, and by chance there was only one double seat open, so I sat next to her, giving her the window. She was pretending to look out the window, but every once in a while she glanced at me. I did the same. In the bus's rear view mirror I could see her knees. We went more than twenty blocks together, and at one point her arm brushed up against mine. Then, in the city center, she got up and left. I thought about getting off at the same corner and talking to her on the street, but I got the feeling that she was watching me the whole trip, so I decided to get off a block later. When I got back to the corner where she got off, she was gone. For three days I wandered around the train station, hoping to see her again, but didn't find a single trace. I saw her a week later. I was at the bar in the arcade, drinking a cup of coffee with a college friend who had been in medical school in Córdoba for six months, and I see her coming up the corridor toward the bar, again in that yellow dress, the copper sheets of hair bouncing on her shoulders. I liked her perky little tits and realized that she had seen me because she started looking bored. She went up to a toy store window. And then Arnoldo Pampiglioni gets up, walks over to her, gives her a kiss, and they start talking. They were five meters away and the fucking son of a bitch couldn't invite her to the table for coffee and instead left me waiting fifteen minutes. Then she turned—not before throwing a sidelong glance at me—and went back down the corridor toward the street, shaking the roundest, tightest—the word is *perfect*—ass I've seen in my life. Arnoldo sits down again and says, *Perlita only gets a pass because we're cousins.* I exhaled and asked who she was. *She's Perlita Pampiglioni,* Arnoldo said. *She got her masters this year.* He told me where she lived and everything. Then he went back to Córdoba. The next day I launched the operation. Based on the address that Arnoldo gave me, I looked for her number in the phone book and found what I was looking for. Her father was José Pampiglioni, and he lived in Guadalupe. There was also a José Pampiglioni downtown, under the heading *Home Furnishings.* So I posted myself a whole afternoon in front of the shop on San Martín until I saw all the workers leave, and finally, half an hour after the shop closed, a fifty-year-old man locked the door, leaving the shop lights on.

The next day, around eleven, I went in and asked the price of a vacuum cleaner, if I could buy it on credit, and if the credit could be in my name, because I was under age and wanted to surprise my mother. The salesman asked if I worked and I said yes, and on top of that I regularly got a two-hundred-dollar-a-month allowance from my mother's brother, a Mister Philip Marlowe, from Los Angeles, California. The salesman told me it might be possible, but in any case I would need an older person, someone with property, to guarantee the loan. Just then I felt something strange behind me; I turned, and she came in: she had on these super tight white pants and a white shirt. She trailed a soft perfume as she passed toward the back of the shop and entered the offices, disappearing inside. Unfortunately we were at the end of the conversation, and it was obvious that the salesman was trying

28

to put me off until I came back with more security. I asked if he could get me a credit application, and if it wasn't convenient I could make my case to the owner, but the salesman took me to the register at the back, gave me an application, and told me it wasn't worth talking to the owner because the situation was perfectly normal as long as I could find someone older, with property, to guarantee the loan. I asked him to show me the vacuum cleaner again, that I wanted to try it out some more. The salesman told me that there was nothing else to see, that he had shown me all the functions and features of the machine, and if I came back with the application in order and had the down payment, I could take the vacuum cleaner home and work it as much as I wanted.

So I left and set up on the corner to wait. I was there more than a half an hour in the sun. Around twelve fifteen, after the rest of the workers had gone, I saw her leave with her father. They turned toward the opposite corner, but as her father was turning back to lock the front door, I realized she was looking in my direction, very discreetly, and was making like she knew I was there. I started following them, for something like thirty meters. Her father had his arm around her shoulder. They reached the first corner on San Martín and turned right toward 25 de Mayo, passing in front of the Banco Provincial, whose round clock read twelve sixteen, and then continued toward the Parque Palomar. The old man had parked his car next to the park. It was sky blue, long, and wide, and must have had at least two or three different climates and indoor plumbing. They talked a second before getting in (I had stopped at the corner, pretending to wait for a bus), and finally I saw the old man give her the keys and she sat down behind the wheel, but not before throwing a sidelong gaze toward where I was standing. Then they left.

I went half crazy realizing that I was up against more than her body, that her body was something frail compared to the element that had just appeared: her car. And so began the long period in which I waited for her to appear in her car. I waited for it so fiercely, with such conviction, that it appeared twice. Once was on the waterfront, a rainy afternoon—I was leaning on the railing, watching how the rain fell on the river, sheltered only by a tree, thinking, *Right now she's going to show up in her car and take me away, right now*, and I turned around suddenly and saw the massive blue car coming slowly up from Guadalupe along the wide, deserted waterfront. It took forever to get there, growing slowly out of the gray horizon, and as it approached I could make out the regular movement of the windshield wipers clearing the drops that were falling on the windshield and blurring the face behind the glass. It passed by and it wasn't her. And the second time, an afternoon in January, I was crossing another completely deserted street, and just as I'm thinking, *Her car is going to turn the corner and come this way*, I hear the squeal of brakes and see the blue car speed around the corner, growling on the boiling asphalt. Again it passed by and again it wasn't her. But I realized that I was developing the ability to manifest the blue car and bring it where I was, no matter where it had been before.

I saw her five more times, always on foot. Even with all the long stakeouts I did around her house, I only managed to see her there once. She came out, crossed the street running, and went into a house on the opposite side. She was wearing the white pants and white shirt. I waited three hours for her to come out, but she never did. Over the three hours it got dark. I saw so many whitish blurs passing quickly in the darkness, between the black trees, that the millionth time I thought I saw her I decided that I was playing the fool and went home to sleep. The second time was at the movies: I walked into the darkness and sat down, and when the lights came up I realized that she was sitting next to me. She had on a leather jacket and her skin was whiter, because it was the middle of winter. I thought I saw her blush when she realized who the guy sitting next to her was. Then the lights went out again, and we spent the whole movie rubbing elbows on the armrest; if on the way out someone had asked me how the movie was or even what it was called, I would have been dumb as a stone. Ten minutes before the end of the movie she got up and left. The third time was at the bar in the arcade. We walked up to the register at the same time, her from the courtyard, me from the street, and I let her order first, even though I had reached the register a few seconds earlier. She ordered an Orange Crush and a hot dog. She took them to her table, and I drank my coffee at the bar, looking at her every once in a while, but she had her back to me and didn't see me. When I turned to look at her for the last time, she was gone. The fourth time I saw her I was on the bus and she was standing on the corner. I watched her from the rear window until she disappeared. A month later I was the one standing on the corner while she passed on the bus. Then I didn't see her for several months, and finally I forgot about her.

When the violin concerto finished I stopped thinking about Perla Pampiglioni and walked over to the window. Ernesto switched off the record player.

—It's so quiet, he said.

We were standing in an illuminated block. Outside there was rain, the black trees, and the lake in the park. I had a momentary feeling that the block of light was covered with a dry clarity, floating in empty space, in a slow drift, not spilling a single ray of icy light into the blackness. Ernesto sat down.

—What have you been doing all this time? he said.

I turned back from the window and sat down in front of him.

—Nothing, I said.

—Read anything? asked Ernesto.

—Yes, I said.

31

—Sleep with anyone? asked Ernesto.

—Yes, I said.

—Meanwhile all I've done is try to translate this goddamned book, said Ernesto.

—And sent several men to prison, too, I suppose, I said.

—No one recently, said Ernesto.

Then we were silent again for about ten minutes. During that time Ernesto didn't take his eyes off me once. He was sunk so low in his chair that it looked like he would never be able to get up again. That he would break in half and die sitting right there. I observed him with a sort of disbelief. His eyes were half shut, and he held his whiskey in one hand. Suddenly he shifted slightly and the ice clinked against the sides of the glass. That clinking terrified me—I didn't know why, but I started to panic and wanted to talk, to say something so that the clinking would be lost in the sound of my words. Ernesto listened, but he seemed absent.

—I've had a bad summer, I said. Really bad. I've spent whole nights in the courtyard, looking at the stars, and I've seen strange things in the sky. I've seen signs in the sky that scared me. I haven't told anyone yet. This is the first time. I've seen the stars moving, and one night I saw the moon fill up with tigers and panthers tearing each other to pieces and staining the sky all around the moon with blood. Then I saw a carriage diving to hell, full of people I knew who still hadn't died.

I hadn't seen any of that, but had hoped to. The only thing I had seen was a million glowing-blue naked women floating in the blackness.

—There are worse things to see, and not just in the sky, said Ernesto, sitting up slightly and taking a drink of the whiskey.

I spent another hour at his house and then went home to sleep. It was still raining. I crossed a dead, black city, and when I passed the Plaza de Mayo I saw the courthouse again, transformed into a

32

dark mass with glowing shades of gray. My shoes filled up with a pink mud, and I had to dry my face and hair and feet when I laid down between the icy sheets. I shivered for a half an hour, not able to sleep, and I masturbated to warm myself up. I only succeeded in staining the sheets, because I was still cold after. Not only were there no panthers or tigers in the moon, but no naked women radiating a blue iridescence into the blackness either. There was only the frozen darkness, and the only thing I could locate in its center—if in fact there was a center—was the illuminated block, drifting, with Ernesto sitting in a chair, and the muted clinking of the ice against the sides of the glass. I turned on the light, looked around the room, then turned it off so it would be dark again.

But I didn't know that would happen when I left the court-house the day before, around noon. I would have to go through an afternoon, a night, and a whole other day and part of a night before drying my hair in my room and then getting in bed be-tween the cold sheets with the image of the illuminated block drifting in the black, empty space of my head. The whole plaza was saturated with the gray sheen of the rain, and several men, blurry, hunched over, crossed it slowly. I went to the paper and found Tomatis drinking coffee with the head printer, a tall guy with glasses who I couldn't stand. Tomatis gets along with every-one because he doesn't care at all about anyone. With cigar smok-ers he smokes cigars; if they take their coffee with cream, so does he; if they don't like salt, he doesn't either. But he isn't easygoing or anything, however much he seems to be. You actually get the impression that there's nothing in the world that could interest him in the least. I don't think anything at all interests him. And because of this, he can do whatever he wants. It's crazy.

When he leaves the printer's office, Tomatis comes up to me and says:

—I challenge you to a game of straight rail after lunch.

—Done, I say.

At the billiard hall, Tomatis takes the white and gives me the spot ball, botches the break, and leaves me to make all the caroms so he can run his mouth all he wants. He stands next to a little table, turning his coffee cup endlessly. The enormous hall is full of cones of light that make the green felt glow and wash the balls with reflections as they move and collide, making that peculiar sound. I count the tents of light—six—then lean over and aim the first carom.

—Hey! Tomatis shouts. I turn around, startled. He had called to the lottery vendor, a gray-haired man who was missing a leg, and whose crutch clicks on the tiles as he moves around.

—Do you have the results? says Tomatis.

—The first ten games only, says the lottery vendor.

—Did two forty-five come up? says Tomatis.

The man takes a list of numbers from his pocket and gives it to Tomatis, who studies it a second.

—Nothing, he says, returning the table.

The man leaves. I take the first shot and set up for the second. Tomatis looks through the window at the street.

—It's going to rain all year, he says.

I finish the game with five strings: one of twelve, one of fourteen, one of nine, one of seven, and one of eight caroms. I make the one of fourteen because Tomatis had left the balls together in a corner—deliberately I think—and I don't let them separate until the fourteenth carom. When I'm shooting the fifteenth the cue slips for lack of chalk, and I miss. Tomatis's cue slips immediately, and I make nine more. I don't think Tomatis saw a single one of the caroms I made, and at least one wouldn't have counted, easily called out in any international competition. Tomatis's gaze passed from the window and slid slowly across the large hall full of sounds and echoes.

—In Buenos Aires, he says, I never left the hotel. I ordered a box of North American cigarettes, and every time the producer came up I had to shake off this paralysis that would set in again the moment he left. The producer would come with the director. They would grab me, take my clothes off, make me shower, dress me in a bathrobe, and sit me at a table with a pencil in my hand. Every once in a while the director would slap me. *Use your imagination*, he would say. *The whole film crew is waiting. We brought three technicians from the US*, the producer would say. *Alright, what is it you want?* I would say. *You have to finish the dialogue between Fulano and Mengano*, the director would say. *Where was I?* I would ask. *At the word "money,"* the director would say. *Money*, I would say, *Yes, exactly, money*, the producer would say. At this point a blonde would walk out of the bedroom in a nightgown, holding two empty bottles, one in each hand. *Haven't I told you more than a thousand times not to leave your empty bottles in the suitcase?* she would say. Sometimes she would come in totally naked. But no one looked at her, not me or the producer or the director. I don't think we even saw her. *Money*, I would say. *Money, perfect*. And I would start scratching my head wondering why I had written *money* the day before and what the hell this movie was about. *Show me what I wrote yesterday*, I would say. *Forget about that*, the producer would say. The last sentence went something like: *I need money*. And I would say, with conviction, *You never say money outright—you use euphemisms, like "cash," "bread," "means." Money isn't said. I couldn't have written that*. And the producer would hit me again, twice. *Don't theorize, Tomatis*, he would say. *I'm not paying you for theory, I'm paying you to write a screenplay*. Finally we would come to an agreement—Fulano asked Mengano for money, and Mengano loaned it to him on the following condition: Fulano had to give way as regards a certain lady. Then we would write the dialogue. As he was leaving, the producer would collide with the waiter who was bringing the first bottle of the day. The producer would start talking to me, and what I could make out over the sound coming from the bathroom, the blonde singing, and the tub filling with hot water for the bath, sounded something like, *You're a good guy Tomatis. A cool guy. I've seen a lot of cool guys but no one as cool as you. If I didn't have this two hundred million dollar company, which feeds cool guys like you, and could get by with my two factories and my cattle, I would spend all my time talking to you. I'm positive we'd get along like crazy. I've even seriously thought about giving you a stipend so you can write your novels and mail them to me. But I swear on my mother's ashes that no movie I ever make again will be written by you.* And then he would leave. I would start laughing, shake my head, and dive into the bath. With the blonde and me inside, it would overflow, and sometimes we'd get off by spitting jets of bathwater on the waiter's ass.

Then I went back to the paper, and Tomatis said he was going somewhere or other. The print shop asked me for a headline for the weather report, which I had forgotten when I sent it in, and after turning it over a hundred times I decided on: *No Change in Sight.* I sent it to the shop and smoked a cigarette without anyone coming around to bother me. Then I went down to the machine room, and when the first copies came out I took one with me to the bar at the arcade. It was full of people, and when I got to the last page—with the comics and the classifieds—it was after seven-thirty. It was dark by then, and it was still raining. The neon signs reflected off the pavement, and since it was too early to go to Tomatis's, and I had no interest in running into my mother at home, I decided to follow the first suspicious-looking guy I saw. I picked one who was dressed fashionably, with a white raincoat and an extremely fancy black umbrella that he had closed and was using as a cane. He was around thirty.

I was set up in one of the entrances to the arcade, protected from the rain falling on the sidewalk, and saw the guy coming south to north on San Martín. He stopped a second in front of the window to a shoe store and then went in the tobacconist that divides the arcade walkway in half. He bought pipe tobacco and left. I followed. He walked four blocks up San Martín and turned right toward the Plaza de Mayo, and after walking around the block he turned back onto San Martín, this time north to south, on the opposite sidewalk. I was following some forty meters back, not losing a step. In the entrance to a shop he took shelter from the rain and lit his pipe, taking three or four deep drags to make sure it was lit well. I stopped no more than two meters away, pretending to look in the window of the shop where he had stopped. When I realized that it was a lingerie shop, I turned away quickly and went ahead a few meters, but I stopped again because the guy was walking so slow that I was already ten meters ahead. I waited on the corner, and he passed next to me, stopping a second to open his black umbrella because the rain was getting heavier every second. The guy went six more blocks north to south on San Martín and then turned back, south to north again, on the opposite sidewalk. I didn't lose a step the whole trip. He was walking so slow it was crazy. He passed by the illuminated walkway of the arcade again and at the first corner turned toward the bus station. At the entrance to the platforms he stopped, grabbed the pipe he had been chewing on the whole time, and with his mouth open gazed at the post office on the opposite sidewalk, where the windows were completely illuminated. The guy looked the building up and down, his mouth open the whole time, raising his head so high that at one point I thought he was going to fall backward. Then he went to the ticket window to Rosario and bought a fare. I went up to the window and got close enough to hear that the

37

ticket was for the next day, at eight-ten in the morning. Then he went out onto the platforms, opened his umbrella again, crossed to the opposite sidewalk, and started walking back the way he had come. On the corner of 25 de Mayo he stopped in front of the windows of the Monte Carlo bar and looked in curiously. Apparently he didn't see anything interesting because he turned around and kept walking north up 25 de Mayo. At the corner he closed his umbrella and went in the Palace Hotel. I went in after. The hotel lobby was incredibly bright and clean. There wasn't a doormat, and yet there wasn't a single muddy puddle on the floor. The guy went to the concierge desk and I followed him.

—Two twelve, he said.

The concierge gave him the key. The guy turned around without even looking at me and got in the elevator. I stood there watching him through the elevator gate as the metal box rose and then disappeared. Then the concierge asked me what he could do for me.

—I'm wondering if a Mister Philip Marlowe is staying in this hotel; I expected him this morning, I said.

—Mister what? said the concierge.

—Philip Marlowe, I said.

The concierge started looking over the registry.

—Arriving from where? he said.

—Los Angeles, California, I said.

The concierge looked carefully over the guest registry.

—He hasn't arrived, sir.

—Thanks, I said, and left.

The clock at the Casa Escassany rang nine times. I passed through the deli, bought two bottles of red wine, and went to Tomatis's place. It had stopped raining now, but the humidity was madman. I caught a taxi on the corner of the central market and gave Tomatis's address. When Tomatis invites you to his house, he means you should go to a tiny apartment he rents for work, in a remote neighborhood, jammed between two avenues. When he says to come to *my mother's house*, he means the house where he lives with his mother and sister, downtown. I actually prefer the room Tomatis has on the terrace of his mother's house, because there's a pullout sofa, a desk, a small library, and a reproduction of *Wheatfield with Crows* over the sofa, on the yellow wall. The apartment on the outskirts is more comfortable, but you rarely find him there. It's likely he won't answer phone calls because he's either working or in bed with someone. Sometimes he invites me over and he's not home when I get there. The city rolled by past the taxi's windows, drenched. The sidewalk in front of Tomatis's house was darker than the bottom of the ocean, but a trace of light escaped through the foot of his doorway. I rang the doorbell twice and waited a long time before anyone opened the door. Horacio Barco was the one who answered. He took up the whole entrance with his bulk, which was stuffed into a wine-colored turtleneck sweater and these wool pants I'll ask to borrow the day I take up begging.

—Hello, he said.

He let me in, and I crossed the threshold into the house. He followed me into the first illuminated room. There were two armchairs and several chairs scattered around, a bookcase, and a desk. A sofa bed was pulled out, and I supposed Barco had been there because only a person of his dimensions could have made a hole like that in a bed. The late edition was on the floor, strewn around. I left the wine on the table and asked Barco if he had some idea were Tomatis could be.

—I'm absolutely certain he's somewhere, Barco said.

—He invited me to dinner, I said.

Barco extended his arm.

—I think there's stuff in the kitchen, he said.

—I can wait a while still, I said.

Barco made a gesture that meant absolutely nothing and threw himself on the bed. He stretched out face up and was snoring two minutes later. I went over to Tomatis's desk and saw an open notebook, full of scribbles in the margin and a handwritten text that went as follows:

> *To catch a rabbit, you need a point the rabbit can't cross;*
> *to make him tired, you need a field for him to run;*
> *to make him die, you need a place, in the open country or in a*
> *tangle of branches, where death can find him.*
> *Only the light he carried inside himself was unreal.*

Then some blank pages I slid back with my forefinger, among them a loose sheet, handwritten, that said:

> *The faint farmhouse, erased, moving away,*
> *the sparse habitations warmly illuminated,*
> *where pale-faced men walk from the table to the window,*
> *the beds filled with an animal smell,*
> *the melancholy bars with sticky floors where turbulent music*
> *plays,*
> *the government office and the police precinct, the courthouse,*
> *the parks abandoned in the rain,*
> *women face-down on mossy, arabesque rugs,*
> *the pavement and the smoke of sad chimneys, mixing with*
> *the rain,*
> *the white city hall, it's dark windows,*
> *the slow buses traveling the empty streets,*
> *the murmur of a million minds constantly running,*
> *a slow disintegration*

The sound of the street door startled me, and I hid the sheet of paper inside the notebook. I left the notebook open on the table, the way I had found it. Tomatis appeared at the entrance to the room, followed by male and female voices. I heard the sound of high heels in the corridor. Tomatis stopped, surprised to see me. I realized that he had forgotten the invitation but remembered it right away. Then he glanced quickly from the bed to the table and, seeing the notebook open, gave me a suspicious look and went and closed it. Immediately behind him were three young women and a guy with glasses who was dressed in a blue jacket and wool pants. The women's faces I recognized. The guy I had never seen in my fucking life. He was holding a raincoat. The women were folding up their umbrellas and one of them, wearing this madman green dress, untied a headscarf and started shaking out her hair, throwing it backward. Tomatis went and shook Barco, who sat up in the bed and looked around. Then he rubbed his hands over his face a few times and got up. One of the women, wearing a white raincoat cinched at the waist, carried a straw bag in her hand. Tomatis took it and put it on the table. He opened it and started taking things out: two bottles of whiskey and a pile of canned food. From the bottom he pulled a loaf of homemade bread. Two of the women disappeared farther into the house, and Tomatis followed them, so in the room the only people left were Horacio Barco, the girl in the green dress, and the guy with the raincoat folded over his arm. The guy was standing near the door; Barco next to the bed, his hands in his pockets; I was resting a hand on the table, near the cans and the bottles of whiskey; and the girl in the green dress stood in the middle of the room, with her green umbrella in one hand and her scarf and handbag in the other. I was about to say something, because no one was talking and the situation was getting awkward, but just then Tomatis and the other two women reappeared and started taking the cans and bottles to the kitchen. Barco crossed the room behind them and disappeared, so the only people left were the guy in the blue jacket with his raincoat folded over his arm, the girl in the green dress, and me.

—Is it raining again? I ask.

—A little, says the girl in the green dress.

The guy with glasses stares but doesn't say a thing. After a second, I gesture to the bed and the chairs and say:

—Should we sit?

The girl in the green dress shrugs and sits in a chair, without letting go of the umbrella or the handbag or the scarf. The guy with glasses stands there as if he was made out of stone. I sit down on the edge of the bed. I take out my cigarette pack and offer, but no one accepts. So I light a cigarette for myself and put the pack away. I bite the filter, my lips apart and head back slightly so the smoke doesn't get in my eyes. If they don't have a filter to chew on, cigarettes don't interest me. What I really like is chewing the filter, not smoking. The girl in the green dress looks at me with her eyes wide open. I'm sitting on the edge of the table, my legs stretched out, my hands in the pockets of my raincoat, chewing the cigarette filter. My eyes are half shut and my head is back. The other guy is still standing there, not moving, and I'm tempted to go over and shake him to see if he's dead or not. Just then Tomatis comes in, holding a glass.

—Make yourselves comfortable, he says, looking at me. I would prefer it if your ass didn't touch the table.

The girl starts laughing.

—Carlitos, she says, where did you get this chair?

—I inherited it from my grandmother, Tomatis says. He goes over to the statue of a man with a raincoat over his arm and slaps him on the shoulder.

—Don't just stand there.

The guy obeys and sits down.

—You can go in the kitchen and serve yourselves what you want, Tomatis says. Gloria and la Negra are getting the food ready and Barco is eating it. He's always hungry. Once he ate a whole cow.

—I don't believe it, says the girl in green.

—Well, he left the horns and the tail, Tomatis says. He nods toward me. Angelito is a friend of mine from the paper. He writes the weather report. He's responsible for this incessant rain.

The woman in the white raincoat comes in and starts taking it off. Underneath she had on a sea-blue dress and a sweater of the same color. She finished taking off her raincoat and throws it on the bed. I saw she had hair on her temples, and I wondered if she would be too hairy underneath her clothes.

—We're eating in ten minutes, she said before going back.

—Negra, said the girl in green, I can help if you need it.

—Barco's helping, said la Negra, and disappeared.

Even though he was sitting, the guy with glasses still had his raincoat folded over his arm. He was on the edge of his chair, leaning forward, his raincoat folded over his arm and his arm resting on his thigh. Not a single muscle on his face was moving. I thought that if you went up behind him and took out the chair, the guy would stay in the exact same position, floating there. Tomatis was still standing, holding a glass. His beard had grown some since the morning, and his cheeks gave off blue, metallic reflections. His hooked nose was shining at the bridge.

—Where were we? he says.

—That he left the horns and the tail, says the girl in green.

—So we were talking about the devil, Tomatis says.

The girl in green laughs. Tomatis leaves the glass on the table and picks up the pages of the newspaper, arranging and folding them up.

43

—Tomorrow's old news, he says, and stands up, his face red from the effort it took to bend over.

Horacio Barco comes in, covering the entire doorway with his body. He's chewing something and has a glass of wine in his hand.

—Carlos, he says. There's no salt.

—Impossible, Tomatis says.

But Barco has already disappeared back into the kitchen. Tomatis goes out behind him.

—Are you a writer as well? says the girl in green.

—No, I say.

—What do you do, besides the paper? she says.

—Nothing. Sometimes I do some work for the police, but not often, I say.

—What kind of work? says the girl in green.

—Follow people, shakedowns, I say. Nothing much.

—How exciting, says the girl in green.

—Not really, I say. It's boring, mostly.

—Yes, I can imagine, says the girl in green, thoughtfully. Everything ends up boring in the long run.

Tomatis comes in just as I'm raising his whiskey to take a drink from it. He waits until I'm done and then takes the glass.

—There are two bottles, in the kitchen, he says.

Then he goes up to the guy with the raincoat folded over his arm, who must have died by then.

—You can serve yourself something in the kitchen, Nicolás, he says.

The guy stands up without saying a word and leaves, taking his raincoat with him. When he disappears I turn to Tomatis:

—Is it sewn to his arm? I ask.

—What? says Tomatis.

—The raincoat, I say.

Tomatis laughs weakly and tells me to go to the kitchen if I want to drink something, and to shout when dinner is ready.

—No, I say. I don't want to drink anything for now. With dinner, in any case.

—Ángel is a character, Tomatis says.

—So it seems, says the girl in green, looking at me with some curiosity.

I throw the cigarette on the floor and jump off the table, crushing the butt with my shoe. The floor is covered with mud stains, and from the center of the room to the kitchen door there's a trail of puddles. The girl in green has her legs open, and her gathered dress shows half of her thighs, which are madman. I try every possible way to not look in that direction, but some crazy force makes me turn my head again and again. She doesn't even notice. I even get the impression that she barely knows I'm there, and the questions she asks come out of her mouth mechanically, as though she has them prepared for whenever she's with someone whose face isn't totally familiar. The last look she gave me was the most vivid, but she grazed my face with it so lightly that it ended up annoying me.

—Your face is familiar, I say.

—Could be, she says. In this city, everyone knows everyone.

—No, I say. I have a feeling that we were talking once before.

—Could be, she says. I talk so much. And with so many people.

—But I have a feeling we were talking intimately, I say.

This has no effect. She makes an ambiguous gesture and shrugs, admitting the possibility. Tomatis stares at me. Just then the guy with the raincoat over his arm comes in holding a glass of whiskey in his free hand. He stops near the door, motionless. He has on these enormous brown shoes with rubber soles so thick that they look like orthopedics.

—Nicolás, you've filled your tank I see, Tomatis says cheerfully.

—We can go to the table now, Nicolás says.

So he *could* talk. It was pretty amazing, considering his striking resemblance to a human being. I thought it possible that he was some plastic android for whom Barco had quickly improvised a mechanism in the kitchen that made it possible for him to formulate the expression, *We can go to the table now.* Or that Tomatis himself was the one who responded, like a ventriloquist. The girl in green got up and left.

—Don't rush off, Ángel, Tomatis said. Pupé doesn't have a cunt. She was born that way. But she's lots of fun, and useful for conversation. In any case, she doesn't understand anything about *anything.*

The dinner was awful. They had opened like fifty cans of peas, boiled them with onions, and ended up with a flavorless, runny stew. I don't know who convinced Nicolás to leave his raincoat on the back of his chair, but his posture didn't change much—the whole time his arm stayed in the same position it was in when he'd been holding the coat. Because there weren't enough chairs, Gloria ate sitting on Barco's lap, from his plate. Apparently they had gotten quite intimate during the cooking, or most likely they already knew each other before. Gloria had on these very tight black pants, and her hair was in a ponytail. She had a long, thin neck, like a pole, and Barco held her back so she wouldn't fall. I sat between Tomatis and la Negra—Pupé was sitting next to Tomatis—and noticed that la Negra's hair even grew behind her ears. I imagined her covered in hair, like a monkey. When he took his first mouthful, Tomatis said that maybe with rotten onions the stew might have come out a little better, but there was still time to dig through the trash for some condiments to add. Then he said a movie producer is easy to recognize right off by the thickness of his cigar, but with a director it's trickier, because behind the frontal bone of a movie director's face there's only air. Then he argued with Barco, who was saying Othello wasn't a jealous man, that Iago was only presenting him evidence of Desdemona's deception, and in the end he was just an easily influenced person. What was more apparent, according to Barco, was his masochism, and Shakespeare's vulgar construction of a tragedy based on the stereotypical idea that all Arabs are jealous and impulsive. From that he starting talking about how the phlegmatism of the English was a product of the intense humidity. Tomatis laughed at Barco's arguments but admitted that Othello wasn't a jealous man, agreeing that it was obvious Othello wasn't jealous because his behavior wasn't typical for a jealous man, since it's common knowledge that jealous men don't beat to death the women who have betrayed them, but rather they dedicate themselves to calculating the dimensions of their banana plantations and examining the path of the shadow cast by the last column in the southeast corridor of their guest house. *It's elementary*, Tomatis shouted, punching the table. *No jealous man beats his wife to death. That's cheap psychology. A real jealous man is a maniac for details. And the one time in my life I felt real jealousy, I had the irresistible urge to find a carpenter's rule and go take the measurements of the queen-size bed where I suspected the deception was being perpetrated.*

In my opinion, Tomatis was exaggerating, but the theory was original. Barco responded that it would have been better to use the carpenter's rule to measure the object for which Tomatis has been substituted. *If you have to unfold it the full meter to measure it*, he said, *then you've found the reason for the deception.* Then they stopped yelling and it was silent for more than five minutes, and I spent the whole time hitting the edge of my plate with my spoon. When the silence started to bother me, I got up and went to take a piss. I crossed a tiled courtyard that led to a yard full of bare trees—behind their branches I saw a whole lot of clouds moving quickly, opening up for the glow of the moon and a section of starlit sky. But there was no wind in the courtyard, and the black, naked branches stayed motionless. I didn't even reach the bathroom. I pissed in the courtyard, standing on the strip of concrete between the red tiles and the dirt. When I got back to the kitchen, it felt like they had been talking about me because I noticed something suspicious in the silence, different from what I had left earlier.

—I was changing the olive water, I said when I came in and noticed the silence. Tomatis asked me to go to the front room and get a pack of cigarettes from the desk drawer. I went and opened the drawer and saw there were two packs of North American cigarettes. I pocketed one pack and took the other to Tomatis. When I gave it to him, Tomatis opened it and offered one to everyone, me included. I bit the filter and lit it, blowing a mouthful of smoke over the table. I raised my head and squinted my eyes, the filter stuck tight between my teeth.

Then we all moved to the front room. Gloria and Barco threw themselves on the sofa bed, head-to-toe, and every so often Barco would tell her to get her feet off his face. Nicolás grabbed the edge of a chair and sat there like a corpse, not opening his mouth or even breathing probably. I was about to sit down on the edge of the desk again, but Tomatis stopped me, saying, *I don't like visitors putting their ass where I work,* so I sat in a chair and Tomatis leaned up against his book case. La Negra and Pupé sat in two armchairs. Pupé didn't even bother trying to cover her legs, while la Negra spent the whole time pulling her skirt down over her knees, and my suspicion that she was hairier than a chimp grew stronger each time. Gloria complained over and over that Barco wasn't giving her any space on the bed and she could fall off any second. Tomatis said that in the hotel where he stayed in Buenos Aires there was a maid so tall that she couldn't get in the elevator, and once when he was going down to the front desk (*because the only time I left the room I went to the front desk to ask them to fix the phone because it was busted,* he said) the elevator opened and there she was, crouched in one of the corners. *I asked the concierge if it wasn't disruptive to have such a tall maid,* Tomatis said, *but the guy said she did a great job cleaning the ceilings and was in bed with the owner, who was crazy for tall women.* Pupé asked if he was writing anything, and Tomatis nodded several times, squinting his eyes, and said, *Yes, I'm writing something.* Pupé asked him what. *I'm not sure yet,* said Tomatis, *I've only written about three hundred pages.* Pupé asked, *But is it a novel or what?* And Tomatis said, *There's only one genre—the novel. It took years to discover this. There's only three things in literature: perception, language, and form. Literature gives form, through language, to specific perceptions. And that's it. The only possible form is narration, because the substance of perception is time.* I applauded. Pupé shook her head two or three times, and Nicolás opened his mouth for the second time all night. *According to Valéry,* he said, *for certain internal states, discourse and dialectics should be reinforced by narration and description.* Tomatis said, *Exactly—he says this in reference to Swedenborg and the mystic state. Which provides us with a wider field for narration. And further, if the mystic state, the state of ecstasy par excellence, is subject to narration and description, then what happens with fleeting moments of consciousness and jolts to the senses? When discourse and dialectics are no longer scientific or philosophical truths, they transform into a narrative of the error and the perspective of the consciousness that imagined them.*

I applauded again. With Nicolás, I was even more convinced that he was some kind of life-size, plastic robot, built by Tomatis to say, *Dinner is served,* and interject the Valéry quote in the conversation to support his argument.

Finally Barco managed to throw Gloria off the bed, and she got back up and sat on the edge, next to Barco, and started slapping

49

him softly in the face. Her long neck was tilted toward Barco, and when she moved her head her ponytail swung crazily over her shoulders. I realized she was the most complete woman of the three there. I couldn't forget Tomatis's warning about Pupé, and with la Negra the idea of going to bed in the dark with a hairy monkey made me shudder with terror. Gloria's tight pants framed an ass that was madman, and when I saw she was letting Barco move his hands complacently along her thighs and back and all that, I realized that any second I was going to end up with a hard-on. I go nuts when I see a woman in pants. A million naked women radiating a blue iridescence could walk past me and I would hesitate about which one to choose at first, but if in that million one comes along in pants, I'm likely to drop on her like a lightning bolt. Gloria was lifting Barco's head and feeding him whiskey in short sips, then she would drink. In an hour not a drop was left of the two bottles. Suddenly Barco got up and said he was leaving. Tomatis didn't even say goodbye. I don't think they exchanged a single word all night, and as far as I know they've seen each other every single day since they were born. La Negra asked if he was going to the city center, and Barco said he was, so she asked him to wait. She went to the back of the house, to take a piss I assume, and then put on the white trench that fit her so well, and probably worked to camouflage that black tangle of monkey hair that I'm sure covered her entire body. *Nicolás*, said Tomatis. *They're going downtown. They'll get you close to the bus stop at least, because it's already twelve thirty. Tomorrow's May first and later tonight it'll be hard to find transportation.* Nicolás got up, grabbed his raincoat, folded it over his arm, and left with Barco and la Negra.

When it was just the four of us, I threw myself on the bed, hoping Gloria would come pour whiskey in my mouth, but she stayed put in the chair la Negra had been in, listening to Tomatis

tell the story of the producer and the director and the blonde in
the hotel in Buenos Aires. If I heard right, in the latest version
there were now two blondes, identical twins who walked naked
around the hotel room while he and the two movie guys tried to
write dialogue. Suddenly, Gloria was asleep. Tomatis and Pupé
had been talking in low voices for at least ten minutes, I'm not
sure about what, then they got up and went to the back of the
house. I fell asleep, for about ten minutes. When I opened my
eyes I saw Gloria kneeling next to the sofa, looking at me intently.
Tomatis and Pupé still hadn't come back.

—I was looking at you, Gloria said.

I sat up.

—You looked dead, Gloria said.

She had a thin, freckled face. She was thin all over, trim, except
that sensational ass. Her hair was pulled tight around her head. I
could see a mole on her left cheek.

—Well, I'm back, I said.

I sat up on the edge of the bed.

—I'm gonna go change the olive water, I said.

I left the room, and walking past the bedroom I heard Pupé's
hushed voice. The door was half open and the room was faintly
lit by a candle.

—So we've gotten naked and gotten in bed, said Pupé, what's
the point of this?

I went out to the courtyard. It was cloudy again and cold, but
it wasn't raining. When I came back in I tried not making noise
and stopped next to the door to listen.

—You should try everything, Tomatis was saying, how could
you not like it?

—I just don't, Pupé said.

I was pressed against the wall, listening, and suddenly I looked
up and saw Gloria studying me from the other end of the hall, her

51

arms folded and shaking her head. I walked toward her and went back into the room with her.

—He can't convince her, I said.

—I can imagine, Gloria said.

Then Pupé and Tomatis reappeared, and when I was about to leave Tomatis said I could sleep there if I wanted. Gloria and Pupé left, and Tomatis showed them out. He told me to sleep on the sofa, that he was going to his room. I got undressed and got in bed. Before leaving, Gloria gave me a kiss on the cheek. I whispered in her ear that she should stay and she started laughing, didn't say a word, and left. I told Tomatis that I wanted to talk to him before going to sleep, but I didn't hear him come back. When I opened my eyes again it was ten in the morning and Tomatis was sitting at the desk, writing. A gray light, opaque and uneasy, was coming in through the windows facing the street.

I looked at Tomatis a long time without him realizing that I was awake. The room was spotlessly clean and put together, and Tomatis had on a gray sweater, from which the collar of a white shirt showed through, and wool pants. He looked perfectly clean and calm. He would look out through the gray window frame, his eyes wide open, without seeing anything, then he would lean over and start writing again. I kept my eyes half shut so he wouldn't catch me looking at him if he turned around. The whole time I was watching him he probably only wrote twenty words. Then I spoke and he startled.

He turned around suddenly. His beard had grown a little overnight, setting off his facial features.

—I didn't realize you were up, he said.

—I just woke up, I said.

—There's coffee in the kitchen, he said.

I got dressed. Tomatis turned toward the window again. Then he leaned over and wrote another two or three words. I left the room and heard Tomatis close the door behind me. I went to the bathroom and sat a while reading an old newspaper that was on the toilet. I looked for the weather report and found the headline: *No Change in Sight*. Then I looked at the date—March fifteenth. Then I washed up and combed my hair and went to the kitchen.

The coffee was cold, so I had to wait around while it heated up. I poured myself a cup and drank it. Then I poured myself another. In a black tin in a cabinet I found some pastries that I dipped in the coffee and which came apart as soon as they touched my tongue. I ate all the pastries, and when I dipped the last one in the coffee cup it came out dry because the cup was empty. I went back to the front room and stopped a second in front of the closed door, hesitating. Then I went in. Tomatis didn't even turn around; he was looking at the gray window frame, his eyes narrowed and his mouth open. I don't know what he saw there that was so interesting. I went to the table to get a cigarette.

—Don't touch it! he shouted.

I jumped back, and Tomatis laughed.

—Sorry, he said. I was distracted.

He sat looking at me without saying anything else. I lit a cigarette, bit the tip, and exhaled a mouthful of smoke.

—I'm almost finished, said Tomatis. Half an hour more and I'm done.

I walked out and closed the door. I went to the courtyard to finish the cigarette. It was a gray day, and the fresh, cold, and gentle breeze made me flush. The sky was covered with a dense, gray sheet. After the cigarette I went back to the kitchen and drank more coffee. There was nothing but black sediment left in the coffee pot, and after the last swallow I had to spit out a mouthful of grounds. Then I got up and opened the door to Tomatis's bedroom. Gloria was lying in the bed, her face flattened against the pillow. She had undone her ponytail and her hair fell in black

53

clumps over the blankets. The black pants and gray sweater she was wearing the night before were folded over a chair. On the floor, at the foot of the bed, were her little black shoes. I tiptoed close to the headboard. Her mouth was open, and next to it, on the pillowcase, a damp stain had formed. I stepped on something soft and looked down; it was a pair of tiny black panties. They must have belonged to her, unless Pupé had forgotten hers the night before.

I shrugged and went back to the kitchen, closing the bedroom door behind me. Just as I was sitting down at the table, Tomatis appeared. He was euphoric, the same kind of euphoria I had noticed at the paper the morning before. He washed the coffee pot and put more water on. He asked if I had slept well.

—Perfectly, I said.

—How did you like the party? he asked.

—Oh, so fun. A dead body was the only thing missing, I said.

—And how did you like the girls? said Tomatis.

—La Negra was appealing, but I'm worried that she's an ape, I said. I didn't really notice the others.

Tomatis brought a finger to his lips and gestured toward the bedroom.

—Gloria's still here, he said.

—I didn't realize, I said.

Tomatis prepared the coffee and offered me a cup.

—I've had enough coffee, I said.

I put my hand in my pocket and felt the pack of cigarettes I took from the desk drawer the night before. It was still sealed shut and had flattened out. I squeezed it hard. Tomatis sat down with a cup of coffee and started sipping it.

—For a week I've been trying to tell you about something that's been happening to me, and I can't get you to listen, I said.

54

—You can't really count on people for much, he said. Besides, it's not my fault that you asked Gloria to stay and she didn't want to. She decides if she stays or not and who she stays with, don't you think?

So she'd told him. I was blinded for a minute. I could hear Tomatis's voice but didn't understand a thing. I felt a shudder in my stomach, and then I asked Tomatis for a cigarette, just to say something, because he was quiet again, and if there's something I can't stand when I'm with someone else it's silence. Tomatis went to his bedroom and came back with two packs of North American cigarettes. He threw one on the table.

—Keep it, he said.

Then he offered me a cigarette from his pack.

I lit the cigarette and told him the situation with my mother.

—In my opinion she's not being fair with me, I said. I'm the reasonable one. I'll let her dress however she wants, but she can't answer the door naked. It doesn't matter that she's my mother or whatever. It's not right. I don't think the milkman, for example, is at all comfortable with her answering the door in a bikini when she exchanges the bottles. And then there's the thing with the gin. She knew it was mine all along, and there was no reason to pretend it was hers and I was the one in the wrong. And even if the bottle *had* been hers, it's still willful ignorance because she knows full well that she steals piles of cigarettes and cash from me and I act like nothing's happening. And another thing: How does she have the right to keep telling me that my brain is going to rot from so much reading, when all she does is read romance novels and a pile of gossip rags? In any case, it's not my fault she turned on the light and saw me with a hard-on. I didn't call her. I'm not in the habit of calling my mother to come see every hard-on I get. Ever since my father got sick I've turned a blind eye each time she went off on one of her nocturnal excursions to God knows where, so it doesn't seem like asking too much to expect her to respect my rights the way I respect hers. There was no reason for her to come and turn on the light suddenly, thinking she'd find me doing who knows what with who knows who. I don't think she heard a strange noise and turned on the light suddenly to scare a burglar or something like that. No: her idea was to surprise me *in flagrante* in who knows what imaginary crime she assumes I commit every night. Another question: How can she hit me for saying that the bottle of gin she had in her room, and which she'd drank two-thirds of, was in fact mine and not hers? She knew full well the bottle was mine. She shouldn't have gotten up from the bed and slapped me. I got angry and hit her back. Then she slaps me twice again and I couldn't take any more; I took off my belt and start whipping and punching her until she surrenders and curls up on the bed crying and all and doesn't look up or say a word when I pour myself a gin and take it back to my room.

—So you gave your mother a beating, says Tomatis.

—Exactly, I say.

Because Tomatis doesn't say anything, I add: She was making life impossible for me. It seemed like the best way to get her to leave me alone.

—I suspect you didn't come to the decision as calmly as you'd now like to make me believe, says Tomatis.

—I probably wasn't thinking ahead when I hit her, I said.

—Yes, said Tomatis. That's the impression I get.

—And what about her? I asked. Does it seem normal to you to get so enraged that it completely changes our relationship because she saw me in the courtyard with a hard-on?

—How old is your mother? asked Tomatis.

—Thirty-six, I think.

—You should be more careful around the house, said Tomatis.

Then Gloria walked in, and Tomatis told her to make break-fast. Gloria looked at me and smiled weakly, but it seemed like she hadn't woken up completely. She had the pale skin and puffy eyes of someone who's just gotten out of bed, and she couldn't focus her gaze on anything. Tomatis shook his head and gestured for me to follow him to the front room, but I had already forgotten the thing with my mother and would rather have stayed in the kitchen checking out Gloria's ass while she got the food ready. Clearly Tomatis was trying to show interest in my problems after making me wait more than twenty-four hours, but when we got to the front room I didn't feel like talking anymore and went to the window to look at the street. No one was out, and the shrubs bordering the sidewalk were frostbitten. Across the street, the sky's tense gray color seemed even more tense and more gray over the skeletal frame of a house under construction.

Tomatis waited for me to say something, and when he under-stood that I preferred to stand there the whole time looking through the window with my hands in my pockets, he said: I'm not going to give you advice, Angelito. It's not something I do. But I suppose you want to find some explanation for what's happening. If we analyze the facts, maybe we can come up with something.

—She's a slutty old bag, I said.

—First off, she's not old, said Tomatis.

—I hope you're not talking about me, said Gloria, coming in just then.

—Not the old part, I said.

—Give me a cigarette, Carlos, said Gloria.

Tomatis handed her a cigarette and lit it. I had an unopened packet in each pocket, and I squeezed them both.

—Come in and eat, if you want, said Gloria, and walked out.

We stood there in silence for a moment, and I could hear Glo-ria's footsteps moving down the corridor toward the kitchen. She looked like she'd woken up completely, and her thin, freckled face, with the mole on the cheek and the lips curved slightly upward, had regained the soft shape of the night before. When we were walking to the kitchen and I started to smell fried onions, I worried that we were going to have to eat that revolting canned soup again, but Gloria had changed out the peas for some pieces of beef liver that must have gone rotten while the cow was still alive. If she'd fried it in jet fuel it might not have been so terrible. And she and Tomatis swallowed it so easily and with so much appetite it was like they were eating rose-flavored milkshakes. It seemed like Gloria didn't know how to do a thing, apart from letting herself get fondled all night by one guy and then jump in bed naked with another one. I couldn't get the image of her out of my head—her face flattened against the pillow, her mouth open, and the little saliva stain forming on the white pillowcase. But she was able to do more than spread her legs all night, the tramp. She played poker a thousand times better than Carlitos and me, and she won more than a thousand pesos from each of us in less than an hour, when we went to the front room to play a game after breakfast. And after winning she said that something must be open despite it being May first, and she went out and bought a kilo of cream puffs to eat with tea. Then she started reading some poems aloud in English, from an anthology Tomatis had just bought in Buenos Aires. The book had a strange odor, which I can't recall without shuddering. When she grabbed it the first time and brought it to her nose and smelled it with her eyes closed, I thought it was a put on, plain and simple. But then she handed it to me so I could smell it, and I realized the smell was something madman. Then she read a section of Robert Browning's "Pompilia," then "The Chambered Nautilus," by Oliver Wendell Holmes, "This Bread I Break," by Dylan Thomas, "To Waken an Old Lady," by William Carlos Williams, Yeats's "Vacillation,"

Eliot's "Journey of the Magi," Pound's "A Study in Aesthetics," and half a million others. It was obvious she knew everything and had perfect taste, the bimbo. That made me even angrier, and I told her not to read any more in English because I couldn't understand a thing (even though I had studied English for four years and could read it easily) and Tomatis cracked up laughing.

—He's mad because you told me he'd asked you to stay last night, he said.

They barely survived that, and only because I wasn't carrying a .45 pistol and a handful of hollow-points. She started laughing and put down the book and walked over and kissed me on the cheek and told me I was a cute kid. Then she put her hands in her back pockets and went to look at the gray sky through the window. Tomatis was lying in the bed, propped up against the wall with his legs hanging over the edge, and I was standing there like an asshole next to the table, squeezing the cigarette packs in my pockets. To punish Tomatis I told him his theory that the novel was the literary genre *par excellence* was nonsense (although when he said it, it sounded right) and that actually everything was theater, that theater was the only real genre, and that *Discourse on the Method* was a long monologue by someone who was playing the role of a philosopher and who spoke in a way that had nothing to do with how he talked in real life, that talking like that he imagined himself a philosopher and was hoping to pass it off on everyone else. But this didn't bother Tomatis at all, and it actually sounded interesting to him, and he came over and slapped me on the back and told me I was an intelligent guy and I was going places. Then I told him I hadn't read *Discourse on the Method*, and he said it didn't matter, that he had read it and that it was accurate more or less the way I had put it. He finally convinced me. Then Gloria went to make tea, and by the time she brought it steaming to the front room, I wasn't angry any more.

It got dark and we turned on the lights. The sky was like a metal sheet. The room was full of smoke, but it wasn't dirty or anything because Gloria kept cleaning the glasses and ashtrays as they got dirty. We sat there a half hour looking at each other, and I got the impression that they wanted me to scram, but since I wasn't sure I stayed till around eight. I realized that they didn't have any problem with me staying when Tomatis said I could sleep there again if I wanted, but I told him I would rather go home. Then Tomatis said he was going to lay down a while and Gloria followed him out. For about fifteen minutes I listened to their voices and stifled laughter, and then everything was quiet. I took out the pack I had grabbed the night before and put it back in the desk drawer. Then I shouted from the corridor that I was leaving. Gloria responded that one of these days we'd see each other again, and I left.

I walked something like thirty blocks. It took me ten minutes to get to the avenue, then I turned onto 25 de Mayo, and when I reached the intersection with the Banco Provincial, whose clock read exactly nine, I turned onto San Martín. I drank a cognac in the arcade and then turned off San Martín and came back to it crossing the Plaza de Mayo, where the courthouse stood, hazy and dark like a dense, black mass glued to the black sky. I stayed at Ernesto's house until well after midnight, and then I went home to sleep.

It was raining the morning of May second, and I stayed in bed late, in a kind of daze, thinking about the double. Since the night of the gin incident with Mamá, I hadn't thought about him. I had forgotten him completely the last ten days. I first saw him on March fifth, after not having left the house for five days. I got on the bus at around nine in the morning, and when it turned at an intersection with San Martín, I saw someone with a very familiar face coming out of an optician. The face was so familiar. When the bus reached the opposite corner, I jumped up and got off. I had realized it was me.

When I got to the corner there was no sign of him. I went in the optician and stood by the register, waiting for one of the workers to recognize me. One of them came up and asked if I needed anything, but he didn't seem to recognize me. I said I was picking up some glasses that had been brought in for a new lens, under the name Philip Marlowe, and the guy looked through a pile of envelopes filled with glasses, with the names of the owners on the back, but he didn't find the one I had asked for. I told him I must have gotten the wrong shop and I left. I walked around the block twice but didn't see him again. Then I went to the paper.

I saw him a second time two days later, coming out of the courthouse. I was walking down the marble steps at the entrance and I saw a guy in shirtsleeves waiting next to a taxi for someone who just then was paying the driver. The guy in shirtsleeves had his back to me, but there was something familiar about him. I didn't associate him with the person I had seen coming out of the optician two days before, and when the passenger got out and the guy got in the car, I was looking up at the sky because I still hadn't done the weather report, and it was crazy hot out. When I looked back down the taxi was accelerating, and I saw the side of the guys face in the back seat, saying something to the driver. It was me. I started shouting, running down the steps, but the only thing that came out was the word *taxi*. The driver, without slowing down or anything, stuck his head out the window and shouted, *Can't you see I'm occupied, numbnuts?* The guy in the back seat gave me a sidelong look (there was something malignant in it), and then I couldn't see his face, because the car accelerated, turned the corner, and disappeared. I ran to the corner, but when I got there the car was already gone. I stood there, stiff as a board, for like half an hour, staring off in the direction the car had vanished. I don't know how I kept from passing out. For the weather report that day I entered 46 degrees in the shade, and I wasn't far off, because the report they gave on the radio had it at 44.8. Then I went back to the paper and found Tomatis on the phone. *Do me one favor,* he was saying to the guy on the other end of the line. *Look at the results and tell me if two forty-five came up.* When he hung up he turned toward me, and I must have looked strange because he asked me what was wrong.

—I saw myself in the street, twice, I said.

—Don't go egomaniacal, Ángel, said Tomatis, uninterested. Then he started typing.

The third time he didn't see me, and I was able to follow him for two blocks. It was during Carnival. A million people were lined up watching the *murgas* and the masquerades, and the guy was standing on the edge of the sidewalk, trying to cross the street. I was moving through the crowd, looking to write a fluff piece about the parade, for some extra cash, and I saw him from the opposite sidewalk, just as he started crossing toward me. I was blown away seeing him there, a cigarette pressed between his teeth, his head lifted, his eyes narrowed to keep the smoke from bothering him. My heart started pounding—he was walking straight at me. But he didn't stop, and he didn't seem to see me, but he passed so close that his shoulder rubbed against mine. I froze up when he touched me. Something turned over in my stomach. He looked so much like me—he had on a discolored blue shirt and white pants, exactly like the ones I was wearing—that on his right arm, exposed through his short-sleeved shirt, I even saw a white scar that was identical to mine, a long, whitish stain that the summer sun hadn't been able to tan. I followed him. It was easy, at first, because he was walking against the wall and everyone else was pressed up to the edge of the sidewalk to get a better

62

view of the parade, leaving a path open between the wall and the crowd. Less than ten meters separated us. He stopped suddenly because a water balloon flew past, exploded against a shop window, and splashed him. Instinctively, I brought my hand to my face to wipe off the drops. The guy took a handkerchief from his back pocket and dried his face and part of his head, then put the handkerchief away. I watched him and started following again when he walked on. Just above the right back pocket of his pants I could see two dark stains and realized they were ink stains I had made, a few months back, putting a pen away in the back right pocket of the pants I was wearing. He crossed the street and I followed him. On the next block I decided to speed up so I could talk to him—I had no idea what to say, but I wanted to talk to him—and I had already cut in half the distance between us when suddenly something blinded me. I felt a torrent of water—like a million liters—hitting me in the face. For half a minute I didn't know if I was on San Martín or at the bottom of the Pacific, and when I opened my eyes I saw this shitty little brat looking at me from a doorway with an empty bucket in his hands, and when he saw my face—Mr. Hyde probably would have looked like Shirley Temple next to me just then—he took off into the house. When I dried my face off and looked up, the guy was gone.

I took a mental note of the address of the house, thinking the Vampire of Düsseldorf might want to pay a visit, and then I went home. I saw my double again in mid-April, but I couldn't follow him because, just as I was catching up to him, crossing the street, a truck almost ran me over. And, in any case, I was sure I wouldn't catch him.

On May second, before getting up, I thought about all of this. I wondered if seeing my double several times in the street, and once wearing the double of my discolored blue shirt and the double of my white pants with two ink stains on the back right pocket,

63

wasn't some feverish hallucination caused by the insane February sun roasting my skull. Because it had been a crazy summer. House roofs were cracking, and the walls had to be mopped up to dry the water pouring in. Millions of mosquitos were devouring anyone who went down to the riverbank to play sports—they lined all the jocks up along a wall and opened up the machine gun on them—and the pavement had turned black with the beetles that crashed against the streetlights and fell to the street with their wings broken. By January, the trees were surrounded by piles of charred leaves, and anyone who spent more than an hour in the sun would spontaneously combust. But I was sure it was real, because he had bumped into me the night of the parade. I was sure he existed. So I pictured him existing in a small world, like mine. Our worlds never overlapped, except through some unlikely accident that occurred three times. His world and mine, limited as they were, ran together if they approached each other, and his realm of experience was unknown to me, but familiar. I knew that the things that could happen to him in his world could be different from what happened to me in mine, but they were still similar. And if they seemed identical—if he looked at the back of his hand on April seventh at ten thirty-five in the morning, for example, at exactly the same moment as I was doing exactly that—they were, nevertheless, different things. Maybe he was following me in his world, along a duplicate and inverted path that I had mistakenly wandered onto the same night of carnival, when I was following him in my world. Or maybe we lived different lives. One thing I was sure of: our spheres—our worlds—were closed and only touched by accident. It could also be that everything has a double: Tomatis, Gloria, my mother, my notebook, my weather report, the *La Región* newspaper, Ernesto's illuminated block where Shönberg's *Violin Concerto* plays. If that was true, something different had to happen in the other world, because

64

an exact replica seemed absurd and deranged to me, especially because it threatened to multiply indefinitely. There couldn't be an identical bed repeated to infinity in which a guy like me, also repeated to infinity, thought about the possibility of the bed and the guy being repeated to infinity. That kind of thing was crazy. But when I got up I thought that it was just as crazy for there to be only one bed and one guy, and that the only horrifying thing about the double was the possibility that he was living a life I couldn't. So I took a hot shower and went to the courthouse.

Ramírez said all the rain was caused by sun spots, which in turn had been caused by the atomic bombs. I said that the sun spots and the atomic bombs must have been what caused the coffee in the press office to taste like ass, and Ramírez laughed as best he could, but didn't manage to hide the infamous, brown sierras that were all that was left of his rotten teeth. Then I went to Ernesto's office and asked for him. The secretary told me that the judge was in a meeting. I told him to say that the *La Región* reporter was here and ask when the inquest we'd talked about would be. The secretary came back immediately.

—The judge says tomorrow at four, because he has to interview the witnesses first, he said.

So I went back to the paper. I typed out the courthouse report that Ramírez had given me on transparent paper, submitted the headline for the weather report—*No Change in Sight*—and then went to lunch. I didn't see any sign of Tomatis in the office, but when I went to the administration to pick up my check, they told me that Tomatis had been in that morning to pick up his check and then had gone off who knows where. When I got back, Tomatis was opening correspondence addressed to the "Director of the Literary Page."

—Regrettably, everyone in the world has feelings, he said. Because of this, everyone makes literature.

—I know a guy who doesn't have feelings but still makes literature, I said.

—Must be a great writer, said Tomatis.

—He writes with his dick, I said. He dips it in ink and writes like that.

—Those must be some broad strokes—his penmanship I mean, said Tomatis.

—I don't know, I said. I never saw the originals.

—Gloria says hi, said Tomatis. She said she's going to call you up some afternoon to play poker and then invite you to dinner with her winnings. And she said you shouldn't have stepped on her underwear and that she was just waiting for you to pull back the covers so she could slap you.

—Some day I'm going to put a bullet in your heads, both of you, I said.

Tomatis laughed.

—Angelito, all grown up, he said.

I don't like to spit in people's faces, so I walked over to the police reporter and asked him if he knew about a guy who had killed his wife in Barrio Roma the night before.

—Yeah, he said, and read me the part where it said that some guy had blasted his wife's face off with a shotgun.

—The inquest is tomorrow at four, I said. The judge told me.

—Apparently they were out hunting and on their way back they had a brawl in a bar, said the police reporter.

—I understand that that's the most humane way to treat a woman, I said.

—I disagree, said the police reporter. A slow death works better. When you're married you'll see.

—I'm not getting married, I said.

—You never know, said the police reporter.

I went back to Tomatis's desk and found him shaking his head over a typewritten poem.

—Some guy shot his wife in the face, twice, I said.

—What for? asked Tomatis without looking up.

—I don't know. It was at a bar in Barrio Roma. A Luis Fiore, I said.

—I know a Fiore, said Tomatis.

Then I went and typed out the weather report. At five, as it was getting dark, I left the paper. I went to a bookstore and bought three books: *Sexual Behavior in the Human Female*, *Modern Sexual Techniques*, and *The Homosexual in the Modern World*. Around eight I went home with two bottles of gin and locked myself in my room. I was sitting down for less than two minutes before I got up and went to my mother's room.

—Mamá, I said. Can I come in?

My mother answered a second later.

—Just a moment, she said. I waited at the door and heard the sound of papers and bare footsteps on the wood floor. Then I heard the bed squeak and my mother's voice again.

—Come in, she said.

She was in bed with the sheets up to her neck.

—I'm in bed like this because I'm naked. I hope it doesn't bother you. I was changing to go out, she said.

—I won't keep you, I said. I just need a minute.

We were silent. My mother's room was the same dump it had been the night of the fight, just with a little more trash. I hadn't been in there since.

I couldn't speak.

—Say what you're going to say, my mother said.

—I brought you a present, I said. I passed by the store and got you a bottle of gin, since I saw there wasn't any.

—You could have found a more subtle way to call me a drunk, my mother said.

—It doesn't bother me if you drink, or even if you walk around naked, if that's what you want, I said.

—I don't see why it *would* bother you, my mother said. Who are you to be bothered by it? I don't think I'm accountable to you for how I dress or what I drink.

—I just wanted to tell you, that's all, I said. One of the bottles is yours. It's in the fridge, for when you want it.

I went back to my room and picked up my book. I could hear her moving around her bedroom, and I got caught up listening to the sounds made by her heels, the rustling of her dresses, the creaking of the bed, the squeak of the her closet door. I got completely distracted from my reading. Then I heard her heels clicking to the bathroom, and the light turned on, and in the silence that followed I imagined her leaning toward the mirror, carefully applying her makeup and pasting on false eyelashes. Then I heard her turn off the bathroom light, and the sound of her heels was softer as it passed by my room, fading away as she walked down the corridor toward her room. When she went in, the sound, echoing off the wood, changed in quality. It deepened, and was drier than off the tiles. Then I heard her turn off her light, close the door to her room, and leave the house. I threw myself on the bed, with the light on, and closed my eyes after putting the glass of gin down next to the bed. Every so often I would turn over and take a drink. I must have been like that for an hour. I had never felt the house so quiet. No boards were creaking, and the rain was falling so quietly that it seemed more like a fine cloud moving over the dark city in a slow rotation. I went out to the corridor and turned on the light. In the lamplight the rain was a dense, whitish mass of floating particles. I stared at it for several minutes. Then I walked into my mother's room.

The door was unlocked, which surprised me, because I had supposed she always locked her door when she left. I turned the handle and I was inside. Without her there the odor was still the same, though less intense. I turned on the light and glanced around: the bed was a mess, with the sheets and blankets bunched up and halfway to the floor. There was still an impression where she'd been lying, and where she'd rested her head. Both night tables, separated by the queen size bed, were covered with bottles of medicine, jars of cosmetics, and glasses with spoons and caked up dregs at the bottom. There was an ashtray on each side full of butts and ash. I touched the impression and realized it was still warm. Then I opened her wardrobe.

A bunch of dresses in every color were hanging from the bar, and opening the side door I saw a small compartment with four drawers and a hanger where three or four pairs of pants were folded. On the inside part of the door, a string was suspended on two nails, from which colored ribbons and hair ties were hanging. Above the string was a picture of Cary Grant, cut from a magazine and pinned up with four thumbtacks. I opened one of the drawers and found a bundle of letters; a worn out Saint Cajetan prayer card; fake pearls from an old necklace, which were scattered around the bottom of the drawer; and some object of unclear purpose, either mother-of-pearl or tortoiseshell, which wasn't for her hair but was too narrow to be a bracelet. Under the bundle of letters I found a book that was missing the first few pages. It was an old edition, worn out and yellowed. When I read the first paragraph I realized it was a pornographic novel—most likely it had been my father's—and flipping through I realized it was illustrated. I closed the first drawer and opened the next. It was full of photos: one was of me at my first communion, in white shorts; in another my father was holding me on his lap and my mother was smiling at me; in a third is my mother, so young she's almost unrecognizable, in a bathing suit, holding onto a swimming pool handrail as she comes out of the water. I closed the second drawer and sat down on the edge of the bed. I imagined my old man reading a chapter from the book to my mother every night before they made love. I was so enthralled by this image that I ended up lying back and looking at the ceiling, which was stained with damp in the corners. Then I got up and opened the third drawer. It was full of bras and panties, and I closed it without touching a thing. Then I turned off the light and shut the door on my way out.

I poured myself a glass of gin, put some ice in it, and sat down to read the book about women's sexual behavior. By the tenth page I was so turned on, and had learned so little about women's sexual behavior, that I went to the bathroom and ran cold water over my head and stood there a while without drying off, hoping it would pass. But just as I was getting ready to leave, I realized that I was much more excited than when I came in, so I masturbated to keep from staining the sheets because I knew that in any case I would be doing it the moment I got in bed. I ended up drinking the gin straight from the bottle, and I know I went to bed because when I woke up the next day I was in bed, fully dressed, with the light still on. If the atomic bomb had fallen on my room instead of Nagasaki, my head might have hurt a little less. I dragged myself to the bathroom and took a hot shower. Then I drank a cup of coffee and I felt better. When I went to look at myself in the mirror to adjust my tie, I saw my three-day beard and shaved. Then I left for the paper. Tomatis was at the typewriter, and you could tell he'd just shaved too. I sat down at my desk, picked up the phone, and told the operator to connect me to the courthouse. When they answered at the other end, I asked to speak to Ernesto. His secretary answered and transferred me.

—I couldn't see you yesterday, Ángel, he said. I had a meeting.

—Don't worry about it, I said. Is the inquest today?

—Yes, at four. I'm interviewing the witnesses, he said. But I don't think you can come. It's not allowed.

I was quiet. Ernesto didn't speak either for a moment, on the other end. Then I heard his voice.

—This is some kind of blackmail, isn't it? he said. Emotional blackmail. Come at four. I'll see what I can do.

We hung up. Tomatis was still typing. He didn't even look at me.

—I tried to talk to my mother, I said. I think things will get better.

—That's great, said Tomatis, not looking up from the keyboard.

—I gave her a bottle of gin and everything, I said.

—Well done, said Tomatis in a distracted way, looking at the keyboard and then going over what he'd written.

—We talked a while last night, I said.

—You see? Everything has a solution, said Tomatis solemnly, not looking at me and striking at the keyboard.

He wasn't listening. So I spent a while sending things down to the print shop, and then I went to eat. Tomatis followed me and caught up in the stairs.

—Let's play a game of pool, after lunch, he said.

—I can't today, I said.

—That's fine, said Tomatis. Let's eat together.

So we ate together. After lunch I felt like a king. Tomatis smoked a cigarette and told me to visit him more often. Then he said if he ended up going out that night he would come past my place to let me know.

—I'll probably be out, I said, but come by in any case.

When we finished I went back to the paper and told the publisher that there was an important inquest at the courthouse and that I was going to attend. He was reading the paper from the day before, marking the news he found interesting for whatever reason with a red box; he didn't even look up when I explained why I was leaving at three thirty rather than at five, like every other day. He told me to go, only be sure to see to my responsibilities, always, no matter the situation, that it would straighten me out and make a man out of me. He said this without once glancing up at me, feverishly looking over the pages of the newspaper and drawing a red box here and there with insane enthusiasm. I left with the impression that he didn't know who I was or what he was telling me. At three forty-five, I was in Ernesto's office. A blond man was with him, around thirty-five years old, with a blond beard and a Jewish face.

—Mr. Rosemberg, said Ernesto. A journalist.

The guy shook my hand.

—Mr. Rosemberg is Fiore's lawyer, explained Ernesto. He turned back to him. As soon as he gives his statement he can speak to you, he said. So you can wait nearby, if you want.

—They're bringing him at four, correct, Your Honor? said the blonde guy.

—At four, that's right, said Ernesto.

—How long do you think it will take, Your Honor? asked the blonde guy.

—An hour should be enough, said Ernesto.

The blonde guy stood up. He was short and thin.

—I'll be back in an hour, then, he said.

He shook my hand and left.

—It's irregular for a stranger to be present at an inquest, said Ernesto. But I've taken care of it. In any case, the accused doesn't need to know that you're not on staff at the courthouse. You shouldn't take notes or anything like that.

—I don't want to take notes, I said. I just want to see. I've never seen a murderer up close, that's all.

—A kind of unhealthy curiosity, I suppose, said Ernesto.

—I suppose so, I said.

We were silent a moment. Then I walked to the window. I had never done that before. It was large, made of four tall pieces of glass separated by a black wooden cross. The Plaza de Mayo was below, and the still palms were being washed by a slow rain that made their broad, jagged leaves more slippery and tense. A woman was crossing the plaza at a diagonal, on the red brick dust path, shielding herself with a bright blue umbrella. From the third floor I could see the blue circle of the umbrella and the woman's legs pressing into the red path. I could feel Ernesto's gaze on me, and I turned toward him.

—Where will the inquest be? I said.

—Here, said Ernesto.

Just then there was a knock at the door. Ernesto gestured toward me and then toward the door, to indicate that I should open it, but at that moment the door opened from the outside. It was the secretary, a man with gray-streaked hair.

—They're bringing the accused, he said.

—You can stay, Vigo, said Ernesto.

The secretary walked in, leaving the door to the corridor open. He sat down at a typewriter and began inserting a long sheet of white paper into the roll. When he finished, he leaned back against the chair and crossed his arms. Ernesto was going over some papers on his desk, so I turned back to the window. The woman with the blue umbrella had disappeared, and another woman, crossing the plaza at a diagonal in the opposite direction, was advancing slowly, shielding herself with a pink umbrella as she slipped over the red earth. I heard steps coming down the hall and I turned. Through the doorway, a sliver of the empty corridor was visible, and, beyond the atrium, the opposite corridor and a closed door. The secretary still sat there with his arms crossed over his chest, and just as I was going to say who knows what to him, a uniformed guard looked in, bowing slightly.

—Pardon me, Your Honor, he said. He had some papers in his hand, and when Ernesto gestured toward him, the guard entered and left them on the desk. Ernesto looked them over while the guard observed him, leaning in respectfully.

—Bring him in, said Ernesto. The guard left. Then Ernesto had me sit on the other side of the desk, behind him and the secretary. From where he put me I could see everything well, especially the secretary's profile and then Ernesto's. Just as I was sitting down, the guy came in with the guard.

He came in first, handcuffed, and the guard followed behind. His beard was at least a week old, and his eyes were dim. It was obvious he hadn't washed his face for three days at least. He wore a sweater that showed a wool shirt with a short v-neck beneath, and filthy, wrinkled pants of some color or other. His shoes were covered with dried mud.

—Take the handcuffs off, said Ernesto.

The guard removed the handcuffs. The guy didn't even look at him, and when his hands were free he let them hang limp at his sides. If he was looking at anything, it was the gray sky through the window. But I'm not sure he was looking at it. He probably wasn't looking at anything.

The guard brought a wicker-backed chair and set it across the desk from Ernesto. The guy stood there until the guard gave him a little shove on the shoulder with the points of his fingers, and then he sat down. Now he was closer to me and the secretary, and facing Ernesto. I was the farthest from everything, but I could see him well. Just his face was obscured, by that mass of black beard that gave off a reddish glitter. The guy looked at me, or at least turned his head in my direction.

—When we finish I'll call you, officer, said Ernesto.

74

The guard bowed and then left, closing the door behind him. Ernesto arranged the papers on his desk and then looked up at the guy.

—Your name is Luis Fiore, correct? said Ernesto.

The guy didn't say anything. His eyes looked like they were covered with a patina of some transparent material, a kind of flat lacquer that clouded them and made them seem blind. Ernesto stared for a moment, directly at his eyes, not blinking, waiting. The secretary leaned over the typewriter and waited, his hands suspended with his fingers over the keys. The guy's gaze—if you could call it that—was fixed on Ernesto, but he didn't move a single muscle on his face.

—I'll repeat the question. Is your name Luis Fiore or not? said Ernesto.

The guy shook his head, but so weakly and with such a distracted expression—his gaze or whatever you want to call it remained fixed on the point where a moment earlier Ernesto's eyes had been—that it was difficult to consider this movement a response to anything.

—The accused responds in the affirmative, said the secretary, inclining his gray-streaked head slightly more and beginning to strike the keys. For a moment the only sound in the room came from the typewriter keys and the hum of the machine—until the secretary stopped typing and it was silent again. The secretary rubbed his hands for a few seconds and then was still. I leaned toward the guy, sliding forward to the edge of my chair.

Ernesto wrote down two or three words, apparently considering something. Then he said:

—Do you know the charges against you, Fiore?

The prisoner's face opened into a weak, cunning smile, and the terrain around his eyes filled with creases and crows feet. But his eyes didn't light up. Or it might not have been a smile, but actually the facial expression of his effort at understanding. I tried to guess his age. Then I remembered that in the piece the police reporter had read to me it said he was thirty-nine. I looked closely at him and guessed he could be anywhere between thirty-nine and a million. Then he opened his mouth, revealing white teeth under his reddish lips and black beard. His mouth stayed open, but he didn't say a thing. Ernesto narrowed his eyes and leaned forward.

—Do you know the charges against you, Fiore? he said.

The three of us—Ernesto, the secretary, and I—waited for him. The guy leaned toward Ernesto and narrowed his eyes as well. His jaw was clenched, as if he was struggling with something, and I realized that his previous expression hadn't been a smile, or if it had been at that moment, it had now become something else, more turbulent and indistinct. When he spoke, his voice was incredibly soft, high-pitched, and weak.

—Judge, he said.

Ernesto didn't respond. The guy leaned farther in, and I saw that his eyes were now squeezed shut.

—Judge, he repeated in a high-pitched voice.

He started to shake his head.

—The pieces, he said. Can't be put back together.

Then he jumped. None of us—Ernesto, the secretary, and I— moved until we heard the sound of the window shattering; the guy disappeared from the room. The three of us stood up at the same time, but he was gone; all that was left was broken glass and the splinters from the window frame, and in the silence that followed—still filled with the echoing crash of the body hitting the window and disappearing—the piece of glass that came loose and fell into the room made me turn faster than if the guy had reappeared at the window, returned from the void. The secretary started running around the room, saying *Oh God* over and over. When the secretary cut him off as he walked slowly toward the door, Ernesto shoved him aside. The secretary fell over a chair and started foaming at the mouth. Ernesto opened the door and walked out. I approached the secretary; he opened his eyes and said *Oh God* twice, weakly. Then I went out into the corridor and ran down the three flights in one second. When I reached the street, a circle had formed on the sidewalk in front of the courthouse, below the window. Others were running toward them across the plaza. Rosemberg was talking to Ernesto. I pushed into the front row of the circle. The guy was in the center, face down, so shrunk up that he looked like a dwarf. The yellow stones under him were stained with blood. The guy wasn't moving. I realized that when someone throws himself through a window and falls to the ground from the third floor, he doesn't break anything at the moment of impact with the glass or with the pavement—nothing—because he's already been broken to pieces and all he's doing is tossing out an empty shell. The guy had hollowed himself out to the bone, then thrown the shell out the window. The rain fell over the shell and the circle of pale faces that were looking at it silently. I pushed my way out and went back to the courthouse. Separated from the group, Ernesto and Rosemberg were talking in low voices. Two guards were starting to push people out of the way. I went straight to the operator's office. She asked me what had happened and I told her. She got up to leave, but I told her to connect me to the newspaper first. She made the call and ran out. The police reporter told me that the page was closed and we'd have to wait till the next day. Then he said he was leaving for the courthouse. Coming out of the operator's office, I crossed the gallery toward the entrance and ran into Ernesto and Rosemberg coming up the steps quickly, two at a time. I touched Ernesto's arm.

—Tomorrow, tomorrow, said Ernesto, not even slowing down. The other guy didn't look at me.

On the street, the crowd of gawkers had doubled. I couldn't see the guards. I pushed through the crowd and saw them in the center of the group, which was pressing closer and closer on the body. The guards were pushing people away. The guy was still face down, even more shrunken than before. He didn't even look like a shell anymore; he didn't look like anything. When I made my way out of the group that was pressing closer and closer, I saw the secretary, alone, next to the wall. He had put on a raincoat and was looking at me.

—Is he dead? he asked.

—I think so, I said.

His gray-streaked beard was stained with dried saliva. It looked like someone had thrown a handful of quicklime on his face. His eyes were wide open.

—Did the judge go up? he asked.

—Yes, I said.

—I didn't even see him jump, said the secretary. I heard the sound of the glass and he was gone.

—It happened fast, I said.

—All I heard was the sound of the glass, said the secretary.

—I don't know how he could have jumped so quickly, I said.

—I didn't see him move at all, said the secretary. I heard the sound, but I didn't see him. I heard the glass breaking. The glass broke. I heard it break, and he wasn't in the office. It must be raining up there, inside.

He leaned against the wall.

—It'll be covered with glass, he said.

It was getting dark, a sunless, blue twilight. I said goodbye to the secretary and went to the bar at the arcade. It was dark by the time I got there; the lights were on. I drank two cognacs but didn't see anyone. Around seven I went home. The light in my mother's room was on. A rectangle of light showed through the transom. I went to my room and turned on the light. Almost immediately my mother came in.

—Someone named Tomatis came looking for you, she said.

—Did you ask what he wanted? I said.

—No. Since you weren't here, he left, my mother said.

Then she went back to her room. I got in bed and turned out the light, but couldn't manage to get the sheets warm. It was like being crammed between two blocks of ice. Around ten I heard my mother leave, and when I realized that I was completely alone in the house, I felt worse. I went to my mother's room and got in her bed, in the dark. It was a little warmer than mine, but I had to force myself to stay awake for fear that she'd find me there when she got back. I stayed there about two hours, then went back to mine. It was like stepping into an ice box. If someone had come by and amputated my feet, I wouldn't have felt a thing. They could have chopped them off and thrown them in the trash and I wouldn't have realized it till the next day, when I tried to put my shoes on. Then I fell asleep enough to see the shrunken body fall a million times and hear the glass shattering a million times in Ernesto's office. I woke up and looked at the clock—it was five in the morning and colder than when I had gone to sleep. I made a cup of coffee and brought it to bed. Two minutes later I vomited. I realized I was sick and wouldn't be going to work that day. I put the thermometer in my armpit and left it there five minutes. When I took it out I saw it read 38.2. I stared at the transom, watching the light change color—black to blue, then a pale green and eventually gray, where it stayed—until the sun came up. I slept. When I woke up again the room was filled with a weak light, and the gray transom was shining brightly. I heard my mother in the kitchen and I thought I was going to die. It was ten in the morning. I called my mother.

—I have a fever, I said when she came in.

She had on red pants and a black sweater, and she'd put a handkerchief on her head. A cigarette was dangling from her lips, and her round face was washed clean.

—You're soaked, she said. She was silent a moment, then asked, Were you in my room last night?

—I was looking for cold medicine, I said.

—Don't leave your nasty handkerchiefs in my bed, my mother said.

—Do you have anything for the fever? I said.

She left without saying anything. A little later she came back with a pink pill and a glass of water. I sat up and swallowed the pill with two or three sips of water. I retched but didn't throw up the water or the pill. My mother saw the vomit on the floor and came back with a rag and a bucket of water. She crouched down and cleaned it up. Then she fixed up the bed and disappeared.

At exactly one she brought me a plate of soup, but I barely touched it. I asked her to call the paper and tell them I was sick, then heard her leave for the corner store to make the call. When she came back and opened my door, I pretended to be asleep. The sweats had started and the bed was getting hot, and an hour later, when I could feel my clothes sticking to my body, I called my mother again and asked for a towel, then dried off and put on fresh clothes. I put the thermometer under my armpit again, and when I took it out five minutes later I saw that I didn't have a fever. At six I heard the doorbell ring, then my mother's voice coming down the corridor toward my room, talking to someone who was cleaning his feet on the doormat. My door opened and Tomatis came in, followed by my mother. Tomatis pulled up a chair, very close to the bed.

—I've come to hear your last words and persuade you to include me in your will, said Tomatis.

—You can all eat shit. Those are my last words, I said.

—Don't be gross, Angelito, my mother said.

—That's what I call disregard for posterity, said Tomatis.

—Can I get you a drink, Mr. Tomatis? said my mother.

—Don't worry, I'm fine, said Tomatis.

—I'll get you a coffee, Mr. Tomatis, it's easy to make, said my mother, and left.

—What's wrong with you, said Tomatis. Yesterday you were fine.

—I couldn't sleep all night and this morning I woke up with a fever, I said.

Tomatis put his hand on my forehead.

—It's gone now, he said, taking his hand away.

—It passed, I said.

—Gloria is on her way here, said Tomatis. We were going to meet downtown, but I told her you were sick and I was coming to see you, so she said she'd come by too.

—I hope you didn't come here intending to get me out of bed so you could use it for all the filthy things you're into, I said.

Tomatis laughed.

—Wouldn't dream of it, Angelito, he said.

—The guy threw himself out the window, I said. He jumped up and disappeared from the face of the earth.

—I heard, said Tomatis. What were you doing there, if I might ask?

—I crashed the inquest. I wanted to see him up close, I said.

—Romantic delusions, said Tomatis. And how did you get into the inquest, if it's illegal?

—I told the judge that the paper was very interested in the matter and since I was a law student and wanted to specialize in imprisonment, I had double the interest in attending the inquest, I said.

—And you convinced him? said Tomatis.

81

—Apparently I did, I said.

—Who's the judge? said Tomatis.

—López Garay, I said.

—Right, said Tomatis. I know him.

—So Gloria's coming here? I said. Haven't you told her this is a respectable household?

—I told her, said Tomatis. Strange that López Garay let you come to the inquest just like that.

—He bought it up, I said.

—He's not stupid, said Tomatis.

—No. He doesn't seem it, I said.

My mother came in.

—Will you have a little gin with your coffee, Mr. Tomatis? she said.

She'd painted her face and changed her clothes; she had on a fitted skirt and a multicolored shirt.

—You don't even need to ask, I said.

—I asked Mr. Tomatis, not you, my mother said.

—If it's no bother, said Tomatis.

—None, said my mother. Just the opposite.

Just then the bell rang and the most extraordinary piece of ass in the world walked in, accompanied by Gloria. She had the afternoon paper with her and was dressed exactly the same as the night at Tomatis's, but now she had a blue umbrella, folded. I remembered the woman with the blue umbrella I had seen cross the Plaza de Mayo at a diagonal the previous afternoon. Gloria gave me a kiss and then took a package from her handbag and gave it to me.

—It's a gift, she said.

I opened it. It was a cheap edition of Thomas Mann's *Tonio Kröger.*

—I was deciding between this and a book on etiquette, said Gloria. Finally I picked this one because I figured that you are impossible to educate.

—I'm surprised you didn't bring me a smut novel, I said.

—I don't want to perpetuate the decay of your imagination.

—She talks like my mother, I said, looking at Tomatis.

—They all have a little mother in them, and a little slut, said Tomatis.

—It hasn't stopped raining all day, said Gloria.

—It's gotten dark, said Tomatis.

My mother served coffee and gin for Gloria and Tomatis and a straight gin for herself, then she brought me a cup of warm milk. She stayed with us more than half an hour, then she went to her room. Gloria suggested we play poker, and I sat up in bed and pushed my back up against the wall; they brought up their chairs and we used the bed as a table and played. Gloria won again. Around nine, Tomatis said he would go out and buy something to eat, but he ran into my mother in the corridor and she told him she was making something, so Tomatis went into the kitchen with her and after a while he came back with a plate full of cheese and another with sardines. My mother came in behind him with bread and a bottle of wine. Then my mother announced that she was leaving and said that whatever we needed we could get from the fridge. Then she said goodbye from the corridor, and a short while later we heard the sound of the street door opening and closing.

—She's behaving, said Tomatis.

—Things are better, I said.

—It's good to slap her around once in a while, said Tomatis.

Then he got up and said he was leaving. Gloria seemed surprised.

—Well, I'm off, said Tomatis.

—I thought we could stay a little longer, said Gloria.

—I didn't say you had to leave as well, said Tomatis, with an edge in his voice. I said I was the one who was leaving.

I asked Gloria to stay. She shrugged and said she could stay a while longer, as long as I could get her a little more gin. I told her there were two bottles in the fridge, so there would be plenty of that. Tomatis gave her a kiss and before going asked if I was planning on getting up the next day.

—I think so, I said.

—Then I'll look for you at the paper, he said, and left.

Gloria walked him to the door and I was left alone for a minute. I could hear them talking in the corridor but couldn't understand what they were saying. Then Gloria came back and sat down on the edge of the bed.

—I'll go get you some gin, I said.

—Not yet, said Gloria.

—You were amazing to bring me that book, I said, gesturing toward the gift.

—It was just a coincidence, she said.

—Gloria, I said. I'm not mad or anything that you went with Tomatis. I didn't know there was anything between you.

—Before that night there was nothing, said Gloria. And now there's almost nothing.

—You can never have much with Tomatis, I said. You can't hope for much with him, right?

—That's what he says, said Gloria.

—I think it's okay for people to be like that, I said.

I grabbed her hand but she shook me off.

—Don't start, Ángel, she said.

Then she asked me if I would like it if she read to me from the book. I said yes.

—I'll open at random and read some, she said.

She read for an hour. Then she put down the book and said she was tired and she was leaving.

—I'll be alone and the fever will come back, I said.

—Not if you go to sleep once and for all, said Gloria, and she disappeared.

I lay there thinking for a while, then I turned off the light.

I had the feeling of not being exactly anywhere. And then I saw, clearly, a slow procession of everyone in my life, everyone who I'd known in the past few years, and at the end of that slow procession was me, advancing from the blackness of my mind into a bright circle, only to disappear again into another blackness outside the bright circle. Then I fell asleep. I woke up at dawn. The rectangular transom was already a pale green. I felt euphoric. I made myself a cup of coffee, got in bed, and started reading *Tonio Kröger*. It was still raining. When I finished, it was nine-thirty and my mother had been up for a while. I could hear her moving around the house, but she didn't come in my room. I shaved, took a shower, and went to the paper. I didn't see Tomatis, and the police reporter asked me if I had read the piece about the guy who threw himself out the window of the courthouse and if it was right. I told him I hadn't read the paper.

—They're saying you were scared sick, said the police reporter.

—I had a cold, I said.

—But you changed your underwear, right? he said.

I didn't smash his face in because he was wearing glasses, but I asked him if he thought he was Philip Marlowe.

—Who? he said.

—An uncle of mine who's always getting involved in murder cases.

He shrugged and I left for the courthouse. I couldn't see Ernesto because he was giving a statement about what had happened, but I ran into the secretary in the corridor.

—The judge is very busy, he said.

—Did they fix the window? I asked.

—Not yet, he said. Did you see how that maniac jumped through it and broke every piece of glass?

—Yeah, I saw it, I said.

Ramírez met me with a cup of coffee—he'd already added sugar to it for himself; he told me that the judge was in a terrible mood because of the thing with the suicide. That everyone in the courthouse was talking about it. I drank down the revolting paste that Ramírez called coffee and left. Downtown I bumped into Tomatis in front of a lottery kiosk. When he saw me he asked if I knew of anyone with worse luck than his.

—Up comes 255 again, he said. But 245? Nothing.

We ate together and went to play pool. Tomatis asked me if I had gone to bed with Gloria the night before, and when I said no he started laughing.

—You weren't insistent enough, he said.

He saved himself from being murdered with a pool cue by being on the other side of the table. Then he said my mother was a good person and I had to treat her better.

—Don't play the *enfant terrible*, he said. You're too old for that.

—Gloria is going to stab you in the back one of these days and I'll testify on her behalf; I'll say it was self-defense.

—Gloria is in love with me, so I do what I want, said Tomatis. In any case, she's not better than me, or anyone else.

—Have you been writing? I asked.

—Something, said Tomatis.

—Smut, no doubt, I said.

—Something like that, said Tomatis.

He did his best to let me win, to little effect. Then we went back to paper and didn't speak again that afternoon, except to say goodbye on the way out. I walked around the city, drank a cognac at the arcade bar, and around eight I went home. My mother was in the kitchen, filling up a glass of gin.

—Are you going out? I asked.

—Yes, she said.

Any more and she would have emptied the bottle.

—I'm hungry, I said.

—There's cheese in the fridge, said my mother.

—Hungry for dinner. A hot meal, like God intended, I said.

—I have to take a shower and then get out of here, she said.

She went out with her glass, and I stayed in the kitchen. I took a piece of cheese and the bottle of gin from the fridge. My mother went in the bathroom and a little later I heard the shower. Then I saw her go by, wrapped in her towel, walking quickly. She crossed in front of the doorway to the kitchen and then disappeared. She looked amazing. When I finished my cheese I poured myself another gin and went to her room. I asked permission to come in. She had put on a gorgeous yellow dress and was painting her eyes in front of the mirror.

—We should go out to eat together one of these nights, I said.

—We'll see, my mother said, slightly resentful.

—It's time we got along better, I said.

—I hope so, my mother said.

I went back to my room, and a little while later heard her leave. I sat down at my desk, took out my notebook, opened to the last page of *Tonio Kröger*, and copied this down: *I look into an unborn, murky world that needs to be shaped and fashioned; I look into a teeming throng of human shadows, who beckon to me, want me to exorcise them and redeem them: tragic shadows and ludicrous ones and some that are both—and I am very fond of them. But my deepest and most furtive love is for the blond and blue-eyed people, the brightly living, the happy, lovable, and normal ones.* Then I closed the novel and the notebook. I didn't feel like staying in the house. I wanted to walk the streets and be with someone, with everyone if I could. When I stepped into the corridor and turned on the light, the procession from the night before flashed across my eyes. The light illuminated the courtyard, where the rain floated in a white mass. It didn't seem to fall, but to have been suspended in the same place for many days. I realized that I had barely noticed it, and felt guilty. This thing, the rain, was happening around me—a mystery that seemed beautiful and full of sadness—and I hadn't even looked at it. Then I remembered the shrunken body on the yellow pavement, outside the courthouse, and I asked myself what kinds of awful things could happen to make someone hollow out his body into a shell and throw it through a third-floor window and smash it to pieces against the ground. It had grown dark over the body, a sunless, blue twilight. I put on my raincoat and walked into the street. No one was out. I walked downtown and into the arcade. No one was there. A cashier in green overalls was staring into space, her hand resting on the handle of the cash register. I drank a gin standing next to the register and walked out. I walked north two blocks on San Martín and then turned. I passed the Banco Provincial and saw that it was eleven. Then I reached the Parque del Palomar and walked a while under the waterlogged trees. I imagined that I was in a deserted city, abandoned by everyone. They'd all gone, and I was alone. And how great that was! I walked along, in the darkness, passing under the streetlights, spheres of weak light dulled by the rain, then plunging again, across the intersection, into the dark streets. Before I knew it, I was at the corner of Tomatis's house. Light poured through the front window onto the street. I approached slowly. The blinds were all the way up, and through the glass you could see the illuminated room with the couches, the bookcase, the table, and the chairs. Gloria was sitting on the sofa, reading. She was wearing the same clothes as always, propped up against the wall with her legs stretched out in front of her. In one hand she held the anthology of English poetry and in the other a lit cigarette. Her lips moved as she read. I watched her for a long time without her noticing. Then I went to the door and tried the handle, trying not to make noise. It opened. I tiptoed down the dark corridor and entered the front room. I was three meters from Gloria, in front of her, in the doorway, and she still hadn't noticed me. A second later she looked up and screamed. I started laughing.

—Don't be scared, I said. It's me. I saw you through the window.

Gloria was pale.

—Carlitos isn't here, she said.

—Splendid, I said. I'm going to change the olive water and come right back.

I left the room and started walking down the hall. When I passed in front of Tomatis's half-opened bedroom door, I saw light coming through it and heard the voice of Tomatis himself, but couldn't make out what he was saying. I stopped suddenly and opened the door. They were naked on the bed together, Tomatis and Mamá. The yellow dress was balled up on the floor. I slammed the door so hard that it sounded like an explosion. I took off running and shoved Gloria, who had come into the corridor, and then went out into the street. I think Gloria called out to me, but I didn't stop. I didn't even look when I passed the illuminated window.

The first three blocks I ran full speed. Then I started slowing down. By the fifth or sixth block I was walking calmly. The city was a cemetery, and except for the weak streetlights it was covered in darkness. When I started crossing an intersection at a diagonal, under the light that reflected the whitish masses of rain suspended in the air, I saw a human figure coming in my direction. It emerged slowly from the darkness; at first it was blurred by the rain, but then it became clearer. It was a young man, wearing a raincoat that looked familiar. It was exactly like mine. He was coming right at me, and we stopped a half meter apart, directly under the streetlight. I tried not to look him in the face, because I had already guessed who it was. Finally I looked up and met his eyes. I saw my own face. He looked so much like me that I started wondering whether I myself was there, facing him, my flesh and bones really holding together the weak gaze I had fixed on him. Our circles had never overlapped so much, and I realized there was no reason to worry that he was living a life forbidden to me, a richer, more exalted life. Whatever his circle—that space set aside for him, which his consciousness drifted through like a wandering, flickering light—it wasn't so different from mine that he could help but look at me through the May rain with a terrified face, marked by the fresh scars from the first wounds of disbelief and recognition.

MARCH,
APRIL,
MAY

MY GRANDFATHER, TOWARD THE END OF HIS LIFE,
would say to me, There are three ways to win at cards, son—a
bankroll, a steady nerve, or a marked deck. But the bankroll, no
matter how large, always runs out. And no matter how well you
play, there will always be someone out there better than you. So,
the best method is to mark cards. That's how my grandfather
would talk toward the end of his life, which went on a long time.

My grandfather knew. He died when he was eighty-two. The
moqoit indians called him father. Two months before every election, my grandfather would sit down at the desk in his general
store in San Javier and wait. The political bosses would show
up, one by one. My grandfather would listen silently, chewing
his cigar and spitting out brown globs. After making their case,
the political bosses would leave, without my grandfather saying
word one. A week later he would call for one of them. Sometimes
the same boss for two or three consecutive elections, sometimes
the party would change every election. He would talk for ten

minutes with the political boss—spitting his brown globs onto the floor—and then would have his carriage prepared and go out to visit the *moqoit* reservations. That year, the political boss he had summoned would win the election.

With that, my grandfather made something of a fortune. In 1945, during the February election, my grandfather lost an eye. He had called in the Radicalist boss, and then had gone to the *moqoit* reservations, where they called him father, begged him for dysentery medicine, and followed his carriage to the edge of the reservation and waved goodbye until the sandy dust it raised had completely settled. But the Peronists won the election. Early the next morning, my grandfather, who lived alone with his desk in the immense shed next to the general store, heard a knock at the door. He asked who it was, and they said there was someone who was very sick. He opened the door and was shot. The bullet emptied his eye socket, but, miraculously, he lived.

So my grandfather retired from politics, sold the store, and moved to my mother's house in the city. In San Javier, when I was a kid, he liked holding me on his lap, but in 1945, when he came to the city, I had already been shaving for years. He put his entire fortune in my mother's name, saying he was going to die soon. But five years later, my mother, who was the widow of a man I never knew, my father I suppose, my mother, who had never once been sick, was serving soup at the table and said she was going back to the kitchen to get a spoon; that was the last time we saw her alive. Because she was taking a long time, I went to look for her and found her dead. She'd had time to open the drawer but not to take out a spoon, because she didn't have one in her hand, nor was there any trace of a spoon in the utensil drawer or anywhere else in the kitchen.

I was twenty-three at the time, and I was left alone with my grandfather. In 1952 I graduated law school, and in 1955 I was married. Five years later I was widowed. I had started playing sometime around 1956, when I got out of prison. I was married on September 16, 1955. I had just finished saying *I do* to the judge and was walking out with my wife to take some pictures with her and the witnesses in front of the building, when Negro Lencina walks up and tells me that the CGT is holding a rally. I ask him if there's time to take some pictures, and he says no. So I leave the ceremony and go to the CGT.

We came in through the roof and went down to the yellow-tiled courtyard. It was ten in the morning. Three or four shots were fired, at most, and no one was injured except for a guy who tripped on the curb when he came out shooting and fell to the ground and cracked his head open. Then the army arrived and we were all captured.

They let me go nine months later. My wife was waiting for me in the same dress she'd worn to the courthouse the morning of the wedding, and all the witnesses were there, some other relatives, and my grandfather. I invited Negro Lencina and Fiore, from the millers union, who had been with me in the south for nine months. They'd spent the whole time telling me that we were getting out in nine months and that I was going to get home the day my first kid was born. I would tell them there hadn't been time for that.

I started playing a month later, at a cookout put on by the union to celebrate the release of five rail workers. After the cookout we sat down to play *siete y medio*. It's a simple game, played with a Spanish deck. Face cards are worth half a point; numbered cards, one through seven, are worth their value. Seven and a half is the highest score. The banker deals out one card to each player, face down. You ask for cards up to seven and a half points and run the risk of going over. When you're dealt a face card, worth half a point, you turn it over and ask for another. If it's a five or higher you generally stand; if it's less than five, you hit. Sometimes you even hit with six and a half, because the banker determines the value of the cards and always has a half-point advantage, so if the banker has seven, he only pays out players with seven and a half. Anyone with less than seven and a half pays the banker. If you go over seven and a half it's called a bust, and you pay the banker. A two and a six make eight, for example. If a player holds a two, hits, and gets a six, he pays the banker.

I won sixty pesos. It was nothing, but what got my attention was that I could predict the cards I got. All I had to do was really want them and they'd come. If I was dealt a face card and then a two I would concentrate, thinking, *now I need a five*, and it would come. I even ended up hitting on six and a half—where a player usually stands—because I was sure I would get the ace. And the ace would come.

I knew I liked the game. Two days later I asked where they played for larger sums, and I learned that at a club downtown I could play monte at one time, baccarat at another, and dice at a third. I chose the dice game. I took out five thousand-peso bills, ate something at a bar, and went to the club. A mass of people were crowded around a craps table. Craps is an incredibly simple game: the player throws two dice from a shaker and combines the numbers that come up; if the first roll is a six, he tries for a six in the next roll; if a seven comes up before the six, he loses. But if a seven or eleven come up in the first roll, then it's a natural and he wins without having to throw again; if he throws a two, three, or twelve, then he's crapped out and can't roll again. A guy standing next to the table, not playing, explained the game to me. When the shaker got to me, I gave two thousand pesos to the banker; I rolled a seven and two thousand pesos became four. I rolled again and came up with a seven again. On the third roll, an eleven; on the fourth, eleven again; on the fifth, eleven again; on the sixth, a seven. I put down the shaker, took 128,000 pesos from the banker, minus the house take, and went home. On the way I realized that craps wasn't my game, that it was ruled by chaos, and that those dice rolling around in the shaker and then over the green felt were too dependent on chance. I wanted a game with some order, a game where the odds had already been fixed beforehand, whether I knew them or not. I needed a game with a predetermined past.

I found that predetermined past in baccarat. The next night I took twenty from the hundred-thousand-some pesos I had won at dice and went to play baccarat. This time it was a long table, with people sitting around it. Cards were dealt from a dealer's shoe, two to the player, two to the banker. Face cards and the tens were worth zero. Whoever got closest to nine won.

I ended up with eighty thousand pesos, but it wasn't as easy as in dice. It took a lot of work to win. I was never losing, but for more than an hour I wasn't able to win more than four or five thousand pesos, until the shoe came around to me and I was playing the banker. I dealt nine hands, all of nines. All I had to do was think, *I'm going to deal a nine*, and I would. It was easy. All I had to do was want it, and believe in what I wanted. By the second lucky night at the game, I had already made a bundle.

I didn't tell my wife, but I told my grandfather. Son, he said, easy come, easy go; it's a *perspetive*. (My grandfather would say *perspetive*, not perspective, swallowing the *c*, and he'd say it often). I don't deny that it's a *perspetive*. But the only sure way to win is to cheat.

Soon after that I realized he had a point. The two hundred thousand pesos I had won disappeared from one week to the next. But I was hooked. I had to go home at dawn, just to sleep. Little by little I abandoned my work, and little by little I lost the fortune that my grandfather had made from the desk in his general store, from which he would order his carriage prepared before going out to the *moqoit* reservations.

Two years later I had nothing except the house and a pile of debts. Luckily, it turned out my wife was infertile, so there were no children to support. My wife never approved of my playing, and what happened in June of 1960 is proof. She didn't approve at all, as will become apparent.

I had been playing poker all night, around the corner from the house. We'd sat down at eleven to play for an hour, and it was three in the afternoon the next day. Someone knocked at the door. The owner answers and comes back. Sergio, it's your grandfather, he says. I call him in. He was very old, and a little senile, and he looked outlandish with his missing eye and his tobacco-stained beard—he chewed the whole blessed day. He leaned in close to me and says, Son, your wife says if you don't come home in half an hour she'll poison herself. Tell her to poison herself, I said. My grandfather leaves and comes back thirty-five minutes later. He leans in close again and says, Son, she poisoned herself. So I asked permission to leave the table early and I went home and found her dead. She'd changed her mind after taking the poison and had come out to the top of the stairs, calling to my grandfather. But it was already too late, and he was a little bit deaf. I found her at the foot of the stairs.

A year later, my grandfather died. He hocked up his last brown glob and departed for the other world. In the end, he couldn't even run a simple errand. I would take him a pack of Toscanos every once in a while. He'd cut the cigars in two or three pieces, with scissors, and chew them. He'd sit on the stoop and spit onto the sidewalk. Once he accidentally spit on the pants of a guy who was passing the house and I had to come out and defend him. Another time some city workers came out to tell us that we needed to keep the sidewalk more hygienic. So he moved to the kitchen door, which led to the back courtyard, and eventually the floor was covered with dark stains that were impossible to erase. He died in the afternoon, sitting in his chair, looking at the fig tree in the back. If they come for you tonight, saying there's someone very sick, don't open the door, he said. And then he died. When the funeral people came, around nine o'clock that night, they asked for a five thousand peso down payment. I didn't have it, and I told them to wait till two in the morning. I actually didn't have a penny. I went to a casino and waited for someone to throw me a chip. No one did. So I leaned close to a guy who was winning thousands. I asked him to put me in for a thousand on his bet. That meant that on his bet of ten thousand, I was in for a thousand. If I lost, I had to pay him the thousand. If he won, he'd give me a thousand. Supposedly I had a thousand somewhere, in case the banker won. It was an impulsive move, because guys who are winning aren't usually in the mood for jokes. It was impulsive, but it paid off. After that it was as easy as riding a sled. Ten minutes later I had the money for the funeral service. I wouldn't have been at all interested in having my dead grandfather sitting at the kitchen door for months and months.

From then on, I was alone in the house. There was no rent to pay, because I owned the place, and the utilities and taxes were negligible. Once in a while I ate. Except for reading and playing, I didn't do anything. Eventually I started writing my essays.

I think the title for the collection was the hardest thing to come up with. First I called them *Essays on Contemporary Society*, then *Keys to Understanding Our Era*, and later *Fundamental Moments of Modern Realism*. I chose the last one, not totally satisfied with it. It seemed like the words *fundamental, moment,* and *modern* didn't mean anything. Whenever you wanted to fill out a conversation or turn a phrase to make it sound deep, you could use any one of these words, or others like *dynamic, concrete,* or *structure*. But

99

all that was fine. The hard thing was the word *realism*. The word had a meaning: the attitude characterized by a disposition toward reality. I was sure about that. What I was missing was knowing what reality was. Or what it was *like*, at last.

It got harder with each of the six essays, because I came up with them after different readings. Each one was inspired by the principal themes or the central characters of the texts I was reading. I gave myself completely to the reading, trying to find hidden connections in the things I read. The first one was the best, I think, because it came to me unexpectedly one afternoon and I wrote it in one sitting. And the title, *Batman and Robin: Confusion of Feelings*, despite being taken in part from a Stefan Zweig novel, sums up, I think, the crux of the argument.

Professor Nietzsche and Clark Kent was the second one, and I think it suffers for making an overly simplistic analogy between two homonymous and famous characters of the modern imagination. But if it has any value, I think it has value in the observation I think is the most intelligent in the text: that a single fundamental ideology determined the construction of both myths.

I wrote *The Magic Realism of Lee Falk* because I was convinced that in Falk's world I had found the aesthetic basis for the modern Latin American novel. The other three essays can hardly be called that. They're brief notes, two-page critiques that set up a theme almost without commentary. The first, *Flash Gordon and H. G. Wells*, is the best, I think. The other two aren't convincing. *Tarzan of the Apes: A Theory of the Noble Savage*, is more a response to Jean Jacques than Rice Burroughs, because in my opinion the best ideas on the issue are already in Rousseau, and *The Ideological Evolution of Mickey Mouse*, I don't even really know why I wrote it. Notwithstanding Mickey's psychological density, I consider it a minor work, and the critic could only be interested in it as a point of view: the systematic expression of the liberal North American worldview. But I'll leave that to liberals to celebrate, if they want.

A year after my grandfather died, I started feeling lonely in the house, so I put an ad in the paper for a woman to clean and run errands. I hired a tiny little fourteen-year-old, who came with her mother. They were from the coast, and I liked that, because I had spent my whole youth there. The mother was missing all her teeth, and she was so fat that she had to come in sideways. I sat her down on the sofa and the girl stayed next to her and kept her mouth shut, then I explained that I lived alone and I needed someone who would live in the house and pay monthly rent. The mother said that was exactly what she wanted; she said that the girl's things were at the bus stop and if we agreed on a wage she'd go get them herself. Eventually we decided on a number, with the condition that I write a letter to the village every two months telling her how the girl was doing. The girl went along to the station and came back an hour later. She had a package wrapped in pages from the newspaper. She was very thin and looked clean. She had started to develop, and she stared at me in this way that made me look away.

For two years the house hadn't been as clean as it was the day after she arrived. I had it cleaned by a maid occasionally, but that wasn't cleaning. She turned everything over, and the white telephone, an extravagance of my mother's from the '40s, which for the past few years had started looking like my grandfather's tobacco, was shining again. She showered every night, before going to bed, and never spoke a word to me. She didn't know how to read or write, so one night when I had won big at baccarat I bought her a radio, but as far as I know she never turned it on. When she would finish cleaning she'd go into the kitchen and, with her belly against the stove and her arms crossed, look out the window until it got dark. There were better windows to look out, the one by my desk, facing the street, for example, but she would always look out the kitchen window, which faced the courtyard. A few branches of the fig tree, the half-rotten thatch roof of a laundry, and, through the branches of the fig tree, and especially in winter, when the leaves were gone, patches of sky were all you could see through it. The girl's name was Delicia. Every two months I had to ask her what she wanted me to write in the letter to her mother, and she would say: That I'm good.

We hardly saw each other, in fact. I would get up very late, usually around noon, and eat whatever I found. Then I would shut myself up in the study until dark; I would come out for dinner and we would eat what she'd made. Then I would go out to play, and I would come back early the next morning.

Mostly I played baccarat, because there my past was predetermined. Once in a while it could change, but it felt more solid than the crazy mayhem of the dice in the shaker, better than the blind senselessness of their flight before they came to rest on the green felt. My heart would tumble more than the dice when I shook the cup and turned it over the table. You can't bet on chaos. And not because you can't win, but because it's not you who wins, but the chaos that allows it.

In baccarat I saw a different order, analogous to the phenomena of this world, because that other world, the one in which the opposite face of every present moment is utter chaos, and in which the chaos, reinitiated, could erase all the present moments behind it, just like that, seemed horrible to me. That's what I felt whenever I shook the dice. In baccarat, my eyes could follow every movement the dealers made as they shuffled the cards and reinserted them into the shoe. First they would spread them out over the table, and then stack them in piles organized in three or four rows. They'd combine all the piles into a single column, two hundred and sixty cards, five decks in all, and drop them into the shoe. Then the game would start. First you had to think about the cards in the shoe. In baccarat, when the player is dealt a five—made up of a face card and a five, a three and a two, a nine and a six, or any other combination—he can choose whether or not to hit in order to improve his score. If the player hits, the entire makeup of the shoe changes. Before, I said that in baccarat I had a predetermined past. But it's probably better to say I had a predetermined *future*. Objectively speaking, the cards in the shoe are actually a past. For me, ignorant of their arrangement, they become the present and then the past as they are dealt, two at a time. At that point they become the future. And the player's decision when he lands a five—hitting or standing—changes the cards. But the present is necessary for that change to take place.

So the dealer's shoe, its cards arranged in a way that could be completely reorganized by a subjective decision to take a single card, is at once a predetermined past and a predetermined future, and at once determined and changeable according to the player's decision to hit on five or stand.

Every hand was the present, but with the shoe there in the middle of the table both the past and the future were also the present. The three coincided. All three overlapped on the table. Once played, the two cards from that hand moved to a pile of cards face up next to the shoe, the cards that had been used in previous hands. They formed, in this way, another past. Several relative pasts were thus formed: the past of the discards piled face up next to the shoe; the past in the shoe, which was also the future; and the pasts of the rearrangements suffered by the shoe according to the gambler's decision to hit on five or stand.

Several futures coincided as well: the future of the shoe as initially arranged, as well as every future determined by the player's decisions to hit on five or stand. Because the decision to hit was always present, always future, until the decision to hit, standing, you could say, was also a rearrangement.

Every hand was thus a kind of bridge, a crossroads where distinct pasts and futures were exchanged, and where, at its center, all the presents were collected: the present of the current hand, momentary, transitory; the present of the past of the pile of discarded hands; the present of the past of the shoe as it had been arranged initially; the present of the past of the shoe, now that, objectively speaking, the shoe was both a determined past and a determined future, and at once a past and a future from which rearrangement could be dealt.

And with each hand the different pasts and futures would coalesce and intermingle: for example, the first four cards dealt, two to the player and two to the banker—which could reach as many as six each if the player and the banker failed to reach the minimum score (four)—belonged to the past, or the future, of the dealer's shoe: they originated from the two hundred and sixty cards stacked up inside the shoe and nowhere else. And the pile of cards face up next to the shoe consisted of cards that had originated in the shoe, and which had briefly been the deal—that absolute, coalesced present, which my eyes had seen on the table. A narrow relationship, therefore, unified all the states.

Also present were the precedent chaos, the coincident chaos, and the future chaos. The three coincided, actively or potentially. The precedent chaos coincided with the organization suffered by the cards in the shoe, and rematerialized as the coincident chaos represented by the cards that were piled face up next to the shoe, which it coincided with. And this chaos would undergo a transformation similar to the first—when the dealers shuffled the cards, organized them into several even piles, and combined them, ultimately, into a single column of two hundred and sixty cards before dropping them into the shoe. The precedent chaos was

104

present in this act, as the organization of the shoe was determined by it. The future chaos, at once active and potential since it took shape from the chaos of the cards piled face up next to the shoe—and therefore consisted partly of this chaos and could only come from it—would ultimately be indistinguishable from this—the precedent—chaos and from the coincident chaos, since chaos is in itself √ indistinguishable and essentially singular. Each chaos was also the future chaos, and the arrangement of the cards and the transitory present of the deal were also part of the future chaos, since they would soon become it. And the three mutually coincident states of chaos, meanwhile, were coincident with the arrangement of the shoe, the present of the deal, and all the intersections of the past and the future that had been, were, or would be coalesced in it.

Each time the shoe resets, having passed through the original chaos in which the dealers' distracted hands spread the cards in random piles over the table, a new arrangement is produced. As many possibilities for its arrangement exist as there are possibilities for arrangement among the two hundred and sixty cards, each one a fragment of the original chaos submitted to an organization by the reflexive movements of the dealers' hands. As I see it, no arrangement could be identical to another, and even if in two of the arrangements the cards fell in the same order, the first arrangement still wouldn't be the same as the second, and for this reason: it would be, in effect, *another*. On the other hand, it wouldn't *seem* the same. There wouldn't be a way to verify it. The task—a tedious and hopeless waste of time—would be dismaying from the start. And in any case, only the initial arrangement would resemble the other's. Which is to say, only a given pathway or portion of the process could resemble a pathway or portion of the process of the other arrangement.

Because the other pathways or parts wouldn't be the same. For that to happen, the following similarities would have to occur:

first, the way the dealers shuffled would have to be *exactly the same* both times, and the way the cards were arranged would have to turn out exactly as before. A five of diamonds that appears in the shoe between a three of diamonds and an eight of clubs would need to come to occupy this location by the same itinerary as before—above a four of spades and a king of diamonds, under a queen of clubs, between an ace of hearts and a two of hearts, for example—something which, of course, is impossible to verify.

Also: every player dealt the five would have to choose the same in every case in each of the arrangements. Bearing in mind that there are players who tend to stand, and players who tend to hit sometimes and other times not, and players who tend to follow their gut when the cards are turned over, the possibility of repetition becomes practically impossible.

Finally: the pile of cards face up next to the shoe would have to be a arranged in the same way as the pile formed by the discarded hands of the previous arrangement. But that arrangement, because no one controls it, is impossible to verify.

In baccarat, ultimately, repetition is impossible.

The cards themselves are also particular. They're at once significant and insignificant, and what they signify isn't always the same. We could say that what they signify varies depending on the context in which they appear. The cards are significant on the obverse and insignificant on the reverse. The pattern on the reverse side, identical on all of them, does not signify anything; or at most one thing: its insignificance in respect to the significance of the obverse. In this way, the insignificance of the reverse signifies something.

The significance of the obverse, meanwhile, varies. The distinct values, one, four, nine, six, zero, change significance according to their location. An ace changes significance if it's with an eight or with a nine. With an eight it signifies zero, with a nine it signifies nine, with an ace, zero. In a way, zero, not nine, is the highest number. Zero is the principal: a nine is a nine from the reference point of the zero—you get nine when the nine incrementally approaches the zero it started from. And the nine, meanwhile, borders the zero. After nine there's nothing, except zero; and zero, after nine, is a complete reset, from which you have to start counting again.

For example, a seven and a six, combined, usually make thirteen. In the game of baccarat they only make three. Counting up, six, seven, eight, nine—I've taken three from the seven, added it to the six, and made nine. After that comes zero, not ten. When I've reached the highest number, nine, the count rests and I go back to zero. I've used four from the seven and have three left. These three start counting from zero and end up at three. Every significance of the obverse signifiers is filtered through the principal signifier, which is zero, the ultimate number in baccarat. It is the reference point for the highest value, nine, and every time the numbers go beyond nine they must return to zero again, erasing everything up to that point and starting over again.

In short, this is the objective aspect of the game. The subject aspect is also important, but first the place where the game is played needs to be described.

It's a long, oval table, with two shallow indentions in the middle, opposite each other, their convex sides facing. Inside these indentions sit the dealers, facing each other, above the players, on chairs raised on platforms. The shoe is located in the center of the table. In some places it moves around from one player to another, passed to the right as the player finishes the round. Here it stays in the center of the table, and one of the workers deals the cards from the shoe, first one to the player, then one to the banker, then another to the player, and then another to the banker. The player receives his two cards first, and doesn't know what the banker has drawn. The whole game takes place on the table, around which, at the perimeter, the players sit. Everything that happens beyond the table, in the space surrounding it, does not affect the game. The cards are turned on the table. This is the place where the game is played. In the city, on any night, eight or ten baccarat tables are active in different places. What happens in one place, at one of the tables, bears no significance on any other. Every place is self-contained, so to speak. Even when two tables are pressed together, what happens at one doesn't signify anything for the other. Each table has its own order of events with their own rhythm, duration, value, and significance.

Someone observing three tables at once would notice these different states. Even if they were to start and end at the same time, the development would be different. After the first hand, the three would be at different points of development. At the first table, a delay in the betting, just as an example, would slow down the game. At the second, a tie slows things down. At the third, a quick game, in which either the player or the banker are first dealt either an eight or a nine—what's called a *natural*—and no further cards are drawn, would have the third table already dealing the second hand while at the first table the first hand hasn't even been dealt and at the second the tie has forced the players to bet again.

If I were betting at two different tables, on the player, let's say, the score at one table would have no value at another, and vice versa. Therefore, viewed from the outside, the space where the rules of the table don't apply, the internal significations are completely erased.

The table, on the other hand, despite resembling a gaming table, has no significance and no development until the shoe is arranged according to the process I described earlier. Before the cards are drawn from the shoe and reveal their significance, nothing happens on the table. Nothing is worth anything. Without the fleeting glow of the cards being dealt, being turned, revealing their significance, and disappearing again, the table is blind and inert. It's nothing in and of itself. It's just there, and that's it.

What remains is the subjective aspect of the game. There are complications, and the only real relationship is between the player and the deal, once the deal has taken place. The rest is pure speculation.

This relationship between the player and the cards has two stages: the hypothesis and the verification. Let's say that as regards the human faculties, the hypothesis corresponds to what they call imagination, the verification to what they call perception.

The player should bet according to his imagination. He bets on the chance that what he imagines, which could happen, happens. He apprehends the hand as it sets up, not as it happens. But once the cards have been arranged in the shoe, the hand has already happened. It could rearrange itself, if in the previous hand the player was dealt a five and asked for another card, but that transformation of the shoe's internal arrangement always precedes the moment of the player's perception of it. If the gambler sees that the player has asked for a card after getting a five, he knows that some change has occurred, but he doesn't know what.

Evidence, meanwhile, in baccarat, is an accessory to the event, not the event itself. It is, furthermore, subjective. The thing is actualized and only then perceived, but it was no less real while it was hidden. The hand doesn't change because I perceive it. I'm the one who changes. When it disappears back into the undifferentiated pile stacked at one side of the shoe, I retain the evidence of the thing itself and also the evidence that it had remained hidden and yet real, having been prefigured before I perceived it. It manifests, therefore, a duplicate evidence.

The gambler can only perceive the hand as it is dealt. The most he can do is realize that all that is real to him is a delayed

109

perception of the event itself. But despite this the hand means nothing to him as it is dealt. He must either bet blind or invent a system to keep track of a given number of hands.

During the game itself many different things can happen, within a strict set of possibilities. This rigid, generic structure determines that each hand can only go to the punto or the banco, or it can push. If it's a push, a tie, the hand is dealt again. It's like nothing happened. In reality, something has happened, but I act like nothing happened simply because no one has won or lost. Ultimately, the better's interest shifts depending on what happens, and he assigns each outcome a different value.

The other factors of interest to the gambler are the punto and the banco. He bets on either of the two, according to his inclination. Let's say he bets a thousand pesos on the punto. If the punto gets the highest score, he, the gambler, wins. The best score is the one farthest from zero, or, to put it optimistically, the one closest to nine.

What makes a gambler bet on one and not the other? The reasons a gambler bets on one and not the other can be separated into two classes: first, irrational reasons; second, rational reasons.

Let's take my case: when I make an irrational bet, it means I've bet based on some kind of feeling. Emotional factors can play a large part. I don't like the guy playing the banco, so I play the punto. Or I'm determined that it will turn out banco, and I feel sure it will. I play the banco. I owe a favor to the guy who holds the cards for the punto. That makes me play punto. I have a habit of chasing the winner. If the guy who's winning has just dealt four hands to banco, it follows, I think, to play the banco, so I play banco. Punto or banco can take the trick, or it can push. There's no other possibility. If my emotions have controlled the reasons for my best, I've therefore made an irrational bet.

Let's move on to the rational reasons. I set up an ideal system for the hands: if punto has been taking it, it will keep doing so, and I should bet on a string of puntos. When it goes to banco, I bet on a string of those. If it goes punto then banco, punto then banco, and so on, I play what's called a chop, and trade off betting punto then banco. If I see that it's going two puntos and two bancos, I play twice on punto and twice on banco, and so on.

There's a second rational reason to bet—on banco let's say. If the punto takes ten tricks in a row, then logic dictates that a banco will follow. Odds favor it, because the overwhelming imbalance of tricks suggest a limit to the string. And so, after the tenth hand to punto, I bet banco.

My reference point is always the past. Each hand, while prepared at the edge of the future, turns, ultimately, toward the past ✓ as it crosses the fleeting horizon of the present evidence. Each present is unique. No present repeats itself. It could, in the end, resemble a different present that's now confined to the past, could bear some resemblance to it. In the last hand the banco beat the punto nine to six, so we think the same thing will happen in this hand. Twenty tricks have gone to punto, and in the past, or our experience of it, strings of punto have tended to be cut short at some reasonable figure by the banco, so in this string of puntos, which is already at twenty, a completely insane number, reason says a banco will cut short the string.

If it's gone to banco twice, logic tells us that, necessarily, it should again. It's gone four hands choppy, so we're sure it'll go four more.

These are the rational reasons I bet with at baccarat. But we already know that repetition doesn't exist. What exists, ultimately, is resemblance, simulation. And because of this, after twenty con- ✓ secutive hands to punto, it could go twenty more, or thirty, or

111

fifty, a thousand, a million more hands to punto. Ten generations of dumbfounded players could observe, passing the phenomenon down from father to son, a string of puntos that lasted a thousand years. This wouldn't stop a rational player from betting banco. And it could happen that after the string of a million tricks to punto the rational player finally learns from his experience, plays punto, and just then they deal the provident hand to banco that they've been expecting for ten generations.

In a choppy game I'll play a punto after a banco and a banco after a punto. But this doesn't mean that a banco can't follow a banco, or a punto follow a punto. I see that a punto game is taking shape and so, shifting around, I'll play punto, which itself doesn't prevent the banco from taking it again and reinitiating the chop. That I can follow a game for ten hands doesn't mean that the past is repeating itself, only that my sense has overlapped with reality. Like if I fire a shot into the air without looking up and a wild duck falls at my feet.

The examples above demonstrate that, in baccarat, all my reasons for betting, the rational ones as well as the irrational ones, are all irrational.

The singular aspect of the game is its complexity. It precludes all rational behavior, and I'm forced to move through its internal confines with the groping, blind lurch of my imagination and my emotion, where the only perception available to me passes before my eyes in a quick flash, when it's no longer useful because I've already had to bet blind, and then disappears.

In this respect, all the bets in baccarat are bets of desperation. Hope is an edifying but useless accessory.

The extent of experience is not brought to bear. Every flash of evidence is separated from every other flash of evidence by an abyss, and the relationship between them exists outside the reach of our comprehension. I don't mean to say that there isn't a relationship—simply that we can't know it. Every bet is desperate because we gamble for one single motive: to see. We leave everything we have at that place where the spectacle is manifest because, although it's no longer useful, we are curious to know, to see what was concealed at the moment we bet. If reality overlaps with our imagination, we're awarded a pile of excrement: money. It's perfectly natural to walk away from a cesspool with our uniforms covered in shit.

On March first I called Delicia to the study. I told her I was going to pay her monthly salary. She didn't say anything to me. She just picked the bills off the desk and went back to the kitchen. She couldn't have been more than two months over fifteen. These days she was having to wear shirts with a bit more room in the front, and her skirt bulged out in the back. I stayed at my desk the rest of the day, writing my seventh essay: *Doctor Sivana and Modern Science: Pure Knowledge or Compromised Thoughts?* At dusk I went out to the kitchen.

It was hot. Delicia had finished cleaning and was looking out at the rear courtyard through the screen door. She asked me if I wanted to eat something, and I said it was still too early. Then I asked her if she had an idea what she was going to spend her salary on. Nothing, she said. Delicia, I said, Would you do me a favor and loan me those three thousand pesos until tomorrow? She didn't say a word; she went to her room on the second floor, an attic, and came back with a tea tin. She stood next to the stove and opened it.

There was a pile of thousand-peso bills inside. She counted them, one by one, stretching them out, because some were rolled up and others balled up. She piled them up in a stack and then counted them, wetting her index and thumb with the tip of her tongue beforehand. It was fifty-four thousand pesos. She had worked for eighteen months without spending a cent. She'd been wearing my wife's old clothes, which had been left in her bureau since the day she died, without me touching them. I supposed she had on her bra and underwear too.

She held out the pile of thousand-peso bills and told me to use what I needed. I asked her how she had managed to live for two years without spending even ten cents, and she said that wasn't true, that she had brought seven hundred pesos with her from her last job. Then I thought back and remembered that in those eighteen months she hadn't gotten sick, she hadn't gone anywhere but the corner store to buy groceries, hadn't talked to anyone but me, unless they were the butcher or the baker, and hadn't listened to the radio or read a magazine (she didn't know how) or done anything outside of cleaning the house during the day or staring out at the courtyard through the kitchen window in the afternoon. I asked if she didn't need the money, and she said no. So I told her ten thousand should cover me and I gave back the rest. She handed me the tin with all the money and told me to keep it in the desk and go on putting her three thousand in there every month.

Then she made dinner. We didn't exchange a word during the meal. When I got up, I passed by her and rubbed her head. The most beautiful creature in the world lives in this house, I said, and went to play.

I lost the ten thousand, and ten thousand more that I promised to pay back the next day. I got up at two in the afternoon and went straight to my desk, read a full Captain Marvel comic, marked up the most important frames, and then sat down to write. It was even hotter than the day before. My eyelids felt heavy, and my shirt was sopping wet and stuck to my back. I fell asleep at my desk. When I woke up it was getting dark. I took a shower and went out to the kitchen. Delicia was sitting in front of the screen door. She was looking at the dark stains in the tiles of the passageway, the stains that even she hadn't been able to erase, the everlasting remains of the my grandfather's brown spit stains.

Delicia, I said. I've decided to teach you how to read and write. Every day at this time, we'll have a class on reading and writing. Does that sound good? She said it sounded good. Alright, Delicia, I said. Let's get to it, then. I went to the desk, brought back a notebook and some pencils, and put them down in front of her. I had to show her how to hold a pencil. With large, neat netters, I drew more than wrote the full alphabet. Delicia watched the traces I left on the lined paper. Then I drew a separation line below, and, skipping a line, wrote the letter A. This is the letter A, I said. Fill two lines with the letter A. While I'm doing that, said Delicia, go and shave.

It had been three days since I had shaved. I went up and shaved. When I got back, Delicia had filled two lines with the letter A. Some were unrecognizable. Nobody would have said they were the letter A. They didn't seem like a letter of any kind. Then I drew the letter B. This is the letter B, I told Delicia. Now fill two lines with this letter. Delicia leaned over the notebook and started writing, with great application and extreme care, the letter B. There have been times that I've bet fifty thousand on a card, when it was my last fifty thousand. And I never wanted my card to come as much as, at that moment, I wanted Delicia to be able to draw the letter B. She stuck out her tongue and bit on it, and she was bent so far over the notebook that I thought that from one moment to the next she going to crush her face against the scribble-covered page. Finally she drew the first one. It must have taken her at least a minute to do it. A minute or more. But finally she wrote it. And then she started filling two lines with the letter B. I figured I had time to take a walk to the other end of the city, and when I came back the next day I would find her there still filling out the two lines with the letter B.

Then I told her that was enough for one day and to make dinner. During the meal she asked me if I wasn't going to give her homework, so when we finished I drew the letter C, left two blank lines and then drew the letter D. I told her to fill two lines with each for tomorrow.

I went to the desk, took out the forty-four thousand pesos that were left, and went to play. I paid the ten thousand I owed and lost the other thirty-four thousand. That night I didn't get credit, so I left early and went to bed. Early the next day I went downtown and negotiated a mortgage on the house. When I left the estate agency, I ran into Carlos Tomatis outside the Banco Provincial. He was talking with a lottery vendor. He shook my hand and asked if I played the lottery, and I said I didn't bet against the Lord.

You're looking thinner every day, Sergio, he said.

I told him that could be his subjective opinion, because he looked fatter to me every day.

He said it was possible. Then he said that God had nothing to do with luck, that the New Testament said that God could see every hair on every last person. And not one at a time, he said, but all at once, and at the same time, one at a time. I told him that was frankly terrifying, that I couldn't imagine God looking at him so closely. But that in any case God had the disadvantage of not being able to play the lottery. I've been chasing two forty-five for over a year, he said then.

I told him that for my part I was tapped out. And that I had just mortgaged my house.

All the better to put the arm on you, said Tomatis.

Then we went to a café for a bite. Tomatis insisted on going to the bar at the arcade, so we walked there. We turned north up San Martín. The province of chance is the devil's kingdom, Sergio, you have to understand that, Tomatis said as we walked.

116

Sergio. It's strange, I said. It's been months since anyone called me Sergio.

We should see each other more often, said Tomatis.

At the bar he asked me if I had written any more essays.

I'm writing one now, I said. I told him about my work on Sivana. Tomatis offered the theory that next to Sivana, Captain Marvel was a secondary character. That Superman had already exhausted the line.

I told him that he was partly right and partly not. If you examined the issue from an ideological perspective, I said, he could have a point; but still, Superman's powers had a certain antihuman flavor. The fact that he comes from Krypton already makes him a beggar at a banquet. It precludes the human possibility for change, I said. Captain Marvel, meanwhile, lives up to the name. He's the apotheosis of the power of the word. It's the magic word, *Shazam*, that allows him access to his powers. It doesn't matter that the word itself is meaningless. At the beginning of language, no word means anything. *Shazam* is at once a magic word and all words. In that sense, Captain Marvel is a symbolic character.

And so what's with Sivana, asked Tomatis.

Sivana represents modern science, I said. The anxiety of power concealed behind the narrative of pure science. In the title I add the question, *pure science or compromised thought?* The thesis of the essay is that Sivana pretends to be a pure scientist, but to be a pure scientist is, in effect, to be compromised. It's an ideological alibi.

Intelligent, very much so, said Tomatis. Then he added that he had been quoting.

We had a bite to eat, and then another. After paying for the food, Tomatis took a five thousand peso bill from his pocket and held it out. He said it was from what he owed me, but as far as I knew he didn't owe me anything.

We separated outside the Casa Escassany, just as the clock struck one. I told him to call me some afternoon, that when the essay was ready he had to read it. He said he would and then he left for the paper.

It was even hotter than the previous days. It was a murderous sun. The rows of houses didn't cast an inch of shade. At a grocery I bought some grapes and then went home. When I got there Delicia asked if I wanted to eat, and I told her that's what the grapes were for. I put them in the freezer so they would get really cold, then I washed my face and went to my desk. I sat for ten minutes reading a few issues of Superman, because the conversation with Tomatis had left me with a few questions. Then I called for Delicia. When she came in, I told her to sit down. My face felt like it was burning, and not from the heat.

Delicia, I said. I gambled your fifty-four thousand pesos, and I lost them.

Delicia was silent. I thought I noticed an expression, something like surprise, on her face. I thought that maybe she didn't know that I gambled, and that I should have told her before asking for the money. But she didn't say a word.

Yes, Delicia, I said. I lost every cent of it.

You had bad luck, said Delicia.

Very bad luck, I said.

Now you don't have anything else to bet? said Delicia.

I've got five thousand pesos, I said. A friend loaned it to me. But I'm not planning to gamble them, but to put them in your savings tin.

I opened the tin, took the bill from my pocket, and dropped it in. Then I closed the tin.

Don't do that, she said. Bet them.

You want me to play the five thousand pesos after I lost all your savings? I said.

I gave them to you thinking you were asking so you could bet them, said Delicia.

So she did know I gambled. She must have overheard a telephone call, because as far as I knew no one had stepped foot in the house since she'd come to work for me. She'd cleaned the entire house except the dark, indelible stains from my grandfather's brown spit, charging me the miserable sum of three thousand pesos a month, without spending a cent for eighteen months, and then she had given me all her savings so I could lose it in two hours. I got up and kissed her forehead.

God bless you, I said. God bless every hair on your head, and may He keep you in His glory for all eternity.

Delicia laughed, and then she said she was going to take her siesta. I told her to eat some grapes, that I had bought them for her, and told her not to polish the door handle, that it wasn't worth it. It's pointless work, I said.

Delicia said that it wasn't pointless for everything to be clean, and she left. I heard the sound of the freezer opening and then closing. I sat down to work. I reread all my copies of Superman, and then marked up frames from Captain Marvel. Then I dug through the filing cabinet and took out the complete Mary Marvel series. Translated onto a female character, the story lost its appeal. Mary Marvel, with her American co-ed attitude, didn't inspire any respect. A dyke, I suspected. Then I started wondering if Clark Kent and Lois Lane slept together. For hours I thought about Superman's sexuality without reaching any kind of conclusion. Clark Kent showed obvious affection for Lois, but it wasn't clear to me if that affection went as far as sexual attraction. In the end, without knowing why, I decided it didn't.

At five, Delicia brought me a bitter *mate*. She knew that I drank one at that hour, but she'd never brought it for me before. I took a sip, and then told her I was three days late sending the bimonthly letter to her mother, and asked if she wanted me to say anything. I assumed the recent events would lead to a change in the content, which for eighteen months had been, That I'm fine, but she said the exact same thing. Then I told her to leave the kettle and the *mate* and I wrote for an hour.

That night we took on the letters E and F. Delicia was writing somewhat quicker, and the rows of letters were getting straighter and the letters more alike. Then I ate and went out to play.

I had the five-thousand-peso bill balled up in my pants pocket. When I got there, the game had just started. A crowd of people stood over the table, above the heads of the players sitting in the front row. I made a space behind one of the workers and started observing the game. To catch up, I looked at the note pad of the player sitting to the left of the worker. Two bancos had just turned over. I thought it had to go banco again, but I didn't play, and it turned out punto. I squeezed the bill inside my pocket into an even tighter, flatter ball. My hand was sweating, and the bill's hard, crisp consistency gave way to something soft and damp.

I told myself that if I could change my luck with those five thousand pesos I would cancel the mortgage.

The next hand went to banco. Logic told me the following: a game of two bancos and one punto is taking shape. One more banco has to turn over before the next punto. If it goes banco in the next hand, in the one after I should play punto.

When it went banco, as I had calculated, I changed the five thousand bill for five red chips of a thousand. I put three on punto, and a third banco turned out.

So the two bancos and one punto game had been broken up in favor of the banco. I put the two thousand-peso chips on banco, and it came out banco. I cashed in the four thousand and waited.

Two more tricks went to banco. Six bancos had now been dealt. That was too many bancos. In my judgment, it made sense to play punto. So I played the four thousand on punto, and it came out punto, and I cashed out eight thousand.

The next hand was a push at six. History teaches that after a push at six it goes banco. I bet five thousand on banco. It wasn't a banco, but a push at seven, and historically a push at seven is followed by punto rather than banco, so I took out the chips I had put on banco and put them on punto, and it turned out banco.

Then I played the three thousand pesos on banco, and it turned out banco, so with that I played five thousand on banco, and it turned out banco again. In my hand I had an oval, yellow chip, worth five thousand, and six rectangular, red chips of a thousand. I went to the bar, drank a cup of tea, and returned to the table ten minutes later. I opened a space between the guys who were standing around the table and set myself up behind the worker, leaning toward the table over his left shoulder.

I didn't even glance at the notebook of the guy sitting to the left of the worker. Now I have to play punto, I thought. I played the eleven thousand on punto, and punto took it. The worker handed me a green, rectangular chip, with 10,000 carved into it in gold numbers. Besides that he gave me an oval, yellow chip, and seven red rectangles.

If I get to thirty thousand, I thought, I'll cancel the mortgage on the house.

Punto had to take it again. Something in my heart told me punto would take it a second time. I bet eight thousand, handing the worker the oval, yellow chip, and three rectangular, red chips. If punto takes it, I thought while the cards were dealt, I'll reach thirty with these eight, and I'll cancel the mortgage on the house. Something in my heart told me again that punto would take it a third time. It's nothing but a third punto, it's not too much to ask it to come. There was a push at eight, and then punto took it again. During the push I thought about pulling out the chips I had put in, but something told me I had to be patient, and trust. The worker gave me a rectangular, green chip, with the number ten stamped in gold numerals, an oval, yellow chip, and a red rectangle. In my hand I had two chips with the number stamped in gold, a yellow oval, and five red rectangles. I left the table and went to the bar. I drank a second cup of tea. I took out a thousand-peso chip from my pants pocket and paid for the tea. I took the change and put it in my other pocket.

My shirt was stuck to my back, and my whole face was damp. I leaned over the tea cup and a drop of sweat fell from my forehead into the tea. When I finished drinking the tea, sweating the whole time, so much so that the sweat was running down my face and my whole shirt was a swamp, and I put the empty cup on the counter and paused for a moment, examining the strange shapes formed by the leaves at the bottom of the cup, I had already made a decision, and I went back to the table.

They talk about vices that are solitary and vices that aren't. All vices are solitary. All vices need solitude to be exercised. They attack in solitude. And, at the same time, they're a pretext for solitude. I'm not saying that vices are bad. They could never be as bad as virtues, work, chastity, obedience, and so on. I'm simply saying how it is and how it goes.

I reached the table at the exact moment when the guy sitting to the left of the worker was getting up and balling up his notes. I took his place, pulled out the chips, and set them on the felt, against the edge of the table. I arranged them in order: first, against the edge, one of the ten-thousand, then the other, then the oval five-thousand, and then the four red rectangles. The worker told me that it was my turn on the banco. I bet the yellow oval. My plan was to leave the yellow oval in the box for the banco until it rotted. It meant that, after the first hand, there would be ten thousand pesos, after the second, twenty, after the third, forty, after the fourth, eighty, after the fifth, one hundred and sixty, and so on.

When the punto turned over his cards, he showed a king of diamonds and a queen of clubs. That meant he had zero. I turned mine over. It was an eight of hearts and a four of diamonds. That meant I had a two, two more than ten. They gave the punto a third card, an ace.

I was a thousand meters ahead. I could win with any card in the deck except a nine, which would mean a push, and an eight, which would mean zero (two plus eight is ten, or zero). They dealt me an eight. So the banco passed to the next player, the guy to the right of the worker. I have to get to thirty thousand again, I thought, so that I can cancel the mortgage on the house tomorrow.

I lost four straight bets of five thousand. The first I played banco, and it was punto, the second I played banco again, and punto took it again, with the third I played punto and it turned out banco, for the fourth I played banco, then I hesitated when there was a push, took the chip from the banco and put it on punto, and the banco took it.

I was sweating so much that I could feel drops of sweat around my ears—from the outside they must have looked like tears. Once in a while, a drop would fall on the felt and leave a damp ring before it evaporated. The last four red rectangles hadn't stayed stacked up against the edge of the table, but were scattered over the felt. I would gather them together, without looking at them, and scatter them again. I wouldn't look at them. With the fingers of my left hand I carried out the same operation over and over. Finally I separated myself from them, piling them neatly and sliding them across the felt into the hands of the worker. Punto, I said.

And it went to banco. I thought about Delicia's tea tin, where she'd been keeping her savings for eighteen months, and I decided that there wasn't the slightest difference between her behavior and mine. They were exactly the same. Only one of us changed it for geometrical, mother of pearl shapes of various colors and the other kept it in a tea tin. I got up and crossed the room, toward the exit. On the stairs I put my hand in my pants pocket and felt the bills they had given me as change for the thousand-peso chip. I stopped in the staircase, took out the bills, and counted them. There were nine hundred and fifty pesos. There were still some coins in my pocket: they were all tens, and added up to sixty pesos. I had ten thousand and ten pesos total. So I went back up the steps. I went straight to the cage and changed the thousand pesos, giving them the nine-hundred-fifty in bills and five coins. I asked for chips of five hundred. The cashier gave me two silver-plated circles the size of quarters. That silver-plating was a luxury, because they were *charamusca*—just eye candy. For protection, I put them in my left shirt pocket instead of my pants pocket, like I had done with the others. My heart was beating so hard while I walked to the table that I thought it would make the chips clink. After the first hand there wasn't any danger of them clinking, because I only had one left. I turned around and took a spot behind the worker, playing over his left shoulder. So I was in the exact opposite location from where I had been before.

For five or six hands I didn't play either punto or banco. I didn't play anything. I didn't even look at what was happening with the cards. I just waited for the pulse. I'll let my mind empty out, completely, I'll open the plug and let everything drain out. Everything: memories, desires, plans, reasons. Everything down the drain and into the black abyss, so my mind is left as blank as the blank page where Delicia wrote her first letter. Just so the pulse writes itself, carved with letters of fire capable of blasting through the rock in the void of my mind. If you know how to empty your mind completely, and especially not lie to yourself, and feel capable of waiting, the pulse comes. When it came, it said banco, so I took the silver-plated circle from my shirt pocket and told the worker to bet it on banco. I got back two silver-plated circles and immediately played them on banco. They gave me back four red rectangles. Then I played one on banco and they gave me back two. I played two and got back four. I now had five red rectangles. I was going to bet them, but just then the power went out.

We formed a line at the cashier and exchanged our chips by the light of a propane lamp. I received a five-thousand-peso bill that was so damp and crumpled that I thought it must have been the same one I had exchanged when I got there. Then I went down the stairs, guided by a worker's flashlight, and went out into the street. I crossed the dark city and went home to sleep, lighting my way with matches in order to open the front door and find my bedroom.

The next day, Delicia woke me up by banging on the door and saying I had a call on the telephone. It must have been six months since anyone had called me. And I think the last one, six months before, had been some guy with the wrong number. It was Marquitos Rosemberg. He told me he wanted to talk that morning. I told him to come over, then I hung up and took a shower. It was even hotter than the last three days.

Marquitos arrived a half hour later, while I was eating the last of the grapes that had been left from the day before. He was in shirt sleeves and had a black briefcase in his hand. I realized he was coming from the courthouse. At the estate agent they'd asked me for references and I had given his name. He lived eight blocks from me, but it had been three years since I had seen him. The last time, we'd seen each other on the street. He was on the opposite sidewalk. We smiled and raised a hand to each other as we passed. That was it.

I took him to the study and offered him some grapes on a plate. There weren't more than five or six, and I deprived myself in order to offer them. Marquitos ate them one after the other, spitting the skin and seeds onto the plate. In my pants pocket I had the five-thousand-peso bill, crushed into a wet ball.

So you're going to mortgage the house, Marquitos said when he finished the last grape.

I told him that, in effect, yes.

Proof that you're not well at all, said Marquitos.

I said that yes, I was not well at all. That never, that I could remember, had I been so bad. But that I didn't know of anyone who was any better off than me unless they were insane or had recently passed. Then I called Delicia and asked, if she had time, could she make us some coffee.

Marquitos said he was going to try to find some way to help me. I replied that the only way to help me was to give me half a million pesos.

Half a million? said Marquitos. His eyes opened wide and he leaned forward. The chair creaked.

Half a million, that's right, I said. My house is downtown, it's new, it's two stories. It's worth five million pesos, at least. I'll put it up as collateral. I want half a million pesos, and everything arranged.

Half a million pesos, said Marquitos. What do you want half a million pesos for, Sergio?

To play baccarat, I said.

Marquitos rocked back in his chair, laughing.

That joke, he said, is in poor taste.

It would be in poor taste, I said, but it's not a joke. I said I want half a million pesos to play baccarat, and I haven't said it as a joke.

Of course, said Marquitos.

I've even gambled away my maid's savings, eighteen months worth, I said.

Don't expect them to write you a check for half a million in gambling money, Marquitos said. Or that your good references will get your house mortgaged for that price.

I don't expect anything, I said. I'm almost forty. I don't have children or any relatives. I live in a house that I didn't swindle away from anyone's helpless, paralytic grandmother. Am I or am I not allowed to mortgage the house if I want to?

You're allowed to, absolutely, said Marquitos.

Alright then, I said. So what's the problem?

That game is self-destruction, said Marquitos.

I told him I hadn't given his name as a reference so he could come to my house and demonstrate the great strides made by the Salvation Army. Then Delicia came in with the coffees. Marquitos looked at her. He didn't take his eyes off of her until she left the room.

You gambled that creature's savings away, he said, staring at me.

She gave them to me herself to gamble, I said.

You lied to her somehow, said Marquitos.

I didn't lie, I said. I went to her honestly and asked to borrow three thousand pesos and she gave me everything she had and told me to do what I wanted with it and hold on to it myself.

Marquitos just shook his head and added sugar to his coffee. For several minutes we didn't say a word. Then I looked him in the face.

Are you going to give me the reference or not? I said.

Yes, he said. I will.

Then he opened the briefcase and took out his checkbook.

I don't want anything, I said. You're the second guy who has tried to give me money in the last two days, apart from Delicia. And don't insist, because I don't have the luxury of protesting too much.

You're a rotten *petit bourgeoisie*, said Marquitos.

Better a rotten *petit bourgeoisie* than a healthy *petit bourgeoisie*, I said. A rotten apple is better than a healthy one, because the rotten apple is closer to the truth than a healthy one. The rotten apple is a mirror in which a million generations catch sight of themselves just before they explode.

That aphorism does not do you credit, said Marquitos.

Probably not, I said.

Then I told him that I needed the mortgage arranged as quickly as possible. He asked me if all the paperwork was in order, and I said yes.

I suppose like any gambler you're under the delusion that you have a sure system for winning, said Marquitos.

I don't have a system for winning, I said. In fact, I'm pretty certain I'm going to lose. But I want to play. If I had a sure system for winning, I wouldn't play anymore.

I don't understand at all, said Marquitos.

I don't play to win. If there's money for food and to pay the bills, that's more than enough. Even if I have to use candles instead and only eat once a week, I'll still play. My departed grandfather used to say that the only way to win at poker was to cheat. Clearly, he was a man of a different generation. And one who didn't enjoy the game, in the end. I would even play against a guy who is cheating me, if the scam allows me some chance. I've played poker against three guys that were colluding and were using a marked deck, and I beat them. There's no scam that's worth a damn if you've got luck on your side. So I've opted to think of scams as just a bit of luck for the other side.

I want that half a million so I can have an easy mind for at least two weeks and enjoy the game without having to suffer over where I'm going to get money to gamble if they tap me out from one moment to the next. If I was looking for a good return I wouldn't play; I would get into business or go back to being a lawyer.

I don't think the mortgage can be arranged in less than two weeks, said Marquitos. And only because I'm good friends with the people at the estate agency, and they owe me favors.

I know it, I said. That's why I went there.

I'll try to get it through as quick as possible, said Marquitos.

I'd be grateful if you would, I said.

Marquitos put the checkbook away, closed the briefcase, and stood up. I stood up too. We stared at each other a few seconds, not blinking.

Sergio, said Marquitos. We should see each other more often. We could go out for a drink.

We'd get bored, I said. Then I tried to smile. You're still in the party, I suppose? ✓

I am, said Marquitos.

That's a vice like any other, I said.

Marquitos shook his head again. He turned and moved toward the door. Suddenly he stopped, stood a moment with his back to me, then turned around. His eyes were full of tears. I thought he must have been in pain. His eyes were red, and he was sweating. But no, he was crying. Not crying, strictly speaking, but his eyes were filled with tears.

You read the papers, last week, I suppose, he said, hesitating at every word.

I told him it had been years since I had read a newspaper.

César Rey, he said. He killed himself. In Buenos Aires. ✓

129

Chiche? I said. I couldn't expect anything less from him.

No, Marcos said. It was an accident. He slipped on the subway platform and was hit by a train.

He was drunk, I suppose, I said.

Marquitos rubbed the back of his hand over his eyes. He wasn't crying anymore.

And Clara? I said.

She's back here again, said Marcos.

Then he left. I walked him to the door and stood there, watching him walk away close to the wall, in order to make the most of the shade that was getting thinner as the morning progressed. I stood in the doorway until he turned the corner. I would have gotten teary too, if I had found out that the guy who ran off with my wife got hit by a train and that my wife was days away from coming back home. I would have sobbed, not just gotten teary. Not because the guy had been my close friend, but because my wife was about to come home. We'd had some good times with Marquitos and Chiche, years back. It had been years since I had seen Chiche. He knew the game too, and liked it.

That night, after teaching Delicia a couple more letters and eating something, I went back to the club. I didn't work at all during the day. After Marquitos left I got in bed and slept until it was dark. I lost the five thousand at the club and didn't get a penny of credit. The next day I got up late and went straight to my desk. At five Delicia brought me a *mate*.

Delicia, I said. I've noticed you don't play the radio.

She said she didn't like it.

Are you sure you're not going to start liking it? I said.

She said she was absolutely sure.

I'm going to take it in and have it checked out, then, I said.

So I wrapped the radio in old newspapers and tied it up with some thick twine and went out to sell it. After two hours I had gone to so many appliance stores, and unwrapped and rewrapped the package so many times, that there wasn't any paper left. The pretense of selling it new collapsed, so I went straight to a pawn shop. They gave me seventeen hundred pesos for it. I bought two kilos of white grapes and went back home. I nibbled on the clusters on the way, and when I got there I found Delicia in the kitchen. She was looking down the corridor to the rear courtyard, at the dark brown spit stains left by my grandfather.

They won't come out, she said.

My grandfather made them, I said. And he's dead.

That night, at the club, they gave me three circular, silver-plated chips, and I lost them one after the other. I didn't even have the satisfaction afterward of saying that I had guessed a single hand right. Nor could I entertain myself, on the way home, in the chances I could have had at any moment in the game. I guessed wrong in three straight hands. There was no chance. I went to bed soaked in sweat, but I slept straight through until the next afternoon. It was murderously hot. I took a shower and went to my desk. For two hours I flipped through a complete collection of Blondie that I had been clipping, or had asked to have clipped, from the magazine *Vosotras* over the past fifteen years. Each week I would cut out the whole comic, which was printed on the last page, and paste it to a sheet of loose paper. Then I would add the page to a school folder and archive it. The last issues had been cut, but I hadn't pasted any down. They were stacked between the last page and the cover. There must have been fifty.

Then I sat for hours without doing anything, with all the sheets spread out over the desk. The whole time I stared at some vague point in space, not seeing a thing. Every once in a while I would clear my throat or narrow my eyes, nothing else. At five, Delicia came in with the *mate*. I recognized her dress; it was an old house frock, flower patterned and faded, that had belonged to my wife.

I saw that she'd just showered and combed her hair, because it was wet and pulled back, and a drop of water was running down her forehead. The dress was still too big on her, but eventually it would fit tight.

Delicia, I said. In a couple of days I'm going to buy you a primer.

She said that first she had to learn to read, and I explained that a primer was for just that, learning to read. Then she left. Ten minutes later I started going through the house, looking for things to sell. I found my grandfather's .38 long Ruby revolver. I went out to sell it and got back after dark, with the revolver stuck in my belt. It didn't fire. I went inside and picked up the telephone. I looked up Marquitos Rosemberg's number and called him. He answered himself.

Marquitos, I said. It's Sergio.

Yes, said Marquitos. Just this morning I spoke with the people at the estate agency. They'll have the money for you on April fifth.

April fifth? I said.

Yes, said Marquitos. April fifth. I was just about to call you to let you know. I supposed you'd be waiting to hear from me, or something like that.

Yes, I said. But I wasn't calling about that.

No? said Marquitos. Then why did you call me?

Because of the check you were going to write me yesterday, I said.

What's going on with the check? said Marquitos.

Nothing, I said. I think I need it. How much were you going to write it for?

I hadn't decided, said Marquitos. I was going to ask you how much you needed and then make it out.

Could you write it for thirty thousand? I said.

Thirty thousand? said Marquitos. Sure, I can. Tomorrow morning I'll be sure to bring it by.

No, I said. I need it now.

Now? said Marquitos. I'm standing here naked, about to get in the shower.

I can come by for it, I said.

Marquitos hesitated a second and then said it would be better if we met at a bar downtown. He suggested the arcade. Then I hung up. I gave Delicia her writing lesson and then I left. When I got to the bar it was nine. Marquitos was sitting at a table and he had the check in his hands. There was an empty cup of coffee on the table. The check was made out to *bearer*, for thirty thousand pesos. Marquitos's signature was an indecipherable scrawl.

Very good, I said, when he gave me the check. There's only one more problem: who's going to change it.

That's easy, said Marquitos. Give me the check.

I gave it to him and he went over to register and started talking to the cashier. The cashier shook her head, and Marquitos came back, saying that the owner wasn't there. He stood for a moment next to the table, thinking, with the check in his right hand and a key ring that he jingled in his left. Then he said he would be right back, and he disappeared for fifteen minutes. He came back with three ten-thousand-peso bills folded up in his right hand. While he was sitting down he dropped them on the table. I put them in my pocket. Marquitos was staring at me, with a sort of gleeful, surprised smirk on his face.

If you hadn't been born with such dark skin, people would realize that the summer sun hasn't touched you once. You're very thin, Sergio.

Then he asked me if I had eaten, and I said I hadn't, so he said he'd take me out.

You had something to do, I said.

I cancelled it, said Marquitos.

That was a mistake, I said. We'll get bored.

133

I'll be in charge of the conversation, said Marquitos.

We went to a grill bar and sat down at a table in the courtyard. From where I sat I could see the grill and the cook working the fire and turning the meat without getting too close to either. Each time he finished some task at the fire, he would turn to a sort of counter where he attended the waiters, and every so often he took a sip of wine. I watched him work the whole time. Then I started to speculate whether or not he would take a drink each time he turned around. I tried to guess the moment it would happen: whether after talking to a waiter, after stoking the coals, or after pulling a strip of meat from a hook near the grill, salting it, and laying it on the grill. Mentally, I started trying to guess the exact moment when his hand would reach for the glass, grab it, and take a drink. I guessed right six times and wrong twice. Marquitos asked me what was the matter, that I wasn't saying a word, and I said that I felt great and I was happy we had gone out to eat. In the courtyard of the restaurant, the heat was subdued. There was a kind of breeze, and the smoke from the grill kept the mosquitos away.

Marquitos asked me if I had read Dostoevsky's *The Gambler*, and when I said I had he asked me what I thought of it. I told him I thought it was good. We finished eating and then went downtown in Marquitos's car for a cup of coffee. It was a small car, sky blue. We had a coffee at the arcade bar, but now even Marquitos didn't try to talk. He asked me if I wanted to go anywhere, and I said that if it was on his way to drop me off at the club. When we got there, Marquitos stopped and turned off the car. He said he wanted to se me in action and was coming in with me. I said he would get bored, and he answered that there wasn't any chance it could be more boring than dinner, and then he got out. By the time I got to the foot of the stairs that lead to the game room, I was already sweating. I told Marquitos to wait for me near the table, and I went to the cage and exchanged one ten-thousand-peso bill for a yellow oval and five red rectangles. I put them in my shirt pocket and joined Marquitos. He didn't even hear me walk up: his eyes were glued to the center of the table.

There wasn't a single seat open, and the gamblers were pressed close around the table. I had to stand in the second row and watch the game over the shoulders of the guys who were standing behind the chairs. Marquitos was standing on his toes, balancing lightly, his eyes wide open. I asked him which way the last hand had turned out, and he said banco. So I reached over the shoulder of a guy standing behind the table and threw out the yellow oval to bet it on banco. Then I waited for the hand, and it turned out punto. Marquitos gave me a disheartened look. The next hand, I threw the five red rectangles on punto. Punto took it. I left the ten thousand on punto and the third hand turned out banco.

I got in line, then changed the second bill for two yellow ovals and went back to the table. Marquitos was staring at me. I pretended not to see him. I looked away. For a few seconds I knew he was looking at me, even though I was looking at the center of the table. Then he looked away, stood up on his toes again, and looked at the center of the table. I had the two yellow ovals in my right hand, pressed tight. They were damp. I was about to throw one on the table when I saw Marquitos opening a path between two guys who were standing next to the table, and then he disappeared. I turned my head around and saw that he had just sat down. His pale face had reddened, and I thought he looked slightly unhinged. I leaned in and asked him what he was doing.

I want to see it close up, he said.

Then I threw the two yellow ovals to punto. I went to the cage, changed the last ten-thousand-peso bill for a green rectangle with the numbers stamped in the center, in gold, and went back to the table and stood next to Marquitos, opening a path with my elbows through the guys who were standing behind him. I leaned in and asked Marquitos how he saw the thing.

Darkly, he said. His pale color had returned.

We didn't speak again for at least fifteen minutes. I defended my green rectangle as best I could, but in they end they took it. With my last five thousand I looked for my pulse, but no matter how much I tried to empty my mind for a full, uninterrupted minute, nothing came to fill the space, and in the end I threw the yellow oval blindly. Nothing happened. They took it. Right then, Marquitos turned around and had me lean in. He asked me if I had finished, and I said yes. Then he asked if he could cash a check here. I told him he could. He got up, tilted the chair against the edge of the table, to reserve it, and followed me to the cage. I told the cashier that Marquitos wanted to cash a check. I introduced Marquitos and stepped away. Marquitos said two or three words to the cashier, leaned over the counter, filled out the check, and handed it to him. The cashier gave him ten green rectangles. Marquitos put them in his hip pocket, then looked at me and shook his head, indicating that I should follow him. We went back to the table, and he told me to sit down. His tone made it more like an order. He stood to my right. Then he dropped three green rectangles on the felt in front of me. I looked up and saw that he was staring at the table with a malevolent smirk, but his left leg was shaking, his heel tapping against the floor.

I asked him what he wanted me to play.

I don't have any preference whatsoever, he said.

So I put the first rectangle on punto, and it turned out punto. I left the two rectangles on punto and they gave me back four. Marquitos leaned in and asked me if I saw how easy it was, and then he picked up the six green rectangles and put them in his pocket. Then he walked away from the table. I got up, tilted the chair to reserve it, and followed him. He was walking toward the cage. I caught up to him halfway there and asked what he was doing.

Cashing in, said Marquitos. He reached the cage, asked for his check back, and gave them ten green rectangles. Then he exchanged the last three rectangles for three ten-thousand-peso bills. He put away the check and handed me the bills.

These are yours, he said.

I took the bills and put them in my pocket. I asked Marquitos if he wanted to wait for me or if he was leaving, and he said he was leaving. I walked him out to the top of the stairs and watched him as he walked down. Then I shouted for him to hurry the mortgage along, and I went back to the table. A guy was sitting in the chair I had reserved, and I tapped him on his right shoulder with the tips of my fingers and he got up. I didn't play a cent until my turn as the banco came around, and just as I was going to bet the first ten thousand on banco, the game ended. So I went home and went to sleep.

The thirty thousand from Marcos lasted me about eight days, so around the fifteenth I was tapped out. I had defended it well, but in the end they took it. I didn't even manage to buy Delicia her primer, but we had plenty to eat, and every couple of days I would go to the central market and pick up two or three kilos of the late-season grapes, which are sweet and hard, and are even better because there won't be any more until the next year. I picked at the bunches on the way home from the market and then put them in the freezer. Then I would shut myself in the study. On the fifteenth, at five in the afternoon, I finished my seventh essay. √ I decided to call Carlitos Tomatis and read it to him.

Then I decided to wait two or three more days, but on the seventeenth it was Tomatis who called me, asking if I had gotten the money for the mortgage yet. I told him firemen could show up and tear the house apart and they wouldn't find a single cent in it. And that the mortgage would be paid out soon, on April fifth. Tomatis said that was a shame, and he was about to hang up when I told him I had finished my essay on Sivana and I wanted to read it to him.

One of these nights I'll come by your house, then, Sergio, said Tomatis.

I'm almost never home at night, I said. The afternoons work for me.

He said that sounded perfect, that he would come by and see me some afternoon soon, and he hung up. I stayed at my desk until after dark, then I opened the window wide and turned off the light. I sat in the dark for hours, until Delicia knocked on the door and told me to come eat.

Between the fifteenth and the fifth of April I only went to the club twice, first the night of March twenty-second, after I sold my typewriter. I made a clean copy of my essay on Sivana, and then I went out and sold it. I had used the typewriter seven times in the last three or four years, once each time I finished an essay and typed it up. I would make three copies and file them in a red folder, which I had specially printed for law school. The folder had letterhead printed on the inside, on the right. It said, Mr. Sergio Escalante, Attorney. They gave me eighteen thousand for the typewriter, and it lasted two nights. After that there was nothing left to sell. We ate like birds, if at all. I spent hours at my desk, going over my comic book collection. Delicia would come in at five with the *mate*. Five on the dot. I don't know how she managed to tell the time, because apart from my watch, which was always on my wrist, there wasn't anything else in the house that did. I didn't need to look at the time to know it was five when she would knock and then come in with the aluminum kettle and the *mate* gourd with its silver base. I knew it was exactly five. She didn't show up a minute before or a minute after. No, she showed up at five exactly. I had once asked her to bring me a *mate* around five, that I liked to have some bitters around that time. And ever since then she had never gone one day without knocking on the door at five. By the twenty-fourth I didn't have a cent left, so on the twenty-fifth I sold the watch. I didn't even get a thousand pesos for it. With a few coins that I found at the bottom of a drawer in my wife's bureau, which I hadn't opened since the day she ate rat poison and fell down the stairs, I put together a thousand pesos, which I exchanged for two silver-plated circles that I lost immediately. After that, between March twenty-fourth and April fifth, the autumn came.

It came with a lot of water, but you couldn't call it cold. It wasn't cold until May. On the twenty-eighth I went to the estate agency to sign a bunch of papers, and the employee assured me that on the fifth I would have the check for half a million. When I got back home it was the afternoon, and I found Delicia in the kitchen eating some water crackers with minced meat. She scooped some on a cracker and offered it to me, but I said I wasn't hungry, and I went to the study. After dark I went out to the kitchen. I asked Delicia if there was anything to eat, and she said no. Then I asked if she was hungry. She said she wasn't. I thought for a while, and then I told her I was going to teach her something new. That for a few days we were going to do without the reading and writing lessons so we could learn something else (Delicia had learned quickly at first, but then she slowed down so much that I realized she had lost interest completely). I asked if that was alright, and she said yes. So I went to my desk, took out five French decks, and a few sheets of paper, and a pencil, and I went back to the kitchen.

She learned quickly. The hardest thing to teach her was how, after nine, the count fell back to zero and you started over. Everything else was simple. At first we kept track of our bets out loud, for low sums, but the amounts kept increasing and getting more complicated, so I started to keep track of them on sheet of paper. Delicia didn't watch me write. She just waited for the next hand to come together, and she was fine with whatever I decided the bet would be. After the hand, I would write. I wouldn't write down the partial amounts, one under the other, and then add them up. Instead, I would add them up mentally, cross out the previous number, and then write the new number below it, greater or less the amount of the bet Delicia or I had made, depending on whether we had won or lost. So there were two columns of crossed-out figures along a thin strip of the page that always ended in a legible figure. After every hand, this figure was crossed out, and a new amount would appear below it. We played so many hands the first night that Delicia and I filled up both sides of the page with columns of crossed-out numbers. After that we abandoned the betting and just guessed.

We would take turns guessing. If you guessed right, you kept going. When you guessed wrong, it was the other person's turn. Delicia never guessed wrong. Seeing her predict every hand so naturally, predict even the sum that would win, and once even the suit of the card that would win the hand, and once the actual cards that would be dealt, I remembered Marcos and I decided that it was necessary to be outside the game in order to see it clearly and predict it. But the gambler couldn't be outside. He couldn't make bets that were both infallible and casual. He had to submit to a continuous exercise, from start to finish, without the possibility of finding distance through occasional dissociations. A distancing could work for an isolated hand, which in the larger game or over the course of the life of the gambler meant nothing. To always guess right you had to be always outside. But of course to always guess right meant always playing, and the person who always played couldn't, because of the rhythm of the game, be outside. It was a circle, though the gambler would tend to think of it as a spiral. But no, not a chance. It's not a spiral but a circle.

Finally it was April fifth. I got to the estate agency at eight in the morning and was signing papers until after eleven. The employee would offer me coffee every so often. I would say no. The agency's office, on the fifth floor, looked out over the city, toward the river. Each time I finished signing a group of papers, I would approach the windows and look out at the city. Except for half a dozen buildings that were more than five stories tall, everything was squat. But there was a kind of harmony in all those red-shingled roofs, where the rain endlessly washed countless abandoned objects that had been ravaged by the weather, and between which, every so often, a tiny woman could be seen walking. Beyond these were the port, with its two parallel jetties, and then the river and all the interconnected streams that formed low islands between them. The rain erased the horizon.

At quarter of twelve they called me into the administrator's office one last time and gave me the check. It had my name on it, and below that it said Five Hundred Thousand Pesos. The figure was also written in the upper right corner of the paper, but in numbers. I folded the check, tucked it into the pocket of my raincoat, said goodbye to the agents, and went out into the corridor. When I got out of the elevator on the first floor and began walking toward San Martín, I realized that the banks must have closed by then. I went home and put the check in the tea tin Delicia had given me. I shut myself in the study and didn't come out until after dark. When Delicia brought me my *mate*, I was marking up frames in *Blondie*. Then I picked up a pencil and wrote, in slow, neat letters, *They say that comedy is superficial because it shrouds the features of the tragedy. But in the thing itself there is no tragedy; there is only comedy, insofar as reality itself is superficial. Tragedy is*

141

an illusion. That sounded perfect at first, but when I read it again it's meaning had disappeared. I opened the desk drawer and took out the tin. The check was still there. I spread it out over the page and looked at it for a while. I compared the writing on it to my own. Suddenly, I felt strange. That piece of paper was worth half a million pesos. The next day, I would go to the bank and they would take the check and give me a stack of papers of different colors, some resembling each other, that were also worth half a million pesos. That night I could exchange the paper from the bank for green rectangles and yellow ovals and red rectangles and silver-plated circles. All those geometric shapes would also be worth half a million pesos. But their sphere of influence would be limited. The chips only had value at the gaming table, the check at the Banco Provincial, and the money itself in the country. It's necessary to believe in certain symbols for them to have value. And to believe in them you have to be inside their sphere of influence. You can't believe in them from the outside. A bank teller would scoff and think I was crazy if I brought him the silver-plated circles and yellow ovals to exchange for cash. We imagine that those closed circles, as they trace the perimeter of their sphere of influence, could somehow intersect, but in reality they never touch. When I went out, I found Delicia in the kitchen. She said she had asked for credit from the grocer, in my name, and that they had given it to her. We ate steak and potatoes. Then we played baccarat until the next morning.

For four days, the check stayed in the tea tin, but on April ninth, around two in the afternoon, Tomatis showed up. He said he had come to hear my essay on Sivana. When I finished reading it he said it was good, but that I was poisoned by Trotskyism, and I said I couldn't be poisoned by Trotskyism because I was a Peronist, not a Trotskyite, but then I realized that he had said that just to say something, that he hadn't even been listening while I read the essay. I knew that he had been thinking about something else, and when he spoke I knew what.

He asked me if I had charged the mortgage, and I told him I had, and then he asked me to loan him twenty-five thousand pesos. I let out a dry laugh, opened the tea tin, and showed him the check. Tomatis looked at it, and his eyes got round like twenty-five peso coins. Then he whistled.

Besides that, I said, there's not a cent in the house.

He shrugged.

You could have listened to the reading at least, I said.

He said he had listened.

You didn't listen, I said.

I listened in parts, said Tomatis.

Not even in parts, I said. While I read you were thinking about how you were going to ask for the twenty-five thousand.

There could be some truth in that, said Tomatis.

I laughed, and so did he. Then he said he wasn't in the mood to hear anything unless it was that special snap of ten-thousand-peso bills. Because they have a distinctive pop, different from the rest, don't they? he said. Also, he added, they give off a glow. It's like they're surrounded by a halo. They emit their own light. Wherever they go, that luster follows.

The overflow of the sign's significance, I said.

Indeed, said Tomatis.

We cracked up laughing.

But there's still a problem, said Tomatis. How do I go about getting familiar with my twentieth of that check?

I'll cash it tomorrow, I said.

So at ten in the morning I took the check from the tea tin and changed it at the bank. They gave me fifty ten-thousand-peso bills, which I put in the tea tin. At five exactly, and I know it was five because Delicia came in the study with the kettle and the

143

mate, Tomatis arrived. It was raining. Since Tomatis didn't have change, I had to give him thirty thousand. He said he would pay me back at the end of the month, when he got back from Buenos Aires, where he was working on a screenplay. I said I didn't want it back, but that at some point in the future, I didn't know when, be ready for me to come asking for it.

I don't want excuses when that time comes, I said. If I'm asking for the money it's because I don't have a single cent left.

It's a deal, said Tomatis.

Then it was quiet for a minute.

I'm ready to listen to that essay now, he said.

You lost your chance already, I said. I read it and you weren't listening.

After Carlitos Tomatis left, I went out and called Marcos.

I got the check, I said. How can I get those thirty thousand back to you?

I didn't give them to you so I could have them back, said Marquitos.

I didn't ask you why you gave it to me, but how I can get it back to you, I said.

I can wait as long as you want, said Marquitos. I don't need the money.

Should I come by your house tonight and drop it off? I said.

That's not necessary, said Marquitos. I'll see you soon, in any case.

I told him the sooner the better, and I hung up. Then I called Delicia into the study. I took out six ten-thousand-peso bills and held them out.

Here's the fifty-four thousand you gave me, plus three for March, and three in advance for April, which makes sixty, I said.

Delicia said to keep them in the tea tin. I took the rest of the bills from the tin, then I put the tin in the top drawer of the desk.

It's not locked, I said. Whenever you want to take it, any time, day or night, it's here.

Then I put the rest of the money in the second drawer. It was already dark out. And it was still raining. Later, we ate. When I left the house, it was after ten. I had two ten-thousand-peso bills in my pocket. The night was blurred by the rain. I got to the club and walked slowly up the stairs, and as I reached the table I realized that the game hadn't started yet. Several chairs were open, so I went to the cage and got two yellow ovals and ten red rectangles, then I sat down to the right of one of the workers. I stacked the chips on the felt, in front of me, and asked for notepaper. Just as the worker was handing it to me, two other workers at the table started shuffling the five decks of cards on the felt. Their hands moved randomly, in vague circles, and they took care to shuffle the decks. The two-hundred-sixty striped versos, themselves meaningless, were mixed up under the workers' hands. Then they started making the short piles. Finally, they stacked them into a single pile, and the worker handed me a joker to cut the deck. So, I had to make the first decision blind. I ran the edge of the joker down the pike and then inserted it. The worker reversed the order of the two sections of the deck, divided where I had inserted the joker, by putting the top under the bottom. Then he put the deck in the dealer's shoe and the game began.

The first hand, I didn't play anything. It turned out punto. I didn't play the second hand either, and punto took it again. The third hand, therefore, I played punto. There was a push at eight, and then it turned out punto. I had put in a yellow oval, and they gave me back two. I put them on punto again and won again. Instead of the two yellow ovals, they gave me back two large green rectangles. I waited a hand and it turned out banco. So I put one of the two green rectangles on banco and it turned out banco. I left the two rectangles on banco and got back four. I waited a hand, which turned out punto. Then I put two green rectangles on punto, and punto took it. I left the four on punto, and punto took it again. They gave me eight green rectangles.

I waited. I felt the way Christ must have felt when he walked on water. Just like that. When he walked on water, he understood he was the son of God. But he contradicted his laws. And because of this he was at odds with God. He was God too, but I was only Sergio Escalante, attorney. I could walk on water without God begetting me. Over the expectant surface. In my case, it was just an accident: the waters chose to not swallow me. But we refer to those exceptional accidents as miracles. And we are filled up with awe and rapture.

So I waited, and while I waited, it turned out banco. So I put three green rectangles on banco, and it turned out banco. I left the six on banco, and it turned out banco. They gave me six more and I waited. Banco took it again. I hadn't lost, but it was a bad sign, a fracture in the surface of the water that I had to watch not to step in.

During the hands I waited the game got mixed up and progressed without any order at all. Then a game favoring the banco began to take shape, and when I saw that it was holding up, I played thirty thousand on banco and it turned out banco. I left the sixty and it turned out banco again.

While they were giving me the twelve green rectangles, which had the number stamped in gold in the center, I decided that at the next hand the game would shift, and I put five green rectangles on punto. And punto took it. They gave me back ten. I left five on punto, and they gave me back ten again. My pile of green rectangles and yellow ovals was so big that when I stretched my hands over them, with my fingers separated, I couldn't cover them all.

Now three hands will turn out punto, I thought, then two bancos. I'm going to play five chips per hand, and after the fifth I'll get up.

I won the first three hands on punto, and on the fourth I played the banco. The dealer turned the cards over on the table, and they showed that I had nine. I thought that the banco probably had a nine too. The banco turned his cards over and showed an eight and an ace. After the push, it turned out banco, and then to banco again. Now the whole circle of players was looking at my pile of green and yellow chips. I started gathering them up, and when I had the pile ready, I got up. I was walking toward the cage, with my pockets full of chips and even more in my hands, when I saw a guy standing next to me suddenly turn his head toward the stairs. I turned around. Then I saw that the police had come in.

There were more than twenty, and three or four had machine guns. They surrounded the table and told everyone not to move. A photographer jumped out from behind one that seemed to be the captain and took two pictures, the flashes bursting, one, then the next. Then they lined us up against a wall and called us over one at a time. When it was my turn, they took every last chip and wrote down my name and address. Then they sent me back to the wall.

When I got back, one of the workers was talking to a group of gamblers. He was saying that he would rather walk around with a chicken spider in his pocket than with a promise from the cops. Then they made us go down the stairs single file and put us in a van that was waiting by the entrance to the club. Less than half of the players made it in. The rest waited in the club. They took us to the police station and put us in a room with high ceilings and a wood floor. A guy was typing out a list with our names and addresses. When it was my turn, the guy asked if I wanted to leave anything in the depository. I said I didn't.

When the last two groups of players came, they made them line up and they took their names and addresses. Then they started dividing us up among the stations. I was sent to the neighborhood precinct with four other guys. One was a fat guy with a single tooth, a manager at the Copacabana cabaret. Another was one of the dealers, a guy who didn't say a word. The third was a guy who sold typewriters. The fourth, I don't even remember anymore. We got to the station around daybreak, and they distributed us all over the building because we were supposed to be sequestered.

The guard who locked me in said to knock on the bars if I needed anything. The door to the cell looked out onto a courtyard where there was a water pump. Beyond the wall, I could make out the bare vines on the house next door. The top of the wall was lined with broken bottles. When the guard left, I threw myself on the cement floor and fell asleep. I woke up because someone was shaking me. It was a guard, but a different one from before. He wore glasses. He said that a family member was there to see me and was asking if I needed anything. I told him I would be right out. I followed him to the courtyard. I looked toward the waiting area at the front of the building, but I didn't see any familiar faces. Then the guard came back and in a very low voice told me to wait a moment. I went back to the cell. The bars were open. Then the guard returned and told me to follow him.

I followed the guard through the waiting area and then into an office. An official was sitting behind the desk. He told me someone had come to see me and even though it was prohibited, they were going to let me speak to the visitor for a few minutes. He reminded me that I was meant to be sequestered, so I shouldn't tell anyone that they had allowed it. He called me counselor, so I assumed he must have known me from somewhere. They took me to another room, and Marquitos was there, sitting behind a table, where there was a folded blanket and a packaged wrapped in butcher paper. Marquitos shook my hand and asked me how I was.

Locked up, I said.

He said there was a cold chicken in the package and that he was trying to get me out. I asked him what day it was.

Saturday, he said.

I told him not to bother, that there was nothing to do until Monday, and to tell Delicia.

Don't tell her I'm in prison, I said.

Don't you think that was a stupid reason to get locked up? said Marquitos.

I told him that any reason for getting locked up was stupid. That if he refrained from sermonizing it would make being locked up more tolerable. Marquitos said I looked awful.

I lost my luck at baccarat, some time ago, I said.

I have to admit I don't understand anything about your life, said Marquitos.

I thanked him for the blanket.

Tonight, at the end of the shift, I'll come back to see how things are getting along, said Marquitos.

I picked up the packet wrapped in butcher paper and turned toward the door. I stopped and turned around.

I sincerely regret my inability to allow you the pleasure of taking my place, I said, and then I left.

When I opened the blanket over the concrete floor, a book fell out. I picked it up and saw that it was Dostoevsky's *The Gambler*. I left the blanket and the package and sat down near the door to read it. When it got dark, a light came on. It started getting cold, so I wrapped myself up in the blanket and sat down in a corner, near the light. At around eight, I had finished the book. It talked a lot about greed, ambition, weakness, the Russians, the French, the British. It even talked about gamblers. But it didn't have anything to say about the game. It seemed like he thought discussing it would be a waste of time. Or, like my grandfather, that he was a man of a different generation. The last page seemed to me like the best in the book. Then the light was shut off. When the guard came by I asked what time it was, and he said it was ten. Then he said someone had come to see me. I told him to say I couldn't be woken up. Over night, I woke up several times, freezing. When I opened my eyes the next day, it wasn't raining, and the sun was coming out. It was going to be a pleasant day. I saw the package wrapped in butcher paper on the floor. I pulled off a drumstick and started eating it. Then I knocked on the bars, and when the guard came I said I had to use the bathroom. It was the same guard from the morning before. He asked me how I had passed the night, and I said I had passed it sleeping. Before nine, Marcos arrived. They made me go to the same room as before, where he was waiting. On the table there was another package wrapped in butcher paper and an orange thermos. He asked how I had slept. Sitting up, I said.

I let the girl know, said Marcos. There's café con leche in that thermos.

What did she say? I said.

Nothing, said Marquitos. I asked if she needed anything, and she said no, that she was fine.

She always says she's fine, I said.

Yes, he said. She seems to be one of those people.

Then I told him to stop bringing food, that the chicken would be more than enough.

Don't you want to shave, said Marquitos.

No, I said.

In any case, you won't be offended if I come back this after-noon to see how things are going, right? said Marquitos.

Absolutely, I said. Speaking of which, if you come back, could you bring me two or three comic books? *El Tony*, if possible. And, if you could, a notebook, or something like that, and a pencil.

Sure, said Marquitos. *El Tony*, right?

That's right. *El Tony*, I said.

Then Marquitos left, and I went back to my cell. I poured myself two cups of café con leche and then I closed the thermos. Out of curiosity I opened the second package and saw that it was full of rolls. I wrapped them back up and left the package on the floor, next to the chicken. Then I sat down next to the door and looked out at the morning sun.

Well, the two circles had touched. While I was doubling my green rectangles, they were talking on the phone, were getting ready, were picking up their machine guns, were leaving the station, were getting in their cars, were approaching the club. They were getting out of their cars, going up the stairs, and entering the gaming hall. Just then I was standing up. I had just won the last hand to banco, the next-to-last, also to banco, there had been a push, and three hands to punto. I could trace the internal course of each sphere, backward, and see how they coincided, despite there being no connection between them. By the time they arrived, the raid had already happened. But it had already happened for them, not for us. I had won all the small bets, of ten, of twenty, of fifty thousand. But the biggest bet, the one that wiped it all away, I lost. That was the hand being played that night, and I bet blind against it. And I lost. For a moment, they pierced the surface of my circle, passed through like a strong wind, but that was enough for me to lose everything.

Marcos came at two with the comics, the notebook, and the pencil, and I told him not to come back. I read the comics, but I didn't use the pencil or the notebook.

They let me go the next day, as it was getting dark, after I gave a statement to a judge's secretary. The secretary knew me, and he said he was going to see if he could take care of things. He also said we were all human.

Some more than others, I said.

Probably, yes, said the secretary. When a guy doesn't know how else to bust his neighbor's balls, recommend police work. Don't worry, counselor, everything here is done with the utmost discretion.

I asked him why discretion was necessary.

He looked at me, but didn't say anything. I didn't look away. When we left the station, the manager from the cabaret shook my hand and told me to come see him some night, for a drink. I told him I didn't drink.

I found Delicia in the kitchen, with her notebook open. She had started drawing the letter A again. I told her I had been in prison, and that I hadn't washed my face in three days. Then I went up to the bathroom, shaved, and took a shower. While I was shaving, I had a chance to look at myself in the mirror. Yes, I was much thinner, and my beard was going gray. But to myself I was always the same. Other people noticed the changes, after they happened. I was getting old, sure. It would happen again, completely, until I disappeared. Another guy looking for something solid would feel that sudden blackout and disappear when he'd only just glimpsed the possibility of finding his way to it. I could live thirty, forty, fifty more years. It made no difference. I had reached the point where it was clear that the territory I hoped to map out was utterly indecipherable. From the outside, I was passing like a meteor, casting off a green tail that was extinguished just as it was igniting. A blackout, and everything would be dark. Quick spark, then darkness. I stared at myself in the mirror. That's me, I said. That's me. Me.

Then I undressed and got in the shower. When I went back down, Delicia was making dinner. We were just sitting down when the doorbell rang. It was Marquitos. I told him to eat something and he started peeling an orange. He asked how I was doing.

Are you really that worried? I said.

Terribly, he said.

Okay. Don't be, I said.

There's something self-destructive in all this, Sergio, said Marcos. I'm honestly worried.

There's no alcohol, I said. I can offer you coffee.

I'll take it, said Marquitos.

We went to the study, where I had left the comics that Marquitos had brought to the station. I pushed them aside and sat down. Marquitos sat on a sofa.

There's your blanket and the rest of your whatnots, I said.

After we drank the coffee, he said he wanted to take a drive. I went along. We got in the sky blue car, turned toward the city center, then onto San Martín, drove around the Plaza de Mayo, passing in front of the government buildings and the courthouse, and then turned back onto San Martín, this time to the north. We passed by the corridors of the arcade, and at the corner turned toward the bus station. The post office was ahead, all lit up. Then we took the harbor road, where the palms glowed in the light of the streetlamps, and we reached the suspension bridge. We stopped on the waterfront. We got out and leaned on the cement wall and looked out at the river.

It must be two years since I've been here, I said.

Sergio, said Marcos. You're not even twenty blocks away.

It's true, I said. But I haven't come.

I realized he was staring at me.

There's something—something heroic in this, said Marquitos.

Don't mythologize, I said.

And something–something . . . , said Marquitos.

Stupid, I said.

No. Not that, said Marquitos. Something–

Absurd, I said.

No, he said. Insane.

A swath of light shone on the river, dividing it. A yellowish, jagged band, with black water on both sides. But the water is never the same, Marquitos said when I showed it to him. Neither is the reflection, therefore.

It's true, I said.

He took me back up the avenue. On 25 de Mayo we turned south, and on the round Banco Municipal clock, in roman numerals, I saw that it was twelve twenty-five. We turned on Primera Junta, passing in front of the building that housed the offices of the estate agency. The clock at the Casa Escassany showed twelve thirty when we passed. When we got to my door I got out and told Marquitos to wait a minute. I went to my desk, opened the second drawer, and took out three ten-thousand-peso bills. I took them to Marquitos and handed them through the window. He took them, saying that he didn't need them. Then he said he missed Rey.

Chiche was always a thug, I said.

No, said Marcos. It's something else.

He always needed forgiving for everything, I said.

Who doesn't? said Marcos.

I wondered if that was an allusion to me. Then he turned on the engine and left. After I got in bed I remembered that I had seen a strip of light at the bottom of the door to the kitchen. I got dressed and went downstairs. When I opened the door I saw Delicia with five decks of cards on the table. Next to the decks there was a disorganized pile of cards, face up. Delicia was drawing them four at a time, in pairs, then she would turn over the first two and see the value.

Two days later I learned that there was a dice game outside of town. It was a clandestine game. I got a telephone call from the worker at the club who never spoke. He gave me the address and said the game started at ten. I would go two or three times a week and always lost. Never very large sums. Twenty, thirty thousand. My heart would start beating hard whenever I picked up the shaker and started to turn it over. Chaos was knocking against the leather sides, I knew, and it was chaos that rolled across the green felt in the shape of those two small cubes. Then the chaos would settle for a moment into a fleeting motionlessness, and then the hands of the worker, who never spoke, erased that moment when he gathered up the dice. It was like an insane force screaming suddenly and then returning to a vague sound. I thought about the dice when I looked at the clouds. They took on shapes that lasted a second, and then, suddenly, with an apparent slowness that confused the eye, they changed. I always lost. On April twenty-third, at midnight, in the rain, I took a taxi from the club, went home, and took out three ten-thousand-peso bills. I had already lost three. I went back in the same taxi. The city, through the windows of the taxi, dripping water, dissolved into a mass of gleaming patches. By April twenty-eighth, I had a hundred thousand pesos left, besides the sixty I was keeping for Delicia in the tea tin. On the twenty-ninth, at three in the afternoon, the club worker called me on the phone. He said that on May second there would be a clandestine baccarat game.

I asked if he was inviting me.

I am inviting you counselor, said the worker. But it's a large game. Five people are coming in for it. With you it'll be six.

I said I would go. But he didn't hang up.

Then he said, I should tell you, counselor, that to play you'll have to stake a hundred thousand.

How much? I said.

A hundred thousand, said the worker.

A hundred thousand? I said. Who's going to stake the banco, Rockefeller?

The worker laughed.

Those are the conditions, counselor, he said. I'm very sorry, but those are my orders.

Give me the address, I said.

I can't give it out over the phone, counselor, said the worker.

Come to my house, then, I said.

He arrived half an hour later and gave me the address. I told him to stay for coffee, and he sat down in an armchair in the study. It was two guys from the Rosario wholesale market, who were coming in specially for the game: one was called Capúa and the other Méndez. Then he named three others, from Esperanza. It's a no-limit game, said the worker. The bets are for millions of pesos.

I asked about a guarantee as regards the police, and he said that without guarantees they wouldn't have the game. But that in any case he would call me on the second to confirm. Then he was gone. He left an odor of cologne that I wouldn't get rid of for the rest of the afternoon and the next day. Even after I opened the window it was still there. It felt like the whole house was saturated with it. I watched the rain through the window until Delicia brought me the *mate*. She had on one of my wife's sweaters. It was fitting well now. She asked if I wasn't planning to shave, and I said that it was possible that one of these days I would shave. Then she went to leave, and I said she should stay. She asked what for.

Just because I want you to stay, I said.

She stared at me and I had to look away. Then I started talking.

Delicia, I said. You know that gambling is my obsession. That if I can't gamble, I can't live. I don't know if that's good or bad, but that's how it is. I've been invited to a large baccarat game. With any luck, I could win millions of pesos. I have a few systems, and if they're not perfect, my odds are as good as anyone else's. It all depends on luck. So, from what I got with the mortgage, the last of what I have, there's only a hundred thousand left. Unfortunately, to play in this game you have to stake at least a hundred thousand. That means I can't show up with less than a hundred thousand, but it also means that if a hundred thousand is the minimum, that amount is just enough to get started. I think I need to take a hundred and fifty, or more. At best, anything I could get together from now till the second. And all I can get together between today and the second is the hundred thousand left from the mortgage. There's also the sixty thousand in the tea tin. That's yours. You don't have any obligation to me. I want to borrow them from you. To be honest, if I lose them, it's going to be very difficult to get them back. Impossible, practically. Here's what could happen: they could take the house, sell it, and give me what's left over. But before that could happen, lots of time will go by. Under those conditions, would you want to loan me the sixty thousand? Again, it would be pretty difficult to get them back to you if I lost.

I told you to keep it and use whatever you needed, said Delicia.

I stood up and kissed her forehead.

Little angel, I said. God love you.

So I waited for May second. It rained every day but the first of the month. And on the first, at around nine at night, it started again. I kept busy writing my eighth essay, *Chic Young: A Modern Hero*. I drew mostly from *Blondie*, but used a lot of material from *Colonel Potterby and the Duchess* as well. My thesis was that, bearing in mind the observations he had made about the daily life of the middle class, anyone else would have committed suicide, or at least would have chosen an easier form, the tragedy. As an epigraph I used what I had written a few days before about comedy and tragedy. I spent all of May first writing out a clean copy, and by the time it was dark out I felt euphoric. I asked Delicia if she wanted to eat out, and she said that was stupid, that it was raining and we could eat just as well in the kitchen, as usual, without taking the table into the courtyard. I was about to say that I hadn't meant it like that, but it didn't seem worth it. In any event, she was right.

After dinner I helped wash the dishes. When we finished, I took out the five decks of cards, shuffled them, wrote Delicia's name and mine in the upper corner of a clean sheet of paper and separated them with a vertical line. For the rest of the night we guessed hands, and so accurately that long stretches of time would pass before we changed turns. Next thing we knew, it was morning, and we went to bed.

The next day I was woken up by knocking at the door. Delicia said there was someone asking for me. I guessed it was the worker from the game. I told her to have him wait in the study. I got dressed, washed my face, and went down. In the study I saw a fat man with gray-streaked hair. He had his back to me, and the skin on his neck was dark. When he heard me come in he turned. It was el Negro Lencina. For a second we just stared at each other.

You've gained weight, Negro, I said.

We shook hands.

Luisito killed his wife, said el Negro.

I sat down at the desk and offered him a seat on the leather couch. Then I asked if he wanted coffee, and he said no.

Alright, I said, looking at him. Luisito killed his wife. But Luisito who?

Luisito, said el Negro. Luisito Fiore.

Fiore? I said. When?

Last night, said el Negro, in Barrio Roma. Pumped two shots in her head. He's totally crazy.

I insisted that he have coffee, and finally he agreed. I shouted to Delicia to bring some coffee. Then I sat back down behind the desk.

Two shots, I said. In the head.

In the head, right, said el Negro. He put two rounds in her head.

Thanks for coming to tell me, I said.

I didn't just come to tell you, said el Negro. I came so you would defend him.

I don't practice any more, I said.

I can see that, said el Negro.

Was he still in the union? I said.

He wasn't, said el Negro. He worked at the mill, but he wasn't in the union.

That's too bad, I said.

I knew it would end up like this, said el Negro. I knew. I told him.

He stood up and turned toward the window. A gray light came from the street. Then el Negro turned toward me.

I told him. Always, he said.

I told him to calm down.

He sat back down on the leather sofa. It groaned under his tense, dark body. For a moment he looked so vigorous that I asked myself what the hell he was feeding himself. His eyes were wide open and his graying hair was starting to look distinguished. There was a time when, after a couple of drinks, el Negro would pick up an accordion or sit down at the piano.

Do you still play the accordion and the piano? I said.

Sometimes, said el Negro. He looked at me severely. You used to defend the workers, he said.

Yes, I used to, I said.

They've told me you live off gambling, said el Negro.

Just the opposite, I said.

Then I asked him to tell me about Fiore. He said that he had gone hunting in Colastiné Norte with his wife and their girl. In the truck from the mill. That on the way back they stopped at a bar. There was an argument, and when they were leaving he shot her, twice. I asked if the argument had been violent. He said he didn't really know. He said that he had used the shotgun.

That could actually help, I said.

They're going to give him twenty years, at least, said el Negro.

He'll be comfortable in prison, I said. Much more than on the outside. It's always more comfortable in prison, in a way.

El Negro stared at me. The skin on his face was thick and taut. Two cords curved from the base of his nose, dropped to the corners of his mouth, and died at his jawline.

I never thought I would find you like this, said el Negro.

Come on, Negrito, I said. We go back. Tell me what you can, because I'm not asking out of curiosity.

I asked if Fiore and his wife got along, and he said that they fought sometimes. Normal stuff, said el Negro. I asked if he often went hunting and if the wife always came along and if he always brought the shotgun. El Negro said that it looked that way. I asked if the wife was cheating. He said it wasn't likely and added that Fiore was a drunk. Luisito is a good kid, but I was always telling him, said el Negro. Then I asked how long Fiore had been out of the union. A long time, said el Negro. Things got bad, and worse, and finally he left completely. I asked if he had been sanctioned, and he said no.

Boozing and hunting. That's all he did, said el Negro. Then he asked if I would defend him.

No, I said.

Just as he got up to leave, Delicia came in with the coffee. Another step and they would have collided. When he saw Delicia, el Negro hesitated.

I'm going to recommend a lawyer, I said. Someone better than me.

He didn't move. Delicia left the coffee tray, walked out, and closed the door. I put sugar in el Negro's coffee, stirred it, and held it out. I took mine black. El Negro drank his coffee. His skin was almost the same color as the drink. His eyes were wet.

Mr. Rosemberg, I said.

A comrade? said el Negro.

No, a friend, I said.

Can he be trusted? said el Negro.

Completely, I said.

El Negro sat back down, the coffee cup in his hand. The sofa groaned. I said I would call him, and I left the study. I dialed Marquitos's number and a woman answered. I said it was Sergio.

Oh, said the woman. This is Clara.

Clara, I said. It's been years since I've heard your voice.

Marcos isn't here, said Clara. He went to the courthouse.

Her voice sounded hoarse.

I'll call back later, in that case, I said.

At noon, said Clara. He will definitely be home for lunch.

Alright, I said, goodbye.

Ciao, said Clara.

We hung up. I went back to the study and found el Negro back at the window. He didn't turn around. I approached him.

He's sequestered, I suppose, I said.

Yes, said el Negro.

Then I asked him if he was still at the mill too. He said no, that he ran a domestic soda delivery. He said he had his own truck. I asked if he had a telephone, and he said no, but that I could call him at the corner store. I took down the number and said I would call him at one.

Things didn't used to be like this, said el Negro, looking at me and shaking his head.

I said that, in effect, they didn't. He asked if I was going to the wake for Fiore's wife, and I said no. He said that he would leave me the address in any case, and if I wanted to go to the cemetery, the burial was the next day at ten in the morning.

Luisito is too hard-headed, he said at the door. I always told him.

Then he left. I followed him to the door and then I went back to the study. I stood exactly where he had stood, facing the window, looking out at the rain. The rain wasn't the same, of course, but it was hard to tell the difference. It was the same gray sidewalk, the asphalt pavement, the tree on the opposite sidewalk covered in shining green leaves, the house behind it with the two latticework balconies and bronze railings. The rain seemed the same too.

At noon I called Marcos and explained the case. He said to tell el Negro to come by his house at three. I called the store and asked for el Negro. Ten minutes later, el Negro picked up, breathless. I gave him the message from Marquitos and the address, and then I hung up. After that I got in bed and took a nap. At five Delicia brought the *mate*, and at six the worker from the game called. He confirmed the address and said the game started at ten exactly. I stayed at my desk until after eight, and when I went out Delicia was setting the table. The kitchen smelled like cooking. Delicia had washed my wife's black sweater, which was fitting her tightly now. It looked good. For the first time, I noticed how long her fingers were, and how dark. We didn't say anything during the meal. Then I got up from the table, took the hundred-seventy-thousand pesos from the desk, and went to the game.

It was downtown, around the corner from San Martín. So I walked toward the avenue, turned at the Casa Escassany at nine forty-five, and walked three blocks north up San Martín. I passed the news ticker at the *La Región* building and stopped to read it, but it didn't say anything about Fiore. I turned east on the next corner, walked a block and a half, and crossed to the opposite sidewalk. I didn't have to look for the number because the worker was standing in the darkness, in the threshold to a house. I recognized him by the smell of the cologne. He shook my hand and told me to go in.

I don't know why, but the room looked like a stage set. Five guys sat around a long table covered with a velvet-bordered cloth. Two chairs were still empty. In a corner, a guy was standing over a little wooden table, organizing a box of chips. Behind him, a discolored curtain covered a sort of arch. That was probably what gave me the impression of a stage. The guys at the table had stacks of chips in front of them. I sat down at a corner of the table, with my back to the curtain, and asked the cashier for a hundred thousand. He brought me ten green rectangles. I reached into my pocket for the money, but he said we would settle up at the end. Then he asked if I wanted a whiskey. I said I didn't drink.

The worker sat down at the empty seat in the center of the table and started shuffling the cards. One of the other guys, who looked vaguely familiar, inserted the joker into the stack and the worker cut it. He separated the two halves of the deck, placed the top one below the bottom one, and then dropped the cards into the shoe. Then he opened the auction for the banco.

I offered ten thousand, and the guy who had cut offered twenty. I let him take it. Then I put twenty on punto and waited for the cards. I got a queen and a nine, both hearts. The guy turned over two black queens, and the worker passed me the four green rectangles. I left them on punto and it turned out punto again.

I left the eight on punto and punto took it. I got sixteen green rectangles, and I waited. It turned out punto again, but at the next hand I was on the banco. I staked four green rectangles. The cards were dealt. I had a nine of clubs and a nine of diamonds. The punto only had six. I made three more bancos and on the fourth I passed it. The worker asked for chips, and the cashier brought him a stack of large golden plaques worth fifty thousand. I got ten of these and eight or nine green rectangles. The guy who had cut asked for two-hundred-thousand from the cashier and got four gold plaques. I kept getting distracted, fleetingly, by how familiar he looked.

He staked forty thousand on the banco, and I bet forty on punto. They dealt the hand and we pushed at six. After a push at six it's presumed the hand will go banco, so I thought about pulling out the four ten-thousand-peso chips. But it seemed like a vulgar move, since I was up. It turned out punto.

See that? said the familiar-looking guy. He takes four hands on the banco, passes it, then he bets on punto and punto takes it.

That was all he said. And not to anyone in particular. He was thinking out loud. After that it went four more puntos, one banco, another punto, and then the banco came back to me. I made five hands and passed it. Then I played punto again and it turned out punto. No one else at the table seemed to have a cent left. They all looked like some guy who needs ten pesos for the bus. Then the familiar-looking guy stood up and whispered in the worker's ear. The worker listened for a moment and nodded. Then he asked me if I would take a check. I said I would. Then the familiar-looking guy asked how much I would take a check for. I said any amount, as long as there were funds behind it. The guy said there were, but that it would be a little difficult to verify at that hour. He would have to call up the manager at the Banco Provincial in Rosario, get him out of bed, ask him to go to the bank and find his account book in the safe. I said I would rather believe him than waste a hundred and fifty pesos on the phone call to Rosario. With that the guy took a checkbook from the inside pocket of his jacket, sat down, and filled out a check. Then he handed it to me. I must have blushed. It was for a million. I counted out twenty gold plaques and took the check. He put two gold plaques on the banco and I took the bet.

He made six bancos and then he passed it. Two guys who were totally tapped out wrote checks to the guy who had given me the one for a million. Ten minutes later we were neck-deep in the bloodiest game I had ever played in my life. By one in the morning I didn't have anything left but the hundred-sixty in my pocket, which I owed a hundred of, and the check for a million. So I gave back the check and the guy handed me twenty gold plaques. Then he had to give back a check for three hundred thousand that he had just gotten, and he got six gold plaques. The green rectangles had all but disappeared from the table. We used them for tips.

Soon, the chips were collecting in front of a guy dressed in gray. He had on a gold watch. Its band was too big for him, and every time he moved his arm it slid down to the back of his wrist. He was the one who had taken back the check for three hundred. He made twelve bancos in a row, then it went around the circle, and when it got back to him he made another eleven. Before I knew it, all I had was the hundred sixty in my pocket. I asked for a hundred thousand more in chips and lost them.

I leaned over to the worker and whispered that I was short forty thousand but I wanted another hundred thousand. He said he could give it to me, if and when I wrote a check, for the next day. Not only did I not have a check, I said, I didn't have a bank account, but by the next afternoon I could get the money. Finally, he agreed. I lost that too, paid the cashier, and walked out into the street. A fine rain covered me and I started walking slowly. The rain refreshed my face. On the corner, I stopped suddenly. I had recognized the familiar-looking guy's face. One night, as I was leaving the game, he had asked me for two hundred pesos for something to eat.

I turned around, quietly went back in, and softly crossed the dark corridor. Before I even reached the door I could already smell the worker's cologne. As I was turning the handle and pushing the door open, I heard the worker's voice and then laughter. When I opened the door completely I saw the full picture. They weren't playing. No chips were out. They were all standing, bent over the center of the table, and the worker was distributing my money.

Listen, fellas, I said. You should take this show on the road, in the countryside. They all turned at once but no one budged. I walked toward them. The guy with the gold watch looked at me with a kind of half smile. The rest were mute and serious. Then the worker reached into this pocket and pulled out a pistol. But I didn't stop. He moved to block me.

These things always end badly, counselor, he said. Every time.

I didn't even slow down as I slapped him. I thought of hitting him with a fist, but I didn't do it for two reasons. First, I didn't want to hurt him. Second, if I tried to punch him and missed they would've beat me down until I was dead. The slap had the intended effect, and not slowing down reinforced it. The pistol fell from his hand and the others spread around the table in a semicircle. The ten-thousand-peso bills were scattered everywhere. I gathered them up calmly, counted them, and put them in my pocket. As I was leaving the worker said, These things always end badly, every time.

I slammed the door and in a second I was in the street. The rain covered me again. I walked so slowly that it took me more than half an hour to get home. I entered in the darkness and went to my desk. Then I turned on the light, opened the first drawer, took out the tea tin, and put Delicia's sixty thousand in it. I put the tin back, dropped the other hundred thousand in the drawer, and closed it. I turned off the light and went upstairs. In the bathroom I undressed and washed my face. Then I went into my room, in the dark, and got in bed. As I was laying down I realized Delicia was there, awake, her eyes open, waiting for me. She didn't say a word. When I touched her I realized she didn't have anything on. She was shaking.

They cheated, Delicia, I said. They don't gamble, they cheat instead. My grandfather knew.

Then we rolled around in bed for the rest of the night. When I woke up, it was the afternoon. I took a shower and went downstairs. Delicia was in the kitchen. She was staring hard at the brown stains in the courtyard.

There must be some way to get them out, she said.

I said I wasn't sure there was and went to the study. I didn't do anything. I flipped through my comic collection, but couldn't find anything to focus on. Then I reread my essay on Chic Young. It sounded pretty insolent. At five, Delicia brought the *mate*. Her sixty thousand was in the first drawer, I said, in the tin. She could take them whenever she wanted. I went into the kitchen after it got dark, ate something, and then shut myself back up in the study. Before midnight, I went to bed. Delicia was there. We rolled around for an hour or so, and then I fell asleep. I woke up before dawn. Delicia was asleep. I got up, washed my face, then I went down to the kitchen and made a *mate*. I went to my desk and looked out at the rain until it was light out. The sky changed color. First it was blue, then it took on a greenish tint, and finally it ended up a steel gray that lasted the rest of the day. At eight I looked up Negro Lencina's number and called him. The

167

shopkeeper picked up and told me to hold on. For ten minutes I didn't hear anything, until finally the shopkeeper picked up again. El Negro was at a wake, he said. That can't be right, I said, the wake was the day before. But the shopkeeper said he gathered that it wasn't the same wake, but another one, and then he hung up.

APRIL,
MAY

THE WIPER BLADES RHYTHMICALLY SKIM THE windshield surface, where rain droplets strike faintly from the off-white mass that surrounds the car and thickens at a distance and through which the dripping wet facades appear at breaks in the fog, the two rows of facades moving backward, away, down the narrow, gleaming street. The side windows are steamed over, and looking through them I can only make out blurs moving slowly through the fog, the mass of wet particles colliding, and the thick gray or yellow smudges of the facades. Ahead on the corner a solitary gorilla, wrapped in a blue raincoat, a hat smashed low on his head, so that his face is barely visible, doubles over, coughing. Then I pass by and leave him behind.

I turn on Mendoza, where the sun should be, and the car glides slowly, and I pass the bus station. Several gorillas pace or stand motionless on the platforms next to packages and suitcases. The platforms, open at the back, fade into the fog and the still-present shade of night that contrasts with it, almost blinding. A smooth shade, polished and dense. And the gorillas who shake their head or wipe a hand over their brow or bring a cigarette to their lips introduce a white smudge that disappears immediately into the dark penumbra. No buses are on the platforms, and the closed windows keep out the sounds. I can't tell whether the loudspeakers that announce the arrival and departure of the buses are on, or if the gorillas' footsteps or their voices, echoing over the oil-stained cement and the platforms' sloped roofs, are loud or soft. All I hear is the steady hum of the engine, which varies only when I slow down to take a corner or accelerate suddenly, and then only for a moment, if from distraction I have pressed down too hard on the gas.

I make a left and pass the already-illuminated post office. Gorillas pass behind the windows on the first floor and behind the large counters. Through breaks in the fog I see their torsos moving past the counters as though by conveyer. Now the car's movement, rumbling over the shining cobblestones of the harbor road, becomes less regular. Through the windshield I see tall palms approach me, wrapped in fog, and the poles of streetlamps that end in white globes that emit a weak light, swallowed now by the morning. The tree trunks drip water. The harbor road is completely deserted. The palms and the globes of the streetlamps approach me and then disappear behind. And the damp cobblestones advance toward the wheels of the car, and when I pass over a dip in the road, where a puddle has formed, they make a liquid murmur that blends with the monotone hum of the engine. Briefly the windshield fills up with thick splatters that the wiper blades sweep away, first spreading them over the glass where they struck and then sweeping them to the edges of the windshield, leaving me just enough space to see the road ahead. The clean space on the windshield blurs at the edges, and the drops that fall ceaselessly over it hold their shape for a moment, emitting a highly delicate shining fringe, and then they disappear.

172

Soon I reach the suspension bridge, which I have seen approach me. Its columns, darkened and gleaming from the water, are only half-visible here and there through breaks in the fog. A gorilla wrapped in a black cloak, his head covered by a watchman's cap, is standing outside a gray sentry box. He is completely still, his eyes fixed on the fog. Then he disappears. He is behind me. Then the bridge too. Now the old waterfront extends ahead, its oil-stained asphalt covered with fractures and holes. Now the concrete railing, its endless, weathered balustrade. Every so often, a missing column breaks the uniformity. And sometimes a broken column has fallen to pieces over the enormous gray slabs of the wide sidewalk. From beyond the waterfront I see the leafless, tall poplars approach me and then disappear. The fog approaches, a solid, white wall. The car moves through it, a shining wedge behind which the fog closes again. Now I'm on the new waterfront, wider, without immediate reference points, and for a moment there is nothing but the car and the fog, in a kind of stillness. Nothing but the solid, off-white mass where particles rotate in space, like tiny planets, and the car moving but with the illusion of not advancing through the uniform density of the fog. Suddenly, the decayed top of a tree appears and then disappears, behind me, and for a moment it's clear that I have been advancing, although the return of the complete fog renews the illusion of motionlessness.

By now the gorillas will be leaving their burrows, vacating their foul-smelling nests, examining their decaying teeth in the bathroom mirror, voiding their excrement, looking at the fog through the window, turning groggily in the beds where they've copulated with their reddish-sexed females, with quiet moans and brutal sobs; the females are looking now at the males in bed, hearing them move through the poorly illuminated kitchens as they prepare breakfast before leaving for work. Then they will shut their eyes, curl up between the warm sheets, and fall back to sleep until midmorning, after which they will get up and go out to the market to buy food while the males write incoherent reports on oversized log books in offices with tall ceilings and wood floors. They open their front doors, belch stupidly, look at the fog, and hunch over as they walk in the rain to the corner to wait for the bus. In the bus they plaster themselves against each other, still puffy from sleep, rubbing their fleshy asses and smearing the scent over their faces. They utter broken sounds, shake their heads, open their eyes enormously wide, and make unintelligible gestures with their hands.

The yellow walls of a bus stop shelter pull me momentarily from the illusory stillness, then they pass and are left behind. The first houses on the new waterfront, opposite the river, start to appear, withered and blurry. On the other side, the river has disappeared. At a spot where the waterfront makes a wide turn toward the river I stop the car and shut it off. The silence of the quiet engine becomes more monotonous than the monotonous hum of the running engine; the sound echoes for a moment in my head and then dissolves. I stare at the fog, toward what I imagine is the riverbank. Slight breaks in the fog allow me to imagine that I see the surface of the water. Suddenly, a shining black blur appears and disappears. It reappears and is erased again. Then it reappears and hangs for a moment. I just make out the back legs and tail of a horse. The tail shakes and then everything disappears again. Once again the fog through the windshield is empty. With the stillness of the wiper blades, the glass is covered with tiny drops that leave a thin trace of their impact. I turn on the wipers and again the droplets gather and disappear and the glass is left clean. For three minutes I wait for the dark blur of the horse to reappear, but nothing does, so I turn the engine on again, harshly, and move on.

I reach Guadalupe, drive through the roundabout, and turn back onto the waterfront in the opposite direction. If not for the memory of having reached the end of the waterfront and having gone through the roundabout, there would now seem not only to be no movement, but no direction. No direction, except that I face something—my face, like the front of the car, looks at something—but without the memory of having gone through the roundabout on Guadalupe, I wouldn't know what. Then the tree reappears, fragmentary and wet, above me, the top branches swallowed by the fog; it approaches slowly and is left behind.

I retake the old waterfront, and when I reach the mouth of the suspension bridge—the gorilla in the police hat has disappeared, only the gray sentry box remains—I turn onto the boulevard instead of continuing on the harbor road. I follow the boulevard to the west, and after passing the tracks I see the old train station, a large, brown building. Its walls are wet, and its broad doors and windows are dim. Two female gorillas with identical pink umbrellas exit from the main entrance. A row of taxis is parked on the street, parallel to the immense facade. In some, I can make out the blurred figures of the gorilla drivers. They are barely distinguishable. On the boulevard, the large trees are still and wet. Now there is a bit more traffic, slow-moving cars and buses. When I reach the first streetlight, ten blocks from the avenue, the fog is already clearing. The light is red and I stop instinctively. The engine hums, and the wiper blades, with a regular, even sound, form semicircles as they gather and sweep the water away. The red light turns off, and by the time it changes to green I'm already crossing the intersection. Above me, out of the fog, the gothic spire of the Adoratrices appears. Five blocks later, just before I reach the second streetlight, I slow down to pass the mill. The light is green. I turn north onto Rivadavia. On the left-hand side stands a row of old, modest, single-story houses, and on the right the rail yard wasteland, and beyond that the long wall surrounding the mill, barely visible through the side window. The long, solid wall of un-plastered brick is bowed at intervals toward the rail yard by some cylindrical structures that, seen through the side window, take on insane proportions. Then I turn left again, onto a rough cobblestone street that makes the car frame vibrate and shudder, and then I turn south onto 25 de Mayo. I drive one block and cross the avenue, still south on 25 de Mayo. As the fog clears the streets fill with gorillas. But the rain continues. I pass the Banco Provincial—its doors are open and gorillas hurry in and out. First I see the round clock, its roman numerals marking eight twelve, then the momentary flash of glass in the revolving door as it swallows and spits out the gorillas. Then everything is left behind. Next I pass the Palace Hotel, and at the end of the same block, on the opposite corner, the Monte Carlo bar. To the left is the back of the post office, and beyond that the plaza, and on the opposite side the bus station platforms. I cross the intersection, still on 25 de Mayo to the south, and everything is left behind. On the next corner I turn right, travel a block, then turn left onto San Martín to the south. Every minute more gorillas flood the streets. Some are driving, others stare stupidly from bus windows, still others crane their necks out of their raincoats as they peer from their doorways, preparing to leave. San Martín looks washed by the rain. Washed, but still dirty, since the days-long rains have turned the streets into dark swamps, thick and wet with mud from the shoes of the thousands of gorillas that walk them. Six more blocks and I reach the Plaza de Mayo. I have to wait briefly at a streetlight; the red light keeps me from moving. Then the red light shuts off, the green light comes on, and I turn right onto the plaza and follow the road around toward the courthouse. To my left are the palms and the orange trees, and then the tall oaks, in between which the reddish paths intersect. Ahead, the front of the courthouse approaches. I cross the intersection and turn into the rear courtyard. I park the car in the thin, cobblestone space and stop the engine and the wiper blades. For a moment I wait inside the silent interior of the car, still hearing the fading echo of the engine and the rhythmic murmur of the wiper blades. A uniform sound. Then I pick up the briefcase from the rear seat, step out of the car, the rain on my face, lock the door, and enter the building.

Gorillas move through the cold corridors, in and out of offices. A few I greet with a nod. I reach the wide lobby and start making my way up the broad marble staircase. The steps are still clean. At the first landing I stop and lean over the railing. A number of gorillas are rushing through the lobby, carrying briefcases and large dossiers. Others talk loudly in groups scattered around the vast, squared-off, black and white mosaic. They look like pieces on a chess board. I continue up the wide marble staircase, and when I glance down at the lobby one last time, from the third floor, the figures of the gorillas have diminished so much, flattened against the black and white board, that the chess piece effect is suddenly perfect. Only every so often a hurried blur will cross the board diagonally or vertically. I move through the cold corridor and enter my office. The secretary is at his desk in the waiting room, studying a document. He looks up and greets me, "Early morning, judge?" I respond that it's almost eight thirty and pass into my office. I leave the briefcase on the desk, take off the raincoat, and hang it on the coat rack. Then I open the blinds. A gray light filters into the office. The trees in the plaza, the tall palms with shining leaves and the shorter orange trees whose fruits mar the green foliage, look flattened against the reddish paths. I sit down at the desk, open the briefcase, and take out the novel, the notebook, the pencils, and the thick dictionary. Then I put the briefcase on the floor, next to the chair.

The page is marked with a blank sheet of paper that's been folded several times. When I open the novel, the paper falls on the desk and the book opens perfectly, its two halves flawlessly smooth and docile. The verso page, numbered 108 at the bottom center, is covered with pen and pencil marks in several colors. Some words are circled and joined to the white margin by a nervous line that ends with a word in Spanish or some other symbol. Others are underlined in red or green ink. One of the paragraphs, toward the bottom of the page, is set apart by a vertical, red line that follows it down the left margin. The other page, the recto side, numbered 109, is only marked up to the first paragraph. It ends with an underlined sentence: *Here was an ever-present sign of the ruin men brought upon their souls.* The phrase *ever-present sign* is underlined and circled in green.

Below this, the rest of the page is completely clean. I open the notebook on the desk, next to the novel. The left-hand page of the notebook is covered halfway down with my tiny handwriting, in black. Here and there a phrase is underlined in pencil, or with green or red ink, and some words are enclosed in a tight circle drawn in ink with one of those two colors. The rest of the page is blank, as is the right-hand page, except for the thin blue rules and the double vertical line at the margin. But the writing does not follow the margin or the rules, and the white space between the rules contains two manuscript lines and sometimes the corrections to these. I set the thick dictionary within reach.

I pick up the telephone, ask the operator for the press office, and wait while the line connects. This happens after the fourth ring. I say who I am. The office manager asks what he can do for me. "If the reporter for *La Región* comes by, tell him to come to my office, that I want to speak with him," I say. "Sure thing, judge," says the press office manager. I hang up.

I pick up one of the ballpoint pens from the desk and set to work. The last sentence written in the notebook is the following: *Ahí había un imborrable (perenne) (siempre presente) (eterno) signo de la ruina (perdición) que los hombres llevaron (atrajeron) sobre sus almas.* I turn to the book and read:

Three o'clock struck, and four, and the half hour rang its double chime, but Dorian Gray did not stir. He was trying to gather up the scarlet threads of life, and to weave them into a pattern; to find his way through the sanguine labyrinth of passion through which he was wandering.

In red, I mark the word *chime.* The dictionary says, *armonía; clave; juego de campanas; repique; sonar con armonía; repicar; concordar.* Then I look up *stir.* It says, *removerse; agitar; revolver; incitar; moverse; bullir; tumulto; turbulencia.* I turn to T and look up *threads.* It says, *hilo; fibra; enhebrar; atravesar.*

I put down the green pen and pick up the black. I write, *Dieron las tres y después las cuatro, y después la media hora hizo sonar su doble repique (teo) (campanada), pero Dorian Gray no se movió. Estaba tratando de reunir (juntar) (amontonar) (hilvanar) (enhebrar) (atravesar) los hilos (pedazos) (fragmentos) escarlatas (rojos) (rojizos) de su vida, y darles una forma, para hallar su camino a través del sanguíneo (sangriento) laberinto de pasión por el cual (que) había estado vagando.*

With the red pen I underline the words *campanada, pedazos,* and *sangriento.* Then I get up and look out the window. The rain is falling on the palms and the orange trees, and the reddish paths of ground brick glow. Three gorillas are crossing the plaza. They are coming from different directions: one is crossing at a diagonal from southwest to northeast, another in the opposite direction, and the third from northwest to southeast. They meet at the center of the square, in the wide reddish circle. They walk with difficulty, hunched over, blurred by the rain and wrapped in their raincoats. One of them, the one walking to the north, carries a black umbrella that partially obscures his body. The black circle moved rigidly, contrasted against the reddish path. Then I go back to the translation. I write, cross out, and make marks in the notebook and the novel: crosses, vertical and horizontal lines, circles, arrows. I return to page 109 and then turn over to page 110. The page fills up around its even printing with my nervous, quick symbols: crosses, vertical and horizontal lines, arrows, circles. I write, *Hace dos días le he dicho a Sibyl que se case conmigo. No voy a quebrar mi promesa (faltar a mi palabra = to break my word to her).* I underline *faltar a mi palabra*. Then I write, "*Ella va a ser,*" and at that moment Ángel walks into the office. I close the dictionary and mark my page in the novel with the red pen and close it. Ángel's raincoat is soaked on the shoulders, and his dark hair is a mess. He is very thin.

"I haven't been able to call you," says Ángel. "I have lots of problems at home these days." Then he leans over the desk and touches the book. His thin fingers brush over the surface of the cover on which there is a face—drawn in white lines on a purple field—that covers most of the surface. The face is obliterated by jagged, white lines. Ángel asks if I've made much progress with the translation. "It doesn't matter," I say. "It's already been translated so many times that it makes no difference if I make progress or not. All I'm doing is traveling a path that others have made. I don't discover anything. Whole passages come out exactly the same as the versions of the professional translators." Ángel is quiet a moment, and then he asks if I have sent many people to prison. "Lots," I say. "Have you ever been in prison?" he says. "I've been a few times," I say. "Visiting." He's thinking that I'm not bothered by sending people to prison just because I've never been locked up. "Try to avoid vulgar ideas," I say. "That's just advice. Thinking vulgar things is anti-aesthetic. No one is better off because they're free, or worse in prison. It's not better to be outside than inside. People who are alive aren't happier than dead people. It's all a shapeless, gelatinous mass where nothing is different from anything else. Everything is exactly the same." "They said you were looking for me," says Ángel. "I wanted to invite you over for dinner tomorrow night," I say. "Alright," says Ángel. "Actually," I say. "I wanted to see how you were." "I'm fantastic," says Ángel. "You don't look it," I say. "You look skinnier every day and you have terrible bags under your eyes." "Well I don't spend all day sitting behind a desk judging people," says Ángel. "I have my own life." I get up and brush my hand over his head. His hair is wet. "Don't make bad literature and everything will be fine," I say. He blushes. I ask if he wants some coffee. He asks if it's the same as the prisoners' coffee from the press office. "Not the prisoners'," I say. "But it's the same as the press office." "I will decline, in that case," says Ángel. Suddenly, he stands up and says he's leaving. I follow him to the door, holding him by the shoulders. "You're getting very cynical and rebellious," I say in a low voice. Then he disappears.

I set the briefcase on the table and start putting things away: the dictionary, the pens, the notebook, and the novel, which I mark again with the folded paper after removing the red pen. Then I close the briefcase, put on my raincoat, and leave the office. The secretary looks up from a document. His hair is going gray. "Leaving already, judge?" he says. "Yes, I'm leaving. It's almost noon." "I have some reports for you to sign," he says. "Tomorrow," I say. "Yes, tomorrow," he says. "There's no rush." I say goodbye and walk out, then down the dark corridor, stopping at the railing to look down at the floors below. The lobby is crowded with gorillas talking in groups or walking across the black and white mosaic in every direction. I make my way slowly down the white marble stairs toward the first floor. As I approach the wide lobby the gorillas' voices grow louder but no more intelligible. They make strange noises in a strange register that blends together and rebounds off the tall ceiling. It's a shapeless blend of sound, and when I start to make my way through the mass of gorillas toward the rear of the building, the sounds reach me charged with vibrations and echoes: some are shrill, others harsh, others guttural, blending with shouts and laughter to produce an incessant crackle. With pale faces, bulging eyes, with fur that covers their heads, wet from the rain, their arms gesticulating strangely, some gorillas cluster in groups and some hurry across the black and white mosaic. The stairs are covered in muddy tracks, and the impressions left by their shoes on the mosaic have filled with water. Finally I reach the end of the lobby and walk into the cold, empty corridor. Office doors open to the corridor, revealing, every so often, shelves piled to the ceiling with documents. I reach the end of the corridor and walk out into the rear courtyard. The rain covers my face. I get in the car. I put down the briefcase, and when I turn on the engine and the windshield wipers I hear their sounds again, the monotone hum of the engine and the rhythmic scrape of the wiper blades over the windshield, soaked from the hours when the car was parked in the rear courtyard. I back up slowly, then steer down the narrow passageway toward the exit until I reach the street. After crossing the intersection I turn right and start driving around the plaza and the courthouse is left behind. On the corner, the traffic light stops me, but the engine keeps running. When the green light comes on I turn left up San Martín to the north. The gorillas, males and females, crowd the sidewalks in both directions, and their number grows as I approach the city center. At the corner of the municipal theater I have to brake suddenly when a bus rushes through the intersection, full speed, just as I'm starting

across. Then I start moving again, observing the old facade of
the theater, its curved marble staircase washed by the rain. Then
I leave the theater behind and continue north. Two and a half
blocks later I pass the corridors of the arcade, cross Mendoza,
and continue up San Martín. The number of gorillas has grown
considerably; they huddle in the thresholds of shops and under
the eaves of houses to protect themselves from the weather. The
female gorillas' colorful umbrellas move stiffly, filling the sidewalks with circular blurs, red, green, pink, yellow, black, and
white. Farther along, as I pass the entrance to *La Región*, I see
Ángel hurrying inside, but he doesn't see me. I'm only just able
to see him stride quickly up the two steps at the entrance and
then disappear. I go on, slowly, block after block, until I reach
the boulevard, then I turn right, then I pass the university, a pale
yellow building, its windows painted green. To the west, through
the portion of open sky above the boulevard, I can make out the
vast, blurred horizon, a gray that grows more dense as it moves
into the distance. The wiper blades sweep across the windshield
glass with an even rhythm while the fine droplets fall and collide
and form strange, momentary shapes. I drive to the west end of
the boulevard, and then, after some fifteen blocks, I turn left
again, to the south, down the Avenida del Oeste. Restless gorillas
wait silently under bus stop shelters. I can see them through the
windshield, and less distinctly through the side windows soaked
by the rain. I go about twenty blocks down the avenue, passing,
in succession, the Avenida cinema, the wholesale market, then
the regimental gardens, until finally I reach the Avenida del Sur
again and turn left, to the east, down the avenue. Eight blocks
and I pass the rear courtyard of the courthouse again. At the
corner I turn right, circling slowly to the south, in front of the
courthouse, and then I turn again at the corner, to the west again,
between the gray facade of city hall and the southern walkway of

the Plaza de Mayo, where the waterlogged palms and orange trees appear momentarily between the reddish paths that crisscross the plaza at angles and arcs. I reach San Martín and turn right, to the south. On my right is the lateral facade of city hall, on my left the historical museum, and at the first intersection the San Francisco church on the left and the row of single-story houses on the right. I move through the rain. The monotone hum of the engine blends with the regular rhythm of the wiper blades sweeping over the glass, where fine droplets of rain collide and explode into strange, momentary shapes. After the convent begin the woods of the southern park. I travel half a block past the second intersection and stop the car on the left side. For a moment I wait inside the car, hearing only the echo of the monotone hum of the engine and the regular rhythm of the wiper blades, which have now stopped but which continue resonating momentarily before they disappear completely. I take the briefcase from the back seat, step out of the car, lock the door and open the front door of the house, go inside, close the front door behind me, and start up the stairs. I go straight to the study and hang up the raincoat that I've been removing since I started up the stairs. I leave the briefcase on the sofa. I open the curtains, and the gray light from outside enters the study, a gray and rain-soaked gleam coming down. I observe the trees and the lake beyond, also gray, and also gleaming. The trees appear to be surrounded by a soft halo, and the drops form an evanescent myriad suspended momentarily around the wet foliage before they fall. What I can see of the park from the window is completely deserted. I turn around as Elvira comes in and asks if I'm going to eat now or if I prefer to wait a while longer. I say I'll wait a while longer and I sit down on the twin sofa, with my back to the window, and soon I'm asleep.

I wake up almost at once. I think it's at once but I look at my watch and see that it's two ten. I get up. I cough. Straightening my clothes, I leave the study and walk to the dining room. Elvira is at the head of the table, which is half-covered with a tablecloth and set with two covered plates and a glass. There's also a bread basket with two or three crackers. "I came in and saw you were sleeping and didn't want to wake you," Elvira says. "I fell asleep," I say. Elvira's gray hair concentrates a gray light that I can't place; ✓ perhaps the hair itself is what produces it. I sit down at the head of the table. Elvira hobbles into the kitchen and disappears. She returns with a steaming soup tureen and serves me a ladleful of simmering, golden broth. She disappears into the kitchen. I take three or four spoonfuls of soup then leave the spoon submerged in the dish. Slowly, the golden broth stops steaming. Gold-colored lumps form on the surface and turn pale. With the edge of the knife I clink the stemmed glass three or four times. Elvira reappears with a bottle of water that she leaves on the table. She takes the plate with the cold soup and returns with a dish containing three potatoes and a piece of meat. She serves me the meat and a potato and leaves the dish on the table. Then she leaves. I take two or three bites of meat but the potato is left untouched. I clink the glass again, this time with the back edge of the knife so as not to smudge the crystal, and when Elvira reappears I look up. "Tomorrow I'm having company for dinner, doña Elvira," I say, "I want you to make something special." Elvira looks at me for a moment. "How about a chicken?" she says. "Yes," I say, "And something more." "I'll see what I can make," she says. Then she looks at my plate and at the silverware crossed over what's left of the meal. "Is that all you ate?" she says. "I'm not hungry," I say. Elvira sighs and gathers the dishes. I get up, go to the bathroom, urinate, and then I brush my teeth and wash my hands. My face is reflected momentarily in the bathroom mirror as I brush my teeth, but when I lean over to spit it disappears. I rinse out my mouth and then I wash my hands. When I straighten up to dry them on the towel hanging from the rack next to the sink, my face reappears in the mirror. Then I turn off the light and walk out. In the study I sit down on the twin sofa. When I wake up, it's dark. Or rather, it's about to get dark.

Through the window I see the blue sky. It rains. A blue penumbra covers the trees in the park, and behind them, through the foliage, the lake is still and blue, but near-black and murky. Two indistinct figures—a female and a male gorilla, surely—walk slowly between the trees, toward the lake. I scratch my head. The telephone rings and I pick it up. It's the same voice as always, high-pitched, like a puppet, pouring out its long, rapid string of insults. It calls me a thief, a slut, a lowlife. It says I'll get what's coming to me soon enough. I listen impassively until it finishes, and when I sense that it has hung up, I hang up too. Then I pour myself a whiskey, neat, and take a sip.

I put on the raincoat and the waterproof hat and go out. I descend the stairs quietly. At the door I stop for a moment, look down the empty street toward the park, and then I get in the car. It's been getting rained on all day and the windshield is soaked. Through it I can only make out a shapeless, blue penumbra, where a few jagged lights glimmer at a distance. I wait a moment, in the silence, before turning the key. The engine hesitates two or three times before finally turning over. I turn on the windshield wipers and wait for the rain to clear before moving. As they sweep the water from the windshield, the wiper blades reveal the curve of San Martín to the south and the trees beyond that seem to intersect the street where the curve of the park follows of the curve of the blue pavement. I turn on the headlights and they pierce the bluish penumbra. A pair of young gorillas is coming up the sidewalk toward me, arm in arm. They blink at the headlights. I wait for them to pass the car, and then I start moving, but so slowly that it takes me a long time to reach the first corner, where I turn

186

right. The rough cobblestones make the car's frame shudder. At the next corner I turn right again, onto the smooth asphalt of San Gerónimo to the north. At the third corner I come out on the Plaza de Mayo. I go on, the plaza to my right and the courthouse, where no lights are visible, to my left. I cross the intersection with the Avenida del Sur and turn right at the next corner, then I drive one block and turn left onto San Martín to the north.

I cross the Avenida del Sur, and at the next corner I turn right, then drive one block and turn left onto San Martín to the north. Ahead I can make out the neon signs on San Martín, growing more varied and dense. Their lights—green, pink, yellow, and blue—tarnish the night sky, nearly black by now. The streetlights are also lit up, and the shop windows are brightly illuminated. The lobby of the municipal theater is lit up, but I don't see anyone inside. Suddenly, the rain thickens. Through the windshield the street becomes a luminous blot, a blot that takes on a clear but unstable form momentarily, and then returns to the luminous blot, where the colors blend violently. I go slowly, at the end of a long line of cars. Another line advances slowly in the opposite direction. After I pass the illuminated corridors of the arcade, the downpour of thick rain returns to the barely perceptible mist of days and days. I drive two blocks, slowly, following the slow line of cars ahead, and then I turn right, leaving San Martín. At the Banco Provincial I cross 25 de Mayo and continue east. I turn onto the harbor road, where the rough cobblestones make the car frame shudder, and drive the length of it and reach the mouth of the suspension bridge. A weak light filters out from the gray sentry box. I turn onto the boulevard, to the west. I cross the tracks and then pass the facade of the train station—the lobby is illuminated—stop at the first traffic light, start up when the light changes, around the Adoratrices convent, briefly catch sight of the mill before crossing the tracks again at the second light, then drive two more blocks and turn again onto San Martín, to the south. As I approach the city center I fall into a long line of cars that moves more and more slowly. Then I pass the *La Región* building, where the only visible lights are from the news ticker, and farther on the brightly lit passageways of the arcade, now to my left, the lobby filling up with gorillas, pomaded and dressed in dark clothing, and female gorillas covered in jewelry and dressed festively, and then finally the Plaza de Mayo, circling on its east side. The city hall building approaches, and through the right side windows, between the foliage in the plaza, appears the dark mass of the courthouse. City hall is left behind. I cross the first intersection, and the second, and finally stop the car halfway down the block, in front of the house. The trees are dark. I step out of the car and close the door, and I can feel the rain falling on my face and on my hat. Over the roof of the car, through the trees, I see the water on the lake shine momentarily and darken again. I make an effort to keep my shoes clean, tiptoeing across the sidewalk and into the house. I lock the door and start up the stairs.

Elvira is in the dining room. "Will you eat now?" she says. I tell her to leave something out, that for now I'm not hungry. Elvira disappears into the kitchen. "Bring some ice to the study," I say. I hang up the raincoat and the hat on the rack in the bathroom, urinate, and go into the study. The curtains are open, so I close them again. Now the only light, a bright circle, comes from the desk. I pick up the briefcase from the sofa, take out the dictionary, the notebook, the novel, and the pens, and put them on the desk. I drop the empty briefcase on the sofa, pour myself a large whiskey, and sit down at the desk, glass in hand. I take a short drink. Then I open the notebook to the first page and study the black handwriting of the manuscript, which is full of strikethroughs and markups in various colors, green, red, blue. Elvira knocks at the door and then comes in with the ice bucket. "I left you some sandwiches in the kitchen," she says. I ask if she has gone shopping for tomorrow, and she says she has. Then she says goodnight and disappears. I put ice in the whiskey and take a slow drink after swirling the glass, making it clink. Then I leave the glass to my right on the desk, within reach, and open the novel to the first page—it's covered in marks in three or four colors. I read from the notebook. The first word, in capital letters in the center of the page, reads PREFACIO. Below this is a line in regular script. It reads, *El artista es el creador de cosas bellas.* The word *El* is in parentheses. I pause a moment and then pick up a red pen and cross out the word *El*, then superimpose an uppercase *A* over the lowercase *a* of the word *artista.* I'm left with, *Artista es el creador de cosas bellas.* The second line reads, *Revelar el arte y ocultar el artista es el fin (propósito) (finalidad) del arte.* I pause a moment and then cross out the word *fin*, to avoid any sort of misinterpretation.

I cross out and correct, line after line, in various colors, green, blue, red, over the black handwriting. The marks, crosses, circles, lines, and arrows are superimposed on the marks made during the first draft. At ten after twelve I get up from the desk, take a last sip of whiskey, and go to bed. I undress slowly and put on my pajamas. The sheets are warm, and the light on the nightstand casts a long cone over the white wall. I cover myself to my chin with the sheets and stare at the ceiling. Then I stretch out my hand, keeping the rest of my body still, and turn off the light. It doesn't start right away. The common thoughts come first, the memories, the pieces of visual or auditory sensation lingering on the retina or the ear drum, the slow, weak murmur, growing more confused, the vast diurnal sound extinguishing. Then the actual murmur begins. For an immeasurable period it blends with the previous sound. The combination of the two is disorienting. At this hour the gorillas begin to undress and slither toward bed. The female gorillas wait, their legs open like enormous carnivorous flowers, their eyes half shut and their hands open on the pillow, palms up alongside their faces. I'm in complete darkness, hearing the two murmurs blending. The real murmur will start to grow, while the other is extinguished, until it completely takes over the inside of my mind. Phosphorescent blurs will rise from the murmur, then pale, then phosphorescent again, until figures will begin to take shape around the murmur, momentarily focused in the dark camera. Fragments of the faces of long-dead gorillas, their furry hands, a meteorite, incandescent and expanding as it falls to the earth through the darkness. But the external murmur remains, extinguishing gradually. The wiper blades sweep rhythmically across the surface of the glass where the drops fall, and myriad brilliant lights decompose into violent shapes, while through the side windows the blurred facades of houses—repeated blurs, yellow, gray, white—slide slowly backward. Dark windows, pale faces. Newspapers in the street, trampled, covered in mud. An empty package of cigarettes, twisted, the silver rim of the inner wrapper sticking out. Dead leaves piled up into a damp blanket under the trees. Coins stacked on the night stand, a glass of water holding a teaspoon. Stacks of thick, dusty files in the courthouse offices, yellowed at the edges, with faded red covers, on the desks or in file cabinets, piled to the ceiling. The gray sentry box at the mouth of the suspension bridge, empty, glowing in the fog. Silent umbrellas, in every color, sliding rigidly, horizontally, in every direction. The solitary train station building, the illuminated lobby. A gorilla wrapped in a blue raincoat, coughing and then disappearing behind me. The green traffic light coming on. The tracks extending, crossing the street. The landscape, still, moving, still, the orange trees and the palms in the Plaza de Mayo receiving the ceaseless rain and glowing momentarily in the darkness.

As the murmur increases there comes a moment when the external murmur, extinguishing, and the internal murmur, growing, have the same intensity, the same quality, the same rhythm. They are the same. This stability of their intensity, their quality, and their rhythm holds, suspended, until finally the external murmur diminishes, but so slightly that it's imperceptible, and the internal grows, suddenly, and like two passing cars superimposed momentarily and then separating in opposite directions, they reveal the distance between them. I'm face up, the sheets to my chin, in the darkness. My eyes are open, and they grow wider as the murmur grows. I see the phosphorescent blurs, the pale blurs, the brilliant, fleeting shapes accompanied by an inaudible shrillness, trying to make out an image that pulls the blurs from the pure fire, and the shrillness from the pure, senseless sound. But for the moment nothing happens, and I wait in the drift. It lights up, quivers, and disappears, and the inaudible shrillness swells and suddenly retreats, sensible yet remote. I step from the jetty to the vessel, unmoored, and as the vessel moves off, the jetty can be seen more clearly, more distinctly, until soon it can be seen completely. But then the images are called up to fill in the darkness and time that make up the black space.

Generation upon generation of gorillas rise from the darkness. Rough hordes drooling, with a mixture of terror and desolation, in the early twilight. Emerald-colored flies land on their open wounds, from bites and scratches, products of the recent battles. The hordes drift uneasily through a clearing in the woods, looking at each other desolately, waiting for the night. The males' genitals dangle between their lower extremities, jiggling. The females' are a reddish gash. They gnash their teeth and narrow their eyes, gazing at the open space around them, the persistent likeness of the trees and the rocks that remain ecstatic night and day and block their view. And when night falls they gather together, excited, rubbing up against each other around the large bonfire they've lit with dry branches and which fills the ridges and hollows of their brutal faces with shadows. When the tom-tom starts the gorillas form circles, concentric rings, rows that thrash relentlessly with an awkward rhythm until the weakest, panting, collapse on the earth, their pink tongues hanging out and licking the corners of their black lips. In the center of the ring, near the roaring, crackling bonfire, which emits a bright glow that dies out as it ascends into the black sky, a female and a male gorilla embrace and fall to the ground. They roll around, sending up clouds of dust. The circle of upright gorillas looks on, clapping. They make a dry sound, multiplied, following the thunderous tom-tom. The female and the male come up and fall again, embracing, punctuating their brutal movement with gasping, muffled shouts, panting, moaning, laughter, pounding. Then the female turns onto all fours, expectantly, and the male gorilla enters her. The female screams. He's entered her completely, to the testicles, which slap against the female's backside. Without coming out, his legs half bent, his bare feet planted securely on the ground, the male gorilla straightens up as much as possible, raises his arms as though to prove there's no sleight of hand, and greets the circle of expectant faces. The clapping explodes, and the circle of gorillas begin furiously stamping their feet in satisfaction. Clouds of dust lift. The rhythm of the tom-tom picks up. To this mixture of clapping, muffled pounding of feet, and the constant resonant explosion of the drum is added a shriek of voices, laughter, and wailing. The pair in the center is jumbled with a mass of other pairs that have formed in the circle and now embrace and fall to the ground and lift a cloud of dust that turns red in the glow of the flames. From out of that blood-splattered dust, a pair rolls across the ground and into the bonfire, lifting a violent shower of sparks. They don't separate, but keep rolling, covering their burns with dust as they roll. The entire clearing has become a shapeless mass of thrusting and howls. They squirm, pile on top of each other, hit, lick, bite, caress, penetrate each other with their genitals. Then the upheaval in the clouds of reddish dust starts to subside. The dust settles and clears. The gorillas settle into strange positions, some thrown face down, flattened against the ground while others lie on top, also face down with their belly on the other's back, forming a cross. Others are on their sides, an arm stretched alongside their body and the other propping up their head. Others are face up, their legs splayed. One quietly moans while masturbating. Their breathing grows deeper and more even, interspersed with sighs and snoring. A sudden burst of laughter rises and falls. Soon, only their breathing is heard. Dawn finds them asleep, bleary-eyed, snorting and sniffling. They shift restlessly and huddle up against the cold of the dew. They grow uncomfortable in the rising light and half sit up, looking around desolately, disoriented. The corners of their mouths are sticky with dried saliva. Not a single ember remains of the bonfire, which is now nothing more than a pile of white ash. Blood-colored stains from the wounds produced overnight blend with the grass and the earth. They barely exchange a fatigued sign or gesture. Every so often some sound escapes their mouth. Some, lazier, toss and turn before they get up. Others caress, mechanically, the arms of the females one last time. From inside their caves—formed by erosion of the rocks—they take pieces of raw meat. As they eat them their beards are covered with bloody stains. Blinking in the sunlight, they take huge bites from the hunks of meat. They've returned to the same clearing, to the squared-off horizon of trees and rocks where their gaze rebounds. The same rocks and the same trees, and above them the same blue sky and the yellow, incandescent disk that crosses it with maddening, mute slowness, dull, that polished blue surface that fills with glimmers and which at midday is impossible to look at directly. It is the same space that every day surrounds them. They move through it, not comprehending. The one who crosses the line of rocks and trees, the motionless, constant, and endless horizon, disappears and never returns. Likewise the animal that crosses the horizon in the opposite direction, into the clearing. The teeth, rocks, spears, and arrows that patrol the clearing they've taken over fall onto it and tear it to pieces. With their spears and rocks and arrows they wait, crouched, for some living thing to make the precarious crossing, and then they fall onto it and tear it to pieces. After the animal has exhausted its last warm breaths and lies still, dead, they carry it to their cave, where it is distributed, the most succulent parts to the chief and the rest to the horde. The emerald flies barely have time to gather, buzzing, over the remains. When they have filled their stomachs, the gorillas squat in the shade, pensively, and survey the horizon, one arm folded over their abdomen with the other elbow propped on their palm and their chin resting on their hand. Every so often they sigh and narrow their eyes to sharpen and clarify the space that separates them from the horizon line, where the trees and rocks bear silent evidence of the other side, witnesses that make evidence from their silence. Other gorillas perform bewildered examinations of their bodies, of the rocks in their knees, their furry vegetation, the dark caves inside their sphincters, the slow, grim life of their genitals swelling or opening, damply, of their own accord. They pass the idle hours in this desolate melancholy until once again the sun begins its descent and the horizon grows red and the darkness falls finally on the bonfire they lit at the twilight, and around which the nocturnal ceremonies begin anew.

I'm lying in complete darkness, my eyes open, motionless in the bed. It's a darkness without breach, without fissure, the room has no windows and the door to the anteroom is closed, so not a single sliver of light enters. Once again the murmur swells among the phosphorescent shapes. Between the internal darkness and the external darkness there is no longer a barrier or distinction, and the shapes float in the direction—if there is such a thing—toward which my eyes focus, and then disappear.

Now the gorillas appear in a long procession, dressed in garish clothing and gold and silver trinkets—with stones that glitter in the sunlight—hanging from their necks, their ears, and encircling their wrists and fingers. The drum has been exchanged for brass instruments that produce a strident noise when brought to their lips. The chiefs march at the head of the procession in long purple tunics hoisted at the ends by half-naked slaves, to keep them from dragging on the stone path. They are followed by secondary attendants, dressed in black, and then the tertiary, in green tunics. They form even rows and march and dance to the rhythm of the music. Behind them are the women, in dresses of every color that reveal their white breasts and some their violet, circular nipples. And father back, behind the women, come the multitude of ragged gorillas that try to catch sight of the ceremony and every so often are driven back by the whiplashes of bodyguards on horseback. As the first ones fall, the ones coming up behind collide with them and fall too, and by the time they begin gathering themselves up, the long procession led by the marching band has moved off a good distance and the bodyguards push their horses into a gallop over the stone path, to catch up with the rear guard of the procession and secure it. The multitude rushes forward, reaches the procession, and is once again driven back by the whiplashes of the bodyguards, so the distance recovered is lost once again. And again, while the multitude of ragged gorillas struggles to incorporate itself, the hooves of the bodyguards' horses sound on the hard cobblestones as they gallop back to the procession. The chiefs, wrapped in purple robes, hold their swollen faces up with dignified expressions. The secondary attendants stare at the necks of the purple-clad chiefs, and the tertiaries, in green, stare at the necks of the black-clad secondaries. The women ceaselessly rearrange their garish clothing and glittering trinkets. Some rearrange their bodices to reveal even more of their breasts. And the bodyguards on horseback, when they are again reasonably close to the procession, turn suddenly, producing a loud pounding over the cobblestones. The bodyguards glare menacingly at the multitude, though the mass of ragged gorillas has not managed to regain even half the distance. They have arrived at the ceremonial place. Suddenly, from the wrought iron railing on the third floor, I see the square courthouse lobby, its empty checkerboard floor. The white staircase that curves downward is empty as well. The railing, curving and forming three sides of a square, surrounds the vast emptiness that falls steeply over the black and white tiled lobby floor.

The ceremony takes place in a vast, high-walled enclosure with tall windows ending in points, with motifs of the gorilla chiefs painted in spectacular colors on their glass surfaces. A long, broad table is set. It has three sides: a central section and two lateral extensions projecting at a right angles from the ends, enclosing a wide, open area. Two rows of bare-chested slaves, carrying torches, flank the procession as they enter. The chiefs in purple enter the cavernous enclosure, their heads held even higher and wearing even more dignified expressions, and they take their places at the central table. To their right, the attendants in black. To their left, the ones in green. The women gather together at the back of the vast open space in the center and wait nervously. The multitude has gathered before the large entrance, fighting for a view of the scene. The bodyguards have dismounted and strike at them from inside the enclosure, forcing them back. But they've been ordered to allow them to watch, and their attacks are softer than their menacing expressions suggest, so that the hordes will understand that they are attempting to gain a forbidden privilege while not denying the chiefs their audience.

Then the banquet begins. Bare-chested slaves carry in large dishes to the central table and start carving up the sacrificed animals under the gaze of the chiefs, who dictate the size of the portions and their recipients. They barely taste the food, and the top chief doesn't even notice the slaves' work. He sits at the exact center of the table, and over his purple tunic hangs a large obsidian medallion on a gold chain. His long bony fingers play with the medallion. The multitude of gorillas stare at him in ecstasy, with a mixture of astonishment, fury, admiration, and terror at the luminous halo that seems to surround his large graying head and the pale face that emerges from behind a carefully tended black beard. When the attendants finish eating, under the negligent gaze of the chiefs, the bare-chested slaves gather the leftovers, carry them to the entrance, and throw them over the multitude of gorillas. In the struggle the gorillas punch, shove, bite, and curse each other. There is scrambling, spitting, blood, shrieking. Back inside, as the gorillas recline under the fading sunlight to chew the last filaments of bloodless meat from the bones, the parade of women has started, to the rhythm of the music. One by one they leave the nervous and anxious cluster pressed into a corner of the room and enter the open space, twisting and moving their hips and jumping in ways that make their multicolored trinkets jingle. Some undress as they dance. Others are already nude when they reach the open space between the tables. The green and black attendants remain still, tense, silent, observing the twisting of the women without speaking. Only the chiefs in purple comment to each other about each woman. Some laugh and point at the dancers. Others make obscene gestures. But the top chief remains silent, ceaselessly fingering his obsidian medallion. Finally he raises his hand toward one, silently, and points to her. The slaves disappear into one of the deep side corridors and return carrying a narrow bed over their heads. They place the bed in the center of the open space. The chosen woman lays down on the bed, nude, her legs open. The top chief stands and approaches the center of the cavernous space. Two naked slaves follow close behind. The top chief stops next to the bed, makes a gesture, and the slaves undress him. One of them applies unguents to his member. The other kisses his medallion. The chief takes one last look around, to make sure everyone is watching him. He makes an imperceptible gesture to the bodyguards, allowing the multitude to approach the entrance. Then he leans over and enters the woman. A roar and cry rises from the multitude and the rows of attendants and the slaves and the group of women crowded into a corner at the moment the chief penetrates the woman. Then the music starts again.

It reverberates inside me, inaudible, and then the confused horde evaporates. Once again my eyes are open, in complete darkness. Not even the shapeless, phosphorescent, sparkling forms pass by. No sound enters from the street, the room is completely silent. I move, not shifting or turning, only shaking my legs slightly, and the bed creaks. I see the checkerboard courthouse lobby again, the black and white tiles. No one is in the lobby. I see the iron railing and the staircase.

The wiper blades rhythmically sweep away the drops that crash against the windshield, producing a monotonous, even sound. Through the side windows, the blurred city passes around me.

A dark, crackling blur emerges from the fog, where I imagine the riverbank to be.

A piece of gray meat, surrounded by boiled potatoes, in the dish, on the table, the murmur of Elvira's skirt as she disappears into the kitchen.

I drive down San Martín, toward the city center. Myriad colors from the neon signs form brilliant, momentary images through the windshield, where the thick rain explodes and distorts my vision before the wiper blades sweep away the water and leave the glass clear again.

The gray sentry box appears and disappears quickly into the fog at the mouth of the suspension bridge.

I turn on the light.

The white marble staircase, descending from the third floor, is illuminated.

I sit up and look around the room. The white walls don't glow because the light from the nightstand doesn't reach them, except for the cone of pale light that softly illuminates the wall where the headboard rests. I remove the spoon from the glass and take a drink of water. I turn off the light again and close my eyes.

I see the trees in the park and the lake flashing suddenly and then disappearing into the foliage. I see the marble courthouse stairs again, the checkerboard lobby, the black and white tiles, from the railing on the third floor, the illuminated corridors of the arcade, the dark windows in the train station, the white marble stairs in the courthouse again, the checkerboard, the black and white tiles, the trees in the Plaza de Mayo, palms and orange trees. The oranges, yellowing among the green leaves polished by the rain.

Ángel enters the *La Región* building quickly, waves, and disappears.

I see the chief fingering the obsidian medallion.

In the open space walled in by trees and rocks, the gorillas wander and pause, resting their palms on their backsides, bewildered, gazing at the mute horizon.

The gray sentry box appears and disappears into the drifting fog. I see the profile of the uniformed gorilla, cut in half by the edge of the door.

Gorillas cough and hunch over as they smoke on the bus station platforms. Their pale hands and faces shift in the early penumbra.

From the third floor, the courthouse lobby looks empty. The black and white tiles are clean and polished. The white staircase descends, forming a wide curve, toward the second floor.

The windshield wiper sweeps away fine droplets of rain that fall on the glass and distort the bright lights of the neon signs as I move north up San Martín.

I wake up. For a moment, I don't realize that I'm awake. The room is gray. Then I turn on the light and look at the clock on the night stand. It's two. I get up and go to the bathroom. I see gray through the skylight. I undress, defecate, and then take a hot shower. Then I go to my room, wrapped in my bathrobe, dry off, and get dressed. In the long mirror over the bureau I examine my face. My beard has grown in two days. After dressing I go back to the bathroom and shave slowly. The electric razor buzzes, monotonously, quietly. I pass the back of my hand softly over my face, against the grain of the hair. Then I unplug the razor, put it away, and leave. I find Elvira in the dining room. "Your mother called," she says. "I'll call her in a minute," I say. "Judge," Elvira says, "It's three in the afternoon. Will you eat?" I tell her to bring some soup to the study and I go up. I open the curtains and a gray, tense light filters into the study.

I dial my mother's number. I hear her voice. "It's been two days since you've come to see me," she says. "I've been very busy Mamá," I say. "Are you alright?" she says. "Perfectly fine. Never better," I say. "You've heard the news about your wife?" she says. "I haven't, nor do I want to," I say. "She's come back to the city, to stay this time. I heard it at the club, yesterday afternoon, that she had been showing up with some new man, all smug," mother says. "That doesn't interest me, Mamá," I say. "And she gets drunk,

Ernesto. She gets drunk and goes around talking garbage about our family," Mother says. "It can't be her," I say. "How can it not be her?" Mother says. "Even after she walks out you still have the nerve to defend her." "I'm not defending her," I say. "I'm just saying it might not be her." "So you're saying the girls don't know my daughter-in-law when she was married to my son for eight years?" Mother says. "I don't know why she would come to this city," I say. "You never know anything," she says. "How's Father?" I say. "The same," Mother says. "Well," she says, "it's about time you remembered that you have a mother and come visit me. I don't even remember your face." "It's the same as always," I say. "Someone from the club might come to your house soon," Mother says. "You might pay him the two months I owe." "Do you need anything?" I say. "Nothing, for now," Mother says. We say goodbye and hang up.

Almost at once, Elvira arrives with the soup. It's the same as always, a thin broth, steaming and golden. I sit down on the twin sofa, my back to the window, and drink the soup slowly. Then I set the empty dish on the desk, walk to the window, and gaze out at the park. The gray light forms a halo over the trees above the ground that slopes slowly downward to the lake. The paths are dark and covered in a decaying bed of leaves. Bare tree branches crisscross in the green foliage. A pair of gorillas sit on a flat stone bench, their backs to the window, gazing at the lake. The female's head is resting on the male's shoulder. They are still. Suddenly they stand up and start walking toward the lake, then they turn right, following the path, and then they disappear.

I take up the corrections to the translation until it starts to get dark. Then I close the curtains and turn on the desk lamp. I work briefly by the lamplight, which casts a bright, warm circle over the desk and the surrounding area. The rest of the room is in a kind of half darkness. Then I get up, put on a blazer, and go to the kitchen. "Is everything ready for tonight, doña Elvira?" I say. "It's getting there," Elvira says. "I'm going out," I say. "I'll be right back." I go downstairs and out into the street. I'm submerged in cold, blue air. Very soon it will be dark.

I have to turn the key several times before the engine starts. After it turns over I wait a moment for it to warm up. Then I put it into first and start driving slowly. At the corner I turn right, and the car begins to shudder and vibrate as it moves over the rough cobblestones. At the third intersection, the Plaza de Mayo appears to my right, the broad facade of the courthouse to my left. I turn onto the Avenida del Sur, heading west. The avenue is illuminated with mercury gas lamps that cast a whitish, cold light from the sidewalks toward the middle of the street. The Avenida del Oeste is lit up with the same lamps hanging from curved columns that extend toward the street. Beyond the flowerbeds in the center island, to my left, are the regimental gardens, and then, also to the left, the yellow facade of the wholesale market, and farther on the Avenida cinema, completely dark, and then the rows of one- and two-story houses until I reach the boulevard. I turn right, driving slowly to the east. By the time I reach the first traffic light, after passing the yellow facade of the university, with its green window frames, it is already dark. I have to wait at the traffic light for the red light to turn off and the green light to turn on, and as I move forward, after passing the traffic light, the train tracks make the car shudder slightly. The mill is to my left. The second traffic light doesn't stop me—the light changes from green to yellow just as I'm crossing the intersection—and I accelerate slightly. The train station lobby is illuminated, as is the ground outside the tall windows that cast patches of light into the dark air. I cross the tracks and reach the roundabout by the suspension bridge. The gray sentry box is lit up inside, and the outline of a uniformed gorilla interrupts the passage of light through the doorway. I turn onto the old waterfront, which is practically deserted—I've passed only two cars on the way to the suspension bridge—and accelerate when I touch the smooth asphalt of the new waterfront, lined with broad jetties. The red tile roofs of the villas on the waterfront stick out between the black foliage. Every so often, a half-obscured light illuminates the wet leaves. I reach Guadalupe, circle the roundabout, and start driving in the opposite direction. Now the river is to my left. I can't make it out. In the distance, the tall columns of the suspension bridge can be distinguished clearly by the four red lights that blink on and off. I'm alone on the avenue. The headlights illuminate a section of the pavement, and when I switch them on, the high beams cause the surface of light to sort of jump and expand abruptly forward and to the sides. When I lower the lights, its surface area diminishes, illuminating only the pavement in front of the car again. Inside the car, the red dashboard light reaches my face weakly. Every so often I can see a fragment of my face reflected momentarily in the rearview mirror, which fills up with light suddenly when a car approaches and passes me quickly. I watch its rear lights, two red dots, shrink until they disappear. Then I reach the old waterfront again and slow down now that the asphalt is less smooth and covered with patches, potholes, and bumps. When I reach the mouth of the suspension bridge, a sky-blue truck with the inscription *Molino Harinero S.A.* on the bed exits quickly from the bridge and forces me to stop abruptly. The truck stops abruptly as well. Inside the dark cabin I can just make out the silhouette of a man behind the wheel and a woman with a girl sitting on her lap. The truck starts up again and quickly disappears up the boulevard. I continue straight ahead and then circle the plaza next to the waterfront and turn onto the harbor road, which crosses at a diagonal toward the city center. The avenue is dark despite the white spheres of the streetlights, shorter than the palms, whose leaves flash momentarily. And except for the complex structure of the central power plant, which is covered with lights, nothing is visible but dark walls half-obscured by the foliage. On the other side, to my left, loom the silver petroleum tanks of the port warehouses and the operations switchyards of the port railway. I reach the city center, pass the dark post office, the sides and deep passageways of the bus station, and then I turn right, drive two blocks, and turn left onto San Martín, to the south. The street is illuminated, but practically deserted. Then comes the darkened municipal theater, and a few blocks later the traffic light at the Avenida del Sur. I stop, waiting for the light to change from red to green. When I start, after the light has changed, I see the city hall approach, and sliding backward, past the right side window, the east end of the Plaza de Mayo, and beyond, between the trees, the dark, blurred facade of the courthouse. I cross the intersection—the city hall plaza is left behind—drive two and a half blocks, and after passing the white arches of the Franciscan convent and the tree line of the southern park, I stop the car next to the sidewalk, in front of my house, and turn off the engine. I turn off the lights as well. Then I get out, lock the door, and go inside. I haven't finished climbing the stairs when the telephone rings. I hurry into the study and pick up the receiver at the same moment as I turn on the desk lamp.

It's the same voice as always, high-pitched, like a puppet's. "Are you there?" it says. "Can you hear me, you bastard? Pay attention, I want you to hear everything well. Your father is a thief and your mother is a whore. Your wife is the filthiest whore of the bunch. Burning homos alive should be legalized. Nasty family! You should vanish from the face of the earth, you're a disgrace to the city. You'll get what's coming to you. Your names should get printed in the paper for everyone to see." There was a pause. "Are you still there, you coward? You pansy. You chickenshit. Son

204

of a rotten whore. Are you there? Did you know your disgraceful wife is going around at the club polluting another man? The few decent people left in this city are going to take action one of these days. Tar and feather you, like they do with the deviants. And to think you're up in the courthouse administering justice! You hear me, faggot? You're there. I'm sure you're there, hearing everything and laughing at me and all the decent people in this rotten city that have to put up with it all. You'll get what's coming to you, you chickenshit. You've been warned before. I'm hanging up, but you'll know me soon enough, you and everyone else in your deviant family." The line goes dead. When I hear the dial tone, I hang up too. Then I turn off the light and lie down on the twin sofa. I lie for a moment in the darkness of the study, breathing quietly, my mind empty, not thinking of anything. Then I sit up, and the desolation comes.

It comes suddenly. It's a shudder—but it isn't a shudder—sharply—but it isn't sharp—and it comes suddenly. Because of it I know I'm alive, that this—and nothing else—is reality and that my body, piercing it like a meteor, is inside it completely. I know that I'm completely alive and that this can't be avoided. But it's not that either, because that's been said before, many times, and if it's already been said then it's not that. The desolation has come many times, but not this desolation, which could only come now, because every millimeter of time has its place from the beginning, every groove has its place and all the grooves line up alongside each other, grooves of light that turn on and off suddenly in perfect sequence in something resembling a direction and never come on or turn off again.

I raise my right hand in the penumbra of the study—I have a right hand and I'm in a place I call my study, and my mind follows the movement, the right hand rising from my thigh, where it was resting, palm down, the fingers slightly bent, to my chest.

Following this moment, all of it, step by step, is the desolation. Something against memory, that splits it, that lets reality filter in and rise through the cracks like a heavy miasma until it coagulates completely. Alright, so, I am somewhere, and I have a right hand, and a mind that follows its movement from my thigh to my chest, because I have a thigh and a chest as well. And with that it finishes.

I get up, walk to the desk, and turn on the light. I call Elvira. When she arrives, I ask her if everything is ready for dinner and she says it is. "Bring some ice, then, doña Elvira, and set up a table with drinks here in the study." Then I sit down at the desk, open the notebook with the translation, and start to work. At nine twenty-five exactly the doorbell rings. Downstairs, I find Ángel at the door. "I was waiting," I say. "It's raining again," Ángel says. "This damned rain won't quit." He follows me upstairs into the study. Ángel goes straight to the desk and leans over the translation. "Tough handwriting," he says. "Tiny and cramped," I say. "Are you making progress?" he says. *"Yes, Harry, I know what you are going to say. Something dreadful about marriage. Don't say it. Don't ever say things of that kind to me again. Two days ago I asked Sibyl to marry me. I am not going to break my word to her. She is to be my wife,"* I say. "I'm just at the word *wife*." "Interesting," Ángel says. "Would you care for another whiskey?" I say. "Your glass is empty." "Yes, actually," Ángel says. "Ángel," I say, "did you know I was separated?" "I heard something like that," Ángel says. "My wife left me," I say. "Did you know that?" "I didn't know who left who," Ángel says. "There's a rumor that you were separated, but that's it." "No, she left me. She walked out. I came home one night and she wasn't there, just a note saying that she was leaving because I didn't have a soul," I say. "What's that about a soul?" Ángel says. "I don't know," I say. Ángel approaches the window and looks out through the glass at the trees in the park. He grips his glass of whiskey, his back is to me. He's thin, but he doesn't seem at all fragile. "Your house is nice," he says. "Yes, very nice," I say. "When I read the note I wondered if she'd expected me to have a soul. She must have believed in the soul," I say. "Maybe it was a manner of speaking," Ángel says. "I understand," I say. "But in any case she was expecting something. If you say someone is missing their soul, what are you asking for?" I say. "I don't know," Ángel says, "that they like me, that they make me feel good." "People don't have souls," I say. "They just have a body. A body that starts at their fingers and ends in their skull, in an explosion. We're just a horde of gorillas that came from nothing. And that's it." "Maybe slightly more than gorillas," Ángel says. "No, nothing more," I say. "Gorillas searching for what to eat and devouring each other in a thousand different ways. The only grace that man has is death," I say. "If I were you I'd be dead already," Ángel says, laughing.

Then we go to the dining room. We stand briefly next to the table. "I've come up with a great theory," Ángel says. "There's only one literary genre: the novel. Everything we can think of, the things we do, what we think, what we say, it's all a novel. And everything that's written down, everything's a novel, the sciences, poetry, the theater, parliamentary discourse, advertisements. Some good, some average, some bad, but all of them better than the novels of Manuel Gálvez. Doesn't that seem like an interesting theory?" "I'm not one for theories," I say. The telephone rings in the study. A completely unfamiliar voice is asking for Justice Ernesto López Garay. "This is he," I say. "Judge," says the voice, "this is Sergeant Loprete, from the courthouse police. They've called from the precinct about a homicide; they're asking if you can interrogate the accused tomorrow morning because there's no space for him at the precinct." "A homicide?" I say. "A man killed his wife in Barrio Roma," says the sergeant, "He shot her twice in the face." "When did this happen?" I say. "I couldn't tell you, Judge," says the sergeant, "but they're asking at the precinct that if you could take his statement tonight rather than tomorrow morning; it would be much better." "Tonight is impossible," I say, "And tomorrow morning I have a hearing. And, in any case, I have to depose the witnesses first, if there are any." "I couldn't tell you, Judge," says the sergeant. "Tell whoever called you from the precinct that I'm not responsible for their lack of space," I say, "And say they can give him a room at the Palace, if they like. Or do they suppose I'm at the disposal of whatever some guard thinks?" "You're right, Judge. I agree with you. You're absolutely right," says the sergeant. "What did you say your name was, sergeant?" I say. "Loprete, Sergeant Loprete," says the sergeant. "Alright," I say. "Tell them what I've told you. And tell them that I may not be able to interrogate the accused until the day after tomorrow. In any case, I'll see what I can do tomorrow afternoon." "As you say, Judge," says the sergeant. "That's fine," I say. We hang up and I return to the dining room. Ángel is taking a drink as I come in. We sit down at the table. Ángel doesn't say a word for a long time. Then I tell him about my phone conversation, and he asks if he can attend the inquest. "It's not easy," I say. "It's not allowed." "They should allow it," says Ángel. "Don't start criticizing the justice system," I say, "It's what puts food on the table." "So this is a *justice* chicken?" says Ángel. "Precisely," I say. "So it's like I'm eating a prisoner," says Ángel.

After dinner, we go back to the study. I put Schönberg's *Concerto for violin and orchestra* on the record player, and we sit down to listen. Ángel takes on a grave expression, sunk in the chair, his legs stretched out toward me—I'm sitting on the twin sofa, my back to the window—and every so often he takes a sip of whiskey. He looks completely absorbed in the music. I don't look away from him for a single moment, but he avoids my gaze. When the concerto finishes, he gets up and approaches the window. I follow, and stop very close behind him. "Now, after the music," I say, "there is an immense silence." I take the whiskey from his hand, brush his fingers with mine, and take a sip. Then I return the glass and pour myself a drink and sit back down. He continues standing in the center of the room, between the chair, the sofa, and the desk. He asks if I've sent many men to prison recently. "None," I say. Then we're silent again. I examine him, completely. Then he starts talking about things he has seen in the sky, in the moon. He's lying. When he leaves, an hour later, I get in bed and turn off the light. No sounds reach me, not a single trace of light enters the room. I'm in complete darkness and silence. My mind is empty.

Then I see wide fields of wheat burning soundlessly. Their crackling is muted. The flames are low, even, and the fire extends to the horizon. There are no trees, or slopes, nothing. Just a flat plain covered with yellow wheat, over which extends the even flames cracking mutely.

I wake up early, before dawn. I get dressed and go out. There's a light rain. The sun is coming up. The inside of the car is freezing. It takes two or three tries before the engine turns over. Finally it does. The blue dawn air is filled with fine droplets of rain that condense and rotate slowly around the spheres of light. The park is deserted, and the motionless trees imprint their complex black patterns against the blue penumbra. I turn on the headlights, illuminating the empty street, their beams of light colliding, at a distance, with a curve in the road. Then I start. At the corner I turn onto the rough cobblestones that make the car vibrate and shudder, then right onto San Gerónimo, to the north. As I pass between the Plaza de Mayo and the courthouse, I see the first gray daylight concentrating around the tall tops of the palms, their broad metallic leaves shining, fragmentary. I turn onto the Avenida del Sur, heading east, drive a block and then, when the green traffic light allows me passage, I turn onto San Martín. I drive north down the empty street. The wiper blades rhythmically sweep the glass. The tiny droplets collide against the glass and break apart, blurring it momentarily. The wiper blades pass again, rhythmically, the glass is cleaned, and the street appears ahead, clear again. If I turn my head I can see, through the side windows, soaked and covered with drops of water, the facades of buildings sliding backward to my left and right. I pass the municipal theater, to my right, and then, father on, the arcade corridors, empty and dark, and farther still the dark windows of the *La Región* building, whose illegible news boards are submerged in the penumbra. When I reach the boulevard I turn right, driving slowly. At the taxi stand on the corner with 25 de Mayo four taxis are parked, their red lights on. The gorilla drivers are barely visible through the half light in their cars. A gray sphere of rain covers the entire city, a hazy transparency of suspended fine droplets concentrated around the tree tops. The red light at the next intersection forces me to stop. Around the light the drops take on a reddish color then turn suddenly green when the light changes. I cross the empty streets and pass the flour mill to my right behind the tall trees of the boulevard's center walkway. The second traffic light forces me to stop. As the green light comes on, a bus crosses the boulevard full speed, forcing me to stop abruptly just as I'm starting up. I move again. An old gorilla in ragged overalls is sitting on a bench in the center walkway, protected from the rain by the trunk of a eucalyptus. He is digging through a bag. I pass very close to him, on his right, alongside the curb of the walkway. The blackish tree bark drips water and glows darkly at moments. Then I see the train station, its tall windows illuminated and its bright lobby casting light onto the street through the enormous main entrance. Its tall, solid facade slides slowly backward, to my right. I cross several streets, watching the suspension bridge approach. Its columns, first visible at their highest point, send out their four red signals that flash on and off. As I advance, the top edge of the windshield cuts off more and more of the bridge. First the red lights disappear, then the first rods that connect the lateral columns. When I reach the mouth of the bridge itself, all that's left is the railings, the base of the columns, the gray stone ramp, the thick, tense cables that rise in a cluster toward the sky, and the gray sentry box, on the sidewalk to the left of the ramp, empty. A weak glow filters into the rain outside. By the time I turn onto the waterfront and begin traveling down the asphalt that's covered in cracks, potholes, and tar patches, the sun has come up. The morning light comes from the river side, and beyond the even balustrade, interrupted ever so often, at regular intervals, by a staircase landing, I briefly make out the silvery glow of the river, where the gray sheen on the surface tends to smooth out the ripples produced by the gentle breeze and rain. The poplars on the central walkway of the waterfront, beyond which the villas project, between the foliage, their red roofs soaked with rain against the gray background of the sky, form outlines with their sharp, brown, wet needles. I enter the new waterfront and to my left the gray river expands, widening, blending with the sky at the horizon. The river and sky appear to be the same surface, without transition. I accelerate slightly. The monotonous hum of the engine intensifies and then stabilizes at the higher velocity. Under the yellow bus stop shelter, in the center of the wide avenue, a gorilla in a raincoat smokes, slowly. Another leans against the wall, its legs crossed at the calves. They look up and follow the path of the car, turning their heads slowly. I pass a bus traveling in the opposite direction, toward the city center. It's almost empty, but I manage to make out the blurry, abstracted faces of three or four gorillas, males and females, looking toward the river through the wet windows. The roundabout at Guadalupe approaches, the gray-colored power plant beyond. Its metallic, fluted blinds are lowered. The gray door is shuttered, and dense, humid, and stationary patches form on the wet facade. I circle the roundabout, leaving the facade of the power plant behind, and turn again onto the new waterfront toward the city center. I pass behind the yellow shelter, to my left now like the river and the slope, where a row of pines glows deep green, contrasting against the gray sky, condensing whitish masses around it. The black trunks grow straight and their branches form perfect triangles curving slightly upward at the bottom ends. Beyond the trunks, the river blends with the sky. I reach the old waterfront and slow down slightly. The sound of the engine returns and stabilizes, monotonous, after it has diminished. The arc of the wiper blades continues, regularly sweeping the small drops that fall and collide on the windshield. In the distance I see the bridge, the full length of it, its tall columns. On the bridge a tiny, green truck advances slowly toward the city. It leaves the bridge, turns, and accelerates toward the harbor road. I pass the mouth of the bridge—at the entrance of the sentry box there is now a gorilla watchman in a black, waterproof cap—and continue toward the harbor road, watching the backward slide of the waterfront plaza, its arbors covered in vines. The red paths of the plaza are covered with dead leaves flattened by the rain. On the harbor road the rough cobblestones make the car shudder and vibrate. The green truck is two blocks ahead. I accelerate slightly and approach behind it. A large puddle of water that covers the street forces me to slow down, and as I cross it I hear the sound of the water under the tires and see the side windows getting sprayed with droplets. The truck has recovered the distance. I accelerate again and soon I'm right behind it. Less than six meters separate us. Then I make a slight movement, shifting the car to the right—we are in the left lane, alongside the center

212

flowerbeds from which the tall palms grow—and accelerating suddenly I come even with the truck and then leave it behind. For two blocks I don't slow down. I sense the intense reverberations in the car as it moves over the rough cobblestones. Then I slow down again. Reaching the city center, I pass the illuminated post office and the depths of the bus station, where many gorillas are gathered, carrying suitcases, or waiting on the platforms or in line at the ticket windows. At the first corner I turn right. Two blocks later I cross San Martín, continuing straight. I pass the central market and farther on the municipal buildings, their narrow front plaza shadowed by the trees. To my left the broad staircase to the entrance slips backward, beyond the trees in the plaza and the empty parking lot. I continue straight, to the west, passing intersection after intersection. Gorillas fill the sidewalks, the entrances to shops, the street corners, their thresholds. Two young gorillas, high school students surely, wait on a corner carrying books and folders under their arms. A child gorilla in a duster crosses the street, holding his mother's hand. She looks fearfully in my direction, afraid that I'll turn toward them, and then decides to cross when she sees me continue ahead. An old gorilla in a bathrobe picks up an empty trashcan and takes it inside his house. Another gorilla, also old, looks out at the rain through a window. I reach the Avenida del Oeste, turn left, and drive past the regimental gardens to my right. Beyond the trees that grow from perfectly manicured flowerbeds, I see a gray building, the armory. The sidewalk is interrupted suddenly at the entrance, where two soldiers, rifles on their shoulders, stand guard, pacing in front of the gate. I leave the armory behind. Next to me, on the seat, is the closed briefcase. At the Avenida del Sur I turn east. Paradoxically, the daylight has faded. I wait briefly for the traffic light to change from red to green and then I cross the intersection. Before reaching the next corner I turn right onto the sidewalk and enter the narrow, cobblestone rear courtyard of the courthouse. Two or three cars are there, empty. I turn off the engine and stop hearing its hum at the same moment as the wiper blades stop. Then I pick up the briefcase and get out. Water hits me in the face, fine, cold droplets that explode on my skin. I reach the lobby, empty but for two gorillas sitting on a bench next to the right staircase. I pass the open doors to the elevator. The operator, sitting on a stool, his hand resting on the control lever, watches me pass and greets me indifferently. I start up the wide marble staircase, resting my right hand on the wooden banister that caps off the iron railing. When I reach the third floor I stop and look down at the empty square of black and white checkerboard tiles and the two figures sitting on the bench, next to the staircase. Then I continue down the corridor and into my office.

It's empty. Beyond the cross-shaped window frame in the waiting room the gray daylight shines darkly. I turn on the light, leave the briefcase on the desk, take off my raincoat, and hang it on the coat rack. I cross the polished wood floor to the window. In the plaza the rain soaks the palms and the orange trees. Their yellow fruit mar the hard, green leaves. The reddish paths are deserted. I turn back to the desk and sit down. From the briefcase I take out the notebook, the novel, the dictionary, and the variously colored pens. Most of page 110, marked with the folded sheet of white paper, is covered with tick marks and lines. I open the notebook, in which the black handwriting is also covered with every kind of markup: crosses, circles, vertical and horizontal lines. There are no markings on page 111 of the novel, only the evenly printed type. I read the first unmarked paragraph of page 110, softly underlining it with dashes as I go. *"Your wife! Dorian! . . . Didn't you get my letter? I wrote to you this morning, and sent the note down, by my own man." "Your letter? Oh, yes, I remember. I have not read it yet, Harry. I was afraid there might be something in it that I wouldn't like. You cut life to pieces with your epigrams.*" The page ends on the word *epigrams.* I also underline, with soft dashes, in blue ink, the first sentence of page 111: *You know nothing then?* In the notebook, I write in black ink with my cramped handwriting: *"¡Tu esposa! ¡Dorian! ¿No has recibido mi carta?"*

By the time the secretary comes in, I've reached the bottom of page 111. I'm translating the third to last line. All of page 111 is now covered with symbols and markups made in variously colored pens and pencils. The secretary approaches the desk, leaning his graying head toward me. "Judge," he says, "I've been given a report from the precinct about a homicide that took place last night in section six." "Yes," I say, "They called me at home last night." "They say there's no space at the precinct, and if you might take his statement," says the secretary. "We have a hearing this morning," I say. "That can be postponed," says the secretary. "And the witnesses?" I say. "There are some," says the secretary. "I can't interrogate the suspect without speaking to the witnesses first," I say. "That's absolutely true," says the secretary. "Tell them to send me the witnesses early in the afternoon," I say. "And if you can postpone the hearing, postpone it. If anyone calls or asks for me, tell them I'm at the hearing." "When do you want the witnesses?" says the secretary. "At four," I say. The secretary leaves. I lean over the third to last line of page 111 and softly underline, in green dashes, *They ultimately found her lying dead on the floor of her dressing-room.* When the secretary returns I'm underlining the thin, green dashes on the third, second, and last lines of page 113, *"Harry," cried Dorian, coming over and sitting down beside him, "why is it that I cannot feel this tragedy as much as I want to? I don't think I am heartless. Do you?"* He comes in just as I'm underlining the last two words. "The reporter from *La Región* is here, Judge," he says. "He wants to speak to you." "Tell him I'm busy with the deposition," I say. "He asked me when the inquest you mentioned is going to take place," says the secretary. "Do you think that by noon tomorrow we'll be done with the witnesses?" I say. "I think so," says the secretary. "Then tell him tomorrow at four," I say. The secretary leaves. I get up and look out the window. The air has cleared up, but the rain continues. In the plaza, the palms glow. Several gorillas, hunched over in the rain, walk across the reddish paths, toward the government buildings. My watch tells me it's ten fifty-five. I sit back down and continue translating until twelve. I put everything away in the briefcase, put on my raincoat, pass the secretary's office, tell him that at four exactly I'm going to begin questioning the witnesses, and walk out into the corridor. I walk to the edge of the stairs, lean over the railing, and look down: the square of black and white checkerboard tiles is filled with compressed figures that swarm in close groups that break apart and reform in different parts of the checkerboard. I start to descend and the voices grow clearer until eventually they become an incomprehensible clamor when I reach the ground floor and cross the lobby toward the rear courtyard. I pass the emptier back corridors and reach the courtyard. The rain covers my face. I close my eyes for a moment and pause, but immediately I continue to the car. I get in, turn on the engine, and back out, slowly, toward the street.

I steer the rear end of the car to the east and then start driving down the Avenida del Sur. When I reach the Avenida del Oeste I turn right and pass the regiment, the wholesale market, the cinema, and then I reach the boulevard. I turn right again, headed east. I reach San Martín after passing the yellow facade of the university with its green latticework incrustations. I turn south. On San Martín the gorillas gather under eaves, in thresholds, and under awnings to protect themselves from the rain. I pass the windows of *La Región*, to my right, the illuminated corridors of the arcade, to my left, the municipal theater, to my left, driving slowly, behind a long line of cars, the progression halted every so often by young gorillas that jump over the puddles and run across the street so as to not get wet. I stop at the traffic light on Avenida del Sur. When the green light comes on I cross the intersection and pass the Plaza de Mayo on my right. The gray government offices approach and then are left behind. Then the convent and finally the trees in the park beyond which the waters of the lake shine. I stop the car along the right-hand sidewalk, in front of the house. I pick up the briefcase and get out.

I go upstairs and straight into the study. Almost immediately, as I'm taking off the raincoat, Elvira comes in. She asks if I'll eat something. "Yes, something," I say, "Bring it here, to the study." Then I tell her that if the manager from the club comes by for my mother's dues, to pay him. I put *Concerto for violin* on the record player and sit down on the twin sofa to listen to it, my back to the window. Soon, Elvira comes in with a tray and softly crosses the room. I gesture with my head for her to leave the tray on the desk. Before leaving she takes the raincoat from the chair and then she walks out. I get up and examine the tray. Some crackers on a dish and a bowl of thin, steaming, golden broth. As the music plays I drink the soup slowly and eat three or four of the crackers. Then I pour myself a whiskey, neat, and finish it in two or three swallows. Then I lay down on the sofa until the concerto finishes. Soon I hear the sound of the return and then nothing.

The room is completely silent. No sound comes in from the street, just the gray, somewhat opaque light, through the window. I start to hear the muted crackling and then I see the vast plain, devoured by the fire. The flames extend evenly into the horizon. There is no smoke. Only sudden sparks rising briefly above the flames before they disappear.

I approach the window. The park is deserted. The waters of the lake can be made out, here and there, between the trunks rising from the earth. Then I turn back and sit down at the desk and open the briefcase. When everything is ready—the notebook, the novel, the dictionary, and the pens—I get up and go to the bathroom and then return to the study to work. At ten to four I underline the third, fourth, and fifth lines of page 115, *One should absorb the colour of life, but one should never remember its details. Details are always vulgar.* Then I get up, leaving everything on the desk. I take the raincoat from the bathroom, put it on, and go out into the street. It's raining. The sky has darkened a bit. I look up. The gray has grown deeper, darker, and the storm clouds have taken on steely edges. I get in the car, and after turning on the engine, I come around slowly onto San Martín and drive north. At the first intersection on San Martín I turn left and drive a block, pass the courthouse, the north side of the plaza moving behind me, and turning onto the sidewalk I enter the rear courtyard. I park the car and get out. I cross the corridors and the deserted checkerboard lobby and climb to the third floor. In the corridor I see a group of gorillas, two of them in uniforms. The ones in uniforms straighten up when they see me. There are two males, two females, and a tiny girl. I enter the secretary's office without looking at them. The secretary is at the typewriter. He looks up when he sees me come in. "The witnesses are here, Judge," he says, "here's the report." He hands me the file—a thin, red folder—and I take it into the office with me. On May first, it says, around nine P.M., outside a store in Barrio Roma, Luis Fiore, thirty-nine years of age, discharged two shotgun rounds into his wife, María Antonia Pazzi de Fiore (aka "la Gringa"), thirty-four years of age, causing her death in the act; that the accused, after committing the homicide, traveled to a bar nearby, had a couple of drinks, and then went home. That he stayed there until the police arrived and surrendered without resistance. That according to the witnesses—Pedro Gorosito, fifty-four; Amado Jozami, thirty-six; Zulema Giménez, thirty; and Luisa Luengas, thirty-two—though the protagonists demonstrated some irregular behavior, there was no apparent cause that precipitated the homicide. I put down the file and turn toward the window. In the plaza, the reddish paths are deserted and the rain falls on the palms and the orange trees. I take off the raincoat and hang it up. Then I call the secretary. "I want to finish everything today," I tell him. "Tomorrow we'll visit the scene." "Should I send the first one in, Judge?" says the secretary. "Yes, bring him in," I say. He disappears and I sit down behind the desk. Then he comes back with one of the male gorillas. He has a gold tooth, and his head and the backs of his red hands are covered with blond hair. I tell him to sit down. The secretary sits down at the typewriter and looks at him. I feel the blond gorilla's fearful gaze fixed on me. "Your name is Amado Jozami and you are thirty-six years old, is that correct?" the secretary says pleasantly. "Yes, sir," says the blond gorilla. "You are Argentine and you own a store with a bar, located on the corner of Islas and Los Laureles, is that correct?" says the secretary in his pleasant voice. "Yes, sir," says the blond gorilla. "That's fine," I say. "Tell us what you know then, just the truth." The blond gorilla perches on the edge of his chair and looks at the secretary and then at me. "We were in the store when they show up in the truck," he says, and at that moment the secretary starts typing. "We heard the sound of the truck from the store and wondered who it was. Then they come in with the shotgun and the two dead ducks. They leave the ducks and the shotgun on the counter and order two rums. He doesn't say a word, and he stands apart, watching us, but she starts shouting. He tells her to be quiet. She opens her bag and takes out a flashlight and starts shining it on him. He says to turn it off. She drops the flashlight on the counter and starts complaining about her life. Then he says they need to leave. She complains, but they leave. Like a minute later, we hear the shots. We go out and she's on the ground and he's starting the truck. He takes off like a bolt and disappears and she's lying there dead." The blond gorilla falls silent. A moment later the striking sound of the typewriter ceases and the secretary pauses, his hands suspended, his fingers pointing at the keys. "Did you know Fiore and his wife?" I say. "Yes," says the blond gorilla. "They were from the neighborhood. But they didn't shop in my store. He would come in sometimes, for drinks." "How did he behave?" I say. "Fine. Sometimes he would just stand at the counter for an hour or two, not saying a word." "Would he get drunk, or look it?" I say. "Well, the same as anyone else," the blond gorilla says. "Sometimes, but you could hardly tell." "Did he cause any problems in the store, apart from last night?" I say. "None, as far as I know," he says. The typewriter follows his words, loudly, and always stops a moment after his voice goes silent. "Do you think the murderer and the victim were intoxicated last night?" I say. The blond gorilla screws up his broad face and presses his lips together. The gold tooth disappears. "I couldn't say," he says eventually, "She was talking a lot and saying things that are, well, indecent for a woman, as I see it, but he didn't say a word. When she put the flashlight on his face, he didn't even move. He closed his eyes and said to turn it off, but he didn't move. I don't know. They might have been drunk." "What did you and the other witnesses do when you heard the shots?" I say. "We took off out the door," says the blond gorilla, "And when we got there he was starting the truck and she was on the ground—she wasn't moving. After he drove off full speed with the passenger door open, we saw the ducks on the ground, and her bag and the flashlight, which was still on. I was the first one to touch her and see that she was dead. Then I telephoned the station. And then the police came. I told them everything in my statement." Then he says his business is respectable and tries to show me his inspection certificate. I tell him it's not necessary, and to go wait in the corridor. He hesitates and then gets up, looking back and forth between the secretary and me. When he leaves, I notice the secretary staring at me. I look at him, but I don't say a word. The guard appears at the door to the waiting room. "Bring the next one," I say. The guard disappears. For a moment, the office is silent. I turn my head to look through the black cross of the window frame at the gray sheen of the sky. It's somewhat clearer out, and brighter, but the rain continues. The secretary shifts in his chair; it creaks. I move my feet and my shoes tap against the wood floor. Then the guard reappears in the doorway. He has the child with him. Her hair is dark and she's so thin that it seems like the guard's hand on her shoulder could break her to pieces with the slightest pressure. She approaches, a serious expression on her face. I tell her to sit down. The guard stands behind her chair. The secretary leans toward the child and sweetly asks her name. "Lucía Fiore," says the child. The secretary asks how old she is, and the child responds that she's ten. Then I lean toward her and ask what she did yesterday. "I went duck hunting with Mamá and Papá," says the girl. I ask her where. "In Colastiné, and we shot two ducks," she says. "And how did you get there?" I say. "We went in the truck from the mill that Papá borrowed because it was May first and there wasn't a bus," she says. "Did you hear your parents talk about anything yesterday?" I say. "No," she says, "nothing." "What time did you come back from Colastiné?" I say. "At night," she says. "And my papá and mamá left me at home because they said they were going to take the truck back. But then they went to Jozami the Turk's store and Papá killed her." The typewriter resonates a moment after the girl's voice has gone silent, and then finally it stops. Its echo reverberates briefly inside my head. I'm looking at the girl, at the way she gazes back with large, calm eyes. "Would they argue sometimes, your papá and mamá?" I say. "Sometimes," says the girl. "Would they hit you?" I say. "Sometimes," she says. "What did you think when your papá and your mamá said they were going to return the truck?" I say. "That my papá would kill her," she says. The typewriter stops suddenly. The guard turns abruptly and stares at me in shock. I pretend not to notice anything. I let a moment pass in silence before speaking. "How did you know?" I say. "Because I dreamt it that night," she says. "I dreamt that I was coming back from Colastiné with Papá and Mamá and then they said they were going to return the truck but they were going to Jozami the Turk's store and Papá was going to shoot Mamá twice in the face. I dreamt it all just like it happened. So when they said they were going to return the truck, I knew he was going to kill her." "And why didn't you say anything, when you knew he was going to kill her?" I say. "Because that's how it had to happen," says the girl. "Did you love your mamá?" I say. "Yes," she says. "And your papá?" I say. "Him too," she says. The sound of the typewriter continues briefly and then it stops. "You dreamt everything that was going to happen?" I say. "Everything," says the girl. "Did they tell you that here you have to tell the whole truth?" says the secretary. The girl doesn't even look at him. The three of us, the guard, the secretary, and I, lean in toward her. She sits stiffly on the edge of her chair, thin as a rail. Now her calm eyes aren't looking at anything. Again the office is completely silent. "Take her out," I say. The girl stands, obediently, and leaves with the guard. When they disappear the secretary looks at me. "What do you think, Judge?" he says. "Nothing," I say.

The third witness is a fat lady who calls herself Zulema Giménez. She's not talking for the sake of talking, she says, but she knew something bad was going to happen with that woman running her mouth so much. "I've got a lot of psychology," she says, "and I knew something bad was going to happen. I expected it from one moment to the next." I ask her what her profession is and she stops suddenly. "My chores," she says. "What are your chores?" I say. "I stay at home," she says. "A stay-at-home woman doesn't go drinking at a bar," I say. She doesn't respond. "Tell us what happened and don't give a single opinion you aren't asked for," I say. Then I turn to the guard standing behind her. "Does this woman have priors?" I say. "Prophylaxis law," says the guard. Then she says that Fiore had been winking at her the whole time and his woman noticed and that's why she shined the flashlight on him. The typewriter sounds for several moments. Then it stops. "Did anyone else notice?" I say. "My friend, and Jozami the Turk, everyone noticed. And that's why she started provoking him, saying he was going around with this one and that one." "Is that literally what she said, that he was going around with this one and that one?" I say. "I don't know," she says. "She meant as much, that's for sure." "Why?" I say. "Because he started winking at me and she shined the flashlight on him. Then he told her to turn it off and she turned it off. And then she said he was going around with this one and that one," she says. "Did you know the accused or the victim, previously?" I say. "I recognized them," she says. "Where had you seen them?" I say. "I don't know," she says. "Their faces were familiar. They were from the neighborhood." "Did you see anything that took place in the courtyard?" I say. "I saw something," she says. "The flashlight turning on and off and then something moving." "What was moving?" I say. "I don't know, a body, a person," she says. "Him, maybe, or her. Then we heard the shots and we ran out to the courtyard." "Was the door open?" I say. "A little," she says. "Barely. It was May first and the store was supposed to be closed." "And what were you doing in the store?" "I was buying some sausage and cheese," she says. "And you stayed for an hour," I say. "We started talking, me and don Gorosito and the Turk and we lost track of time," she says. I look up at the guard. "Bring in Mr. Jozami," I say. The guard leaves. A moment later he comes back with the blond gorilla. He stands next to the woman. "This young lady claims that the accused was winking at her the whole time, and this infuriated the victim," I say. The blond gorilla shrugs. "I didn't see anything," he says. "He was winking at me, me and Zita," she says. "Who is Zita?" I say. "My friend," she says. "And that's why she—'the victim'—got infuriated. She started saying she was more of a woman than anybody. And when he told her to shut up, she started shining the light on him. She was shining it in his eyes and he put his head back, like this, and he told her to shut it off. And then she shut it off." "This man says he didn't see the accused winking at you," I say. "He must not have seen," she says, and she turns toward the blond gorilla. "Probably you didn't notice, Turk. But didn't you hear her saying she was more of a woman than anyone and he wasn't saying a thing and just standing at the counter?" "He wasn't talking, I saw that, and I heard the things she was saying, but I didn't see him winking at anybody," says the blond gorilla. "Where were you standing?" I say, looking at the blond gorilla. "Behind the counter," he says. "Was the place lit up?" I say. "Yes, there was plenty of light," says the blond gorilla. "Could he have winked at the young lady without you noticing?" I say. "Maybe," says the gorilla, and he shrugs. Then he says his store is a respectable place and that he has a license to sell drinks from the counter. I tell the guard to take him away. When they disappear from the office I turn back to the woman. "You heard the shots and went out. What did you see?" "First I saw the truck pulling out and then Jozami bent down where she was sprawled out. The flashlight was on, pointing at her. Then the truck slammed on the brakes, skidded, and it disappeared. The door was open. Oh, and the ducks were on the ground too. Jozami grabbed the flashlight and shined it in her face and then he stood up and said she was dead." "And then what did you do?" I say. "'Magine," she says. "It was real scary for a minute. That animal had killed her." "Were they carrying anything when they came into the store?" I say. "She had this big bag, and he came in with the shotgun and the two ducks and he put everything on the counter," she says. The guard comes back in just then and stands by the door, looking at us. "Take her out," I say. "Should I bring in the other woman, Judge?" says the guard. "Yes, bring her in," I say. They disappear and soon the guard reappears with the other one. Her lips are painted red and the powder she has on doesn't quite hide the blue veins under her translucent skin. Her name is Luisa Luengas, she says, she's married, and she's thirty-two. She says that what she saw made her blood run cold. That she never could've imagined it. Just like that, from one minute to the next, that man had killed her. And they'd left that poor innocent child alone in the world, you know, this kind of thing happens in the world and you just don't want to go on living. "What is your occupation?" I say. "My chores," she says. I look over her head at the guard, who is standing behind her. "Does this witness have any priors?" I say. "Prophylaxis law," says the guard. "Alright," I say. Then I look at her. "What were you doing in Jozami's store?" I say. "I was there with my friend buying some things for dinner." "Were you drinking?" I say. "One drink, which Jozami offered," she says. "Was there anyone else in the store when you got there?" "Jozami and don Gorosito," she says. "Did you know them?" I say. "Of course I knew them," she says. "Me and my friend live half a block from the store and don Gorosito is always there." "You live with your friend?" I say. "Yes," she says. "I'm separated." "How long have you lived in the neighborhood?" I say. "Four months," she says. "Did you know the victim and the accused?" I say. "I think so," she says. "But I'm not sure. They were familiar." "Tell me what you saw in the store," I say. "We were having a drink and were about to leave when we heard the truck and then the doors opening and closing. Don Gorosito asks Jozami who it might be and Jozami says he doesn't know. The door opens and they come in, her first, with the bag, and then him, with the shotgun and the two ducks. He put the ducks, they were dead, and the shotgun on counter. They say hello to everyone and they order two rums. He stands at the end of the counter and he's not saying anything, but she's shouting. Once it looked like he was laughing, but I'm not sure because of his beard. I saw his white teeth. She starts talking about how she's more of a woman than anybody. I thought she was trying to provoke us, me and Zully, and I didn't say anything. He tells her to shut up. 'Shut up, Gringa,' he says. 'Shut up, Gringa.' Then she takes the flashlight from the bag and shines it on him. He tells her to shut it off. You could tell it was bothering his eyes. He put his head back and closed them and told her to shut off the flashlight. She shut off the flashlight and started talking about what a bad life he made for her. 'He's always chasing after *las negras*,' she says. 'He goes crazy if he sees a *negra*.' Then he said they were leaving and they walked out. Not even a minute goes by and we hear the shots. We run out to the courtyard and she's lying on the ground with the flashlight pointing at her face. He's starting the truck and then he takes off fast. He peels out and disappears. The door was open. Jozami said she was dead and went and called the police. Then they came and took us all in to make a statement." "Apart from the incident with the flashlight, did anything else happen in the store that would make the accused decide to shoot the victim?" I say. The secretary's typewriter follows my words. Then it stops. She hesitates. "I don't know," she says. "Maybe they'd already gotten loaded someplace else." "What do you mean *loaded*? What does that word mean?" I say. "Maybe they had been drinking someplace else, or they'd been fighting on the way there," she says. "Besides saying hello, he didn't say a thing. Maybe he was angry." "Did the accused look at you at any time, or make any gesture with his face, anything significant?" I say. "At me?" she says. "At you or anyone else," I say. "At me, no, but Zully says that he was winking at her," she says, "that she saw it perfectly well and pretended not to 'cause she didn't want problems with the woman. But apparently the woman noticed and then started saying she was more female—um, more of a woman than anybody." "Did she use that exact word, *woman*?" I say. "No, she said female. She said she was more female than anybody," she says. "Then he told her to shut up and she took out the flashlight and shined it on him. He told her to shut it off and then they left. And they'd just walked out when we heard the shots and ran out and found her on the ground with the truck pulling out full speed. The door was open, and I saw that it still was when it passed under the light at the corner." "Did anyone touch the shotgun while it was on the counter?" I say. "I didn't see anything," she says. I look up at the window. It's getting dark, a greenish half light. It's still raining. I look at her again. "You can go for now," I say. I can feel the secretary's gaze on my face, but I pretend not to notice. The guard disappears with her and returns with the other gorilla. He has on an old, black suit, shiny at the elbows and knees, and a black hat. He's very thin, and pale. It smells like alcohol when he talks. He smiles constantly, and when he reaches the desk he leans over and holds out his hand. "Good to meet you," he says. I don't hold out mine, and I tell him to sit down. "Your name?" says the secretary. "Pedro Gorosito, ex-sportsman, fifty-four years, at your service," he says. "Nationality," says the secretary. "Argentine, and proudly so," he says. I have him tell me everything he saw in Jozami's store.

He takes off his hat and sets it on his knee. His hair is combed back with pomade, so polished and slicked to his skull that it looks like a lacquered helmet. His face, which is covered with fine wrinkles, twitches constantly, staring weakly now at the secretary, now at me. He say that he's seen lots of things in his life, that he's a man of experience. That he was a goalkeeper for Club Progreso in the forties and that he's seen lots of strange things with his own eyes, that he could fill up a book with all the experiences he has to tell about. That from what he can tell, and he doesn't mean any disrespect, there's a lot going wrong with this country and what it needs is a strong hand to *take the horse to the post without throwing the jockey.* That he goes for humble folks, and being humble himself despite the glory he's known, *not to brag,* he knows his place and knows how to be country with country folks, a gentleman with gentlemen, a roughneck with roughnecks. That nobody knows the city like he does, that he's worked every job and walked every neighborhood and that's why he knows everybody who's anybody to the people or to the sport. With don Pedro Candioti, for example, he's got to be like a brother, and he was with him when he swam the ten kilometers between Baradero and Santa Fe, *without forgetting my place of course.* That few men of experience from the old guard are left, and that the few that *are* left are outraged by the way things are *nowadays.* That he aims to be of service to the judge, sir, and the secretary, sir, because he doesn't have anything to hide and this isn't the first time that destiny has placed him at the service of the law. That with regards to what happened at the Turk's bar he has plenty to contribute because what happened there was something really *tremendous* and it goes to show you what happens when people don't know their *propers* or their place in the world. That as soon as he saw them coming, he knew something strange was going to happen but he didn't want to open his mouth because that wasn't his house and he's always known his place in another man's house. That it was obvious that man had some *devilish* intentions because he went and stood at the end of the counter and was looking at the *clientele* with an ugly face and listening to the conversation and not saying a single word. And it wasn't good for that lady to be saying things unbecoming for a good woman, *specially* considering that there was other women present she might offend. He says that, as he sees it, with the flashlight stuff she was also looking for trouble, because shining it on her husband and making a fool of him in front of the *present company* showed very bad manners. But even with all that he doesn't judge anybody, and if that woman was complaining that her husband made her life miserable, there was a reason for it. "So when I heard the shots I didn't even flinch, because I'd seen it coming already," he says. I ask him what he saw when he went out to the courtyard.

"What could I have seen?" he says. "What I supposed was going to happen since they walked in. 'Specially when he let her talk and say all those things, laughing all the while. I saw him laughing. And she was laughing too. I even thought that it was all a show and they were pulling our legs. When I went out to the courtyard, I saw the truck passing under the streetlight, quick as you like, and then it disappeared. Jozami the Turk was shining the light on the woman's face, and then he stood up and said she was dead. I'm the kind of man who's used to this sort of tragedy. I didn't even flinch. When Domingo Bucci died, I was his mechanic. And I say, Domingo, I got an ugly *preminishin* about the next lap. I don't like it a bit. And he says, *You have to die from something, Pedrito, and the quicker the better.* Just like that, señores. Soon as I saw them come in with the shotgun and the ducks, I wouldn't have bet a single cent on that woman's life." I look up at the guard. "Take him out," I say. He stands up and leans over, reshaping his black hat. "Not bragging or any of that," he says, "but the devil's wise like the devil he is, but even more so like the old man he is. Good day, your honorable," and he holds out his hand. "That's fine, go on," I say. He leaves. Then the officer comes back. "Bring the accused at four tomorrow," I say. "In the morning the secretary and I are going to the scene." After the guard leaves I stand up and go to the window. It's completely dark above the trees in the plaza. Behind me, the secretary continues typing. I put on my raincoat and walk out. The corridor is empty. I reach the top of the stairs, and looking over the railing, I see the group of witnesses crossing the black and white checkerboard square and then disappear toward the entrance. I go down the stairs slowly. When I reach the first floor, the lobby is deserted. I cross the dark, empty rear corridors and come out into the darkness of the courtyard. The rain hits my face, softly. The car is a dense mass in the penumbra, rising out of the rainy darkness. I feel its coldness when I touch the door handle. I sit down behind the wheel and start the engine. The red dashboard light reaches my face weakly, and I just manage to see it reflected in the rear view. I turn the car halfway around, slowly, and drive slowly across the narrow courtyard, coming out onto the Avenida del Sur. The rain condenses in whitish masses around the white light from the mercury gas lamps. I head west, and as I'm reaching the first intersection, the red traffic light turns green and I turn left and drive down the dark street of rough cobblestones. Small colonial houses with yellow walls and barred windows begin appearing to my left and right, crowded together on the sidewalk between more modern buildings. A dog slowly crosses the empty street, under the streetlight at the corner, and stops at the steps to a store. A blurred light filters through its doorway onto the street corner, and as I pass I make out the vague shapes of two or three gorillas, males and females, standing out against the background of crowded shelves. Then I see the mass of trees in the park advance toward me—black silhouettes attached to the more diffuse darkness of the night sky, rising out of the black horizon. I turn left when I reach the park, driving with the park on my right. Its paths descend in steps between the trees toward the lake; its lamps cast a weak light, revealing the condensed rain as it passes through the foliage. I follow the soft curve of the park and then follow San Martín until I reach the row of houses. I wait for a tractor trailer to pass. It's coming in the opposite direction, its headlights illuminating the inside of the car. Then I cross and park the car in the middle of the street, pointing north. I shut off the engine, get out, and start up the illuminated stairway. I hang my raincoat on the rack in the bathroom and go to the study. I turn on the desk lamp and a sphere of light surrounds the desk while the rest of the room is left in a weak penumbra. I sit down briefly on the twin sofa, with my back to the windows, the curtains open. I close my eyes and rest my neck on the velvet arm. I stay in that position for a moment. Then I see the vast expanse of even flames again, spreading silently.

I see the empty checkerboard lobby of the courthouse, the empty corridors and offices, and then, for a second time, the even flames rippling softly, the flat, uninterrupted expanse that contains the entire visible horizon.

I open my eyes, shake my head, and sit up. I stand, pour myself two fingers of whiskey, neat, and drink it in a single swallow. Then I sit down at the desk. The notebook is open. The last sentence, written in cramped handwriting, in black, reads, *Los detalles son siempre vulgares.* The third, fourth, and fifth lines of page 115 are underlined with a light dashes, in green. The dictionary is open and the pens are scattered over the desk between the dictionary and the notebook. I start to work. I mark up, with crosses, vertical and horizontal lines, and circles in various colors of ink, the cramped handwriting that fills the white space on the page between the blue rules. When Elvira comes in I'm writing the sentence, *El único encanto del pasado es que es el pasado.* I look up after writing the word *pasado.* Elvira says that the man from the club came by, and that my mother called again, and she asks if I would like to eat. She stands motionless next to the desk, her hands alongside her thick body, her graying head tilted slightly to one side, at the outer edge where the sphere of warm light cast by the lamp begins to lose its intensity and blend with the penumbra in the room. I tell her to bring something to the study. When she leaves, I underline two sentences: *They always want a sixth act, and as soon as the interest of the play is entirely over they propose to continue it. If they were allowed their own way, every comedy would have a tragic ending, and every tragedy would end in a farce.* At that moment the telephone rings.

It's the same voice as always, forcibly high-pitched, shrill, like a puppet, to keep from being recognized. It calls me the same names as always: son of a bitch, thief, faggot. It tells me to say something, to not keep quiet, that it knows full well that I'm there, listening. I don't open my mouth. It says the day is fast approaching when I'll pay for it all with blood and tears. It says that this afternoon while I was at the courthouse everyone got a scandalous view of my wife taking one of her studs to a motel room. It asks if I wouldn't have wanted that stud for myself, *isn't that true?* It laughs, sharp and jagged. Then it hangs up, and I do too.

At two in the morning I go to the window and watch the rain falling over the park, and then I go to bed. I lay down face up, in complete darkness, and fall immediately into a quick, vertiginous, and fragmented dream in which a horde of gorillas attends a ritual sacrifice. I'm the victim. I see a bloody knife shining in the sunlight but I don't feel myself die. I know I've died because the knife is bloody, but I can't see myself, alive or dead. Then I see an open space enclosed by a horizon of rocks and trees. The sun glimmers in the hollows and reflects off the leaves, flashing briefly. In the distance, an indistinct body is lying against a tree. I see the body and the horizon but I can't see myself. I wake up and turn on the light. It's not even three. I don't go back to sleep.

I get up when it seems like five thirty and walk slowly to the bathroom. I listen to the monotone hum of the razor as I shave. Then I shower. I stay under the hot water for a long time. I get dressed, drink a cup of hot milk in the kitchen, and then I walk out.

It's raining. Through the trees in the park I can see a sliver of light. I have to try the ignition a few times before the engine starts. The windshield wiper starts as the engine does. Each time the engine is about to turn over and fails, the wiper blades flutter tensely, trembling, and then are static again. Finally the engine turns over and the wiper blades move. I cross San Martín to the boulevard, turn right, reach the suspension bridge, cross the old and the new waterfronts, circle the Guadalupe roundabout, and drive back in the opposite direction, toward the city center. At the mouth of the suspension bridge, I turn right onto the boulevard, heading west. When I reach its end I turn left onto the Avenida del Oeste and then left again at the end onto the Avenida del Sur, heading east, and when I reach the courthouse I turn onto the sidewalk and into the rear courtyard. I stop the car and get out and feel the cold rain on my face. I cross the empty corridors, the empty checkerboard lobby, and start up the white marble staircase with my right hand on the banister. On the third floor I look down at the lobby. It's empty, and the black and white tiles appear tiny, regular, and polished. I enter my office, passing first by the secretary's unoccupied desk, and turn on the light. I approach the window and see the palms and the orange trees in the park and the white masses of rain that condense around them. The white raindrops seem to rotate slowly. An anemic, gray light enters the office. The Plaza de Mayo is deserted. Its red paths crisscross under the foliage.

When the secretary arrives he stops in front of my desk, his graying head tilted toward me. "I need to say something," he says.

I look up. He hesitates. "I've noticed . . . I've noticed a certain unwarranted severity with the witnesses. And also certain irregularities in procedure," he says. "And?" I say. "I think, Judge, that you're very tired and should take a vacation. You don't look well. Pardon the impertinence, but I'm sure something bad is happening to you." "Don't worry, Vigo," I say, "I'm perfectly fine." "Another thing, Judge," says the secretary. "This morning we get paid for April." "That's great," I say. "Have a car readied and look for a clerk. We're going to the scene in a minute." "It's all set," says the secretary. "You're very efficient, Vigo," I say. "You should be here instead of me."

We leave for the crime scene. The driver and the clerk are in the front seats, and the secretary and I are in the back. The car is waiting outside the front entrance to the courthouse. We find it—the secretary and I—after crossing the square lobby where the first groups are gathering in the center of the checkerboard space, talking in loud voices. The clerk and the driver are already inside the car, waiting for us. We turn at the first corner, onto the Avenida del Sur, heading west. At the next corner the red traffic light stops us. When the light changes, and the green shimmer colors the swirl of droplets around it, we cross the intersection and continue on. We turn west at the Avenida del Oeste and soon the regimental gardens and the gray armory building pass to our left. We turn at the market onto a cobblestone street and pass alongside its lateral wall. Through the side window I see the wall of the wholesale market interrupted suddenly by the large entranceway. In the stone courtyard, which is bordered by two long rows of stands crammed with fruit and vegetables, in bags or crates or simply piled up on the ground, a mass of trucks circles slowly with gorillas behind the wheels or standing with their legs apart on the wooden beds. Several gorillas sit atop immense piles of vegetables, bags of potatoes, or crates of fruit loaded onto the

backs of the trucks. Then the wholesale market is left behind.
We drive six blocks and turn left again. At the next corner we
stop. There aren't even cobblestones, only rubble from construction jobs packed down on the street. Weeds are growing from a
ditch full of water next to the road. We get out and walk to the
dirt sidewalk—mud, really—after crossing over a tiny bridge, that's
barely wide enough for a single truck, and then we come to a
rectangular building of un-plastered brick with an open wooden
door in the center and a tiny open window above it and to the
right. A guard is standing in front of the door. Between the sidewalk and the front of the building there's a wide plot of bare land,
without a single blade of grass, covered in footprints. A narrow
path of half-buried bricks leads from the sidewalk to the door of
the building. We cross the path, balancing, under the rain. The
secretary goes first, and I follow, and behind me come the clerk
and the driver. When we reach the door the guard stiffens up and
stands aside to let us pass. We enter the store.

It's a square room with a zinc roof supported by several joists
above us. The counter is to the left of the entrance, and beyond
the counter are the shelves. In the center of the room, to the right
of the counter and almost in line with the entrance, is a pyramid
of canned products. A small doorway covered with a cretonne
curtain opens between the shelves and leads to the interior rooms.
The blond gorilla is behind the counter, and he stands up suddenly when we come in. He greets us and asks if we'd like something to drink. "He was standing over there," he says eventually,
gesturing with his head toward the end of the counter that's next
to the front wall, where a meager light falls through the window.
"The rest of them were more or less there, where you are. And
I was standing where I am now." I look at the secretary. "Have
the reconstruction done by tomorrow afternoon," I say, and then
I look at the clerk. "Map out the place," I say. "It's two squares,"

says the clerk, smiling and looking around, "One filled and the other empty. We just passed through the empty one. Now we're in the filled one. When we leave, we'll pass through the empty one again." "Yes," I say, "but make it just the same." I turn back to the blond gorilla. "No one came in or out while they were here?" I say. "Not as far as I know," says the blond gorilla. "How is it you reached the courtyard first if you were behind the counter?" "I ran," says the blond gorilla, "And they were standing there and then followed after me." I walk toward the door. The guard, who is watching us, steps aside. I look out. A group of onlookers gather on the sidewalk. The square courtyard is empty, covered with tracks that swirl around and tighten into crisscrosses, forming an intricate pattern in the area near the straight, muddy path of half-buried bricks. The courtyard is empty now. The blond gorilla has come around the counter and is standing next to me. The secretary is behind him, and the clerk is drawing out a map on the counter. "He drove the truck into the courtyard," he says, "and parked it facing that way." He makes a gesture indicating that the truck was parallel to the un-plastered brick wall, over the path. "When we came out she was over there," says the blond gorilla, and he points to an empty space about three meters from the door, on the brick path. "Then he turned the truck around, over there, crossed the bridge, and turned the corner. The door was open."

The courtyard is empty.

It's raining. When we head back to the car and cross the bridge I watch the fine rainfall as it pocks the surface of the dirty water in the ditch. The bridge is covered in mud. The onlookers step aside to let us pass. Among them, in passing, I notice the gorilla in the black hat who gave a statement. We get in the car and head back to the courthouse. We pass the lateral wall of the wholesale market again, this time to our right, then alongside the front entrance to the market and the regimental gardens, to our right, and when we reach the Avenida del Sur, we turn left and head west. We cross at the light, turn on the next corner, and stop in front of the courthouse. We get out. The secretary walks next to me. We go up the wide marble steps and cross the lobby at an angle toward the stairs. The secretary veers off and says he's going to take the elevator. The roar of voices echoing in the lobby quiets down as I move up the stairs. When I reach the third floor, they're no longer audible. I lean over the railing and look down at the flattened shapes on the black and white floor, which is almost completely covered by the mass of them. When I reach the office the secretary is sitting behind his desk. I go straight into my office and to the window. In the Plaza de Mayo, a number of flattened gorillas wrapped in raincoats walk in different directions, blurred by the rain. I sit down at the desk. Ángel calls and asks if he can attend the inquest. He insists, and finally I say he can. We hang up. Almost at once a worker enters with the payroll and has me sign three copies. He hands me the envelope. Without opening it, I put it in the inside pocket of my jacket. I walk out and tell the secretary that I'll be back at exactly half past three. I cross the corridor, go down the stairs, and across the checkerboard lobby, through the roar of the voices of the multitude, and out into the rear courtyard. The rain hits my face. I get in the car, steer slowly toward the street, and then turn west onto the Avenida del Sur. When I reach San Martín I turn right just as the green light changes to yellow. I drive toward the government buildings, cross the intersection, pass the San Francisco convent, and a block and a half later I stop the car next to the sidewalk, in front of my house. The rain falls over the trees in the park. Water pours from their black and fissured trunks. I go up the stairs and into the study. Elvira comes in as I'm taking off my raincoat. She says it's barely eleven fifteen; would I like to eat now or wait? I tell her to bring something to the study.

I sit down with the novel, the dictionary, and the open notebook and the pile of pens and pencils of various colors scattered over the desk. I don't even have time to start writing before I fall asleep. Elvira shakes me awake. She's brought a dish with a piece of boiled meat, some bread, and a bowl of golden, steaming soup. "You have to sleep more at night," she says. She puts down the tray and leaves. I eat the boiled meat and the bread and swallow two or three spoonfuls of soup. I leave everything on the desk, draw the curtains—in the park two young, male gorillas, one with glasses and crooked legs, the other older and fatter, with a bulging belly, are walking slowly under an umbrella, reading a book out loud, one of them holding the book and the other the umbrella, the one with glasses, who's holding the book, gesturing as though he's reciting—and the room gets dark. I lay down on the velvet-covered twin sofa and close my eyes.

The desolation comes just as I'm laying my head down on the velvet cushion, and then it passes.

Then the phosphorescent blurs appear, drift, and disappear. Then I don't see anything, and I hear, but don't see, the muted crackling of the flames growing and then fading away. Then the fire appears, and the immense wheat field burning to the horizon and going out silently.

I fall asleep. When I wake up it's three fifteen and I barely have time to wash my face before leaving for the courthouse. I park the car in the rear courtyard, and when I get to my office the secretary is there with a thin, blond gorilla, waiting for me. He says he's Fiore's lawyer. "He's sequestered," I say. I have him sit down in a chair in front of my desk. "They've got him in some awful room in the precinct," he says. "I'm sorry," I say, "but that has nothing to do with me." "Yes, I suppose not," he says. We're silent. I hear Ángel's voice in the secretary's office. He comes in and shakes my hand. I introduce him to the lawyer. "As soon as he gives a statement, the sequestration will be lifted," I say. The thin, blond gorilla with a blond beard stands up and leaves, saying he'll be back in an hour. I tell Ángel that nothing can be published about the inquest, and not to say a word or take notes of any kind. The secretary comes in and says they're bringing the prisoner. Suddenly, the murderer appears in the doorway. His beard is several days old, his eyes are dull, and his hair is a complete mess. The guard follows. He gives him a soft push into the chair, then he hands me the police docket and leaves. The murderer looks out the window, from which a gray light comes in. "Your name is Luis Fiore?" I ask. He nods. Then he looks me straight in the face and says *Judge* and then he says something or other and jumps out the window. There's a shattering of glass and then nothing. I get up and walk toward the corridor, moving quickly. Before reaching the door to the office, I collide with the secretary and push him aside. I go down the stairs and out the front door. A group of people has gathered around the crushed, bloody body. The blond gorilla who was in my office a minute before approaches me. "How could this happen?" he says. "He jumped," I say. "He's dead," he says. "You know this is terribly serious, Your Honor." "Come to my office," I say. At the entrance to the courthouse we pass Ángel. He says something or other and I say something and keep going. The blond gorilla walks quickly, forcing me to keep pace. He goes straight to the elevator and we go up to the third floor. We cross the corridor and go into the office. The secretary has disappeared. We're standing in the middle of the office. He says, "I was standing at the bus stop, and I saw him fall from up here. I could hear the sound." "Typical for a falling body," I say. Suddenly, he slaps me. "That was the body of a person," he says, staring at me with his burning, sky blue eyes. "That's your opinion," I say. "You're a coward," he says, and he leaves.

Cold air and rain enter through the hole that used to be covered in glass. When the secretary returns I tell him to take care of everything and not to bother me until the next day. "They may want to take a statement today, Judge," he says. "Well, they won't find me, in any case," I say. "Just do as I say: have everything ready for tomorrow morning." Then I leave, go down the stairs, and cross the checkerboard lobby. The black and white tiles are clean and polished and the lobby is empty. I cross the corridors on the first floor and go out to the rear courtyard. It's getting dark, and it's raining. I turn onto the Avenida del Sur, heading east, with the Plaza de Mayo to my right, and then turn at the corner, where the green light allows me through. Then I leave the government buildings and the convent behind and park in front of my house. I hang the raincoat in the bathroom, walk to the study, and turn on the desk lamp. I pour myself a whiskey and sit down with the notebook and the novel open on the desk, then I pick up one of the pens. The dictionary is closed. The telephone rings. It's the same voice as always. It insults me and laughs and then it's gone. It hangs up and I do too. I work until after midnight. I underline a last sentence—*You call yesterday the past?*—and go to bed.

I lie down in utter darkness, face up.

At first nothing happens.

Then, almost inaudibly, the crackling begins. But it's more than a wheat field burning, wide as it is. It's a much deeper crackling, a much larger fire. I see hills, cities, plains, jungles burning, slowly incinerating, the even flames extending like a yellow blanket over the surface of the planet, devouring it. And nothing is heard because there's no one to observe it, to know this giant fireball that's burning silently and spinning slowly in the blackness, which it mars with a weak glow. Sometimes the faraway sound of an explosion echoes, at some vague point on the surface,

240

arriving completely silently, or brief sparks from a short burst are perceived. But *perceive* is wrong, because there's no one to perceive anything. The horde of gorillas that rose laboriously from the nothing, clinging to the dried crust with its teeth and claws, has returned to the nothing, without a sound. It was like some awful mirage, a sickening nightmare crashing against the motionless rocks in the middle of a bright and maddening space. I see the ball of fire spin, and then the fire dies down and goes out completely; the first clear breezes form thin whirlwinds with the cold ashes of the finally pacified horde. The white dust sparkles in the air, in the weak light of a dead sun.

It's almost dawn when I get up. I go out. It's raining. I haven't slept. I approach the first corner slowly, then turn right. The headlights illuminate the shifting masses of fog that condense as they move away from the car. Iridescent circles of water take shape around the lights. The fragmented trees in the Plaza de Mayo extend their foliage through the white clouds. Streetlights reflect off the dense, shifting masses. The wiper blades rhythmically skim the windshield surface. I turn north on San Martín, then on the boulevard, to the suspension bridge. Water pours from the gray sentry box at the mouth of the bridge, its painted wood walls barely visible. On the old waterfront I see, through the blurry right side window, the concrete railing with its concrete balustrades repeating infinitely and sliding backward. They're wet, surrounded by fog. For a moment I have the feeling of not moving, of being completely motionless. All I feel is the monotone hum of the engine and the rhythmic sweep of the wiper blades on the glass, where drops collide and explode into strange, fleeting shapes. Suddenly the monotony of the engine is torn; I hear two or three brief explosions that shake the car. Then the explosions continue, and the hum is replaced by a series of explosions and the car starts to slow down. I steer it to the right, coasting on its momentum. Then there's nothing. The wiper blades stop and the car rolls a few meters farther and stops as well. I look at the gauge. The red needle indicates an empty tank. I stop the engine. The sun is coming up, but the wet fog surrounds the car so closely that all I can see is the inert body of the car and the slowly drifting whitish masses that have erased the waterfront, if there really is a waterfront, and which completely obscure my vision, if—beyond the fog—there really is anything for my eyes to see.

MAY

WHOEVER FINDS ME FIRST SHOULD KILL ME.

I wake up. My eyes are closed. I'm on my side, with the sheet to my shoulder. When I open my eyes, there's the light. It's gray, filtering in through the blinds. There's the bureau and the oval mirror. She's in bed, awake, with her back to me. I can hear her breathing.

—Shouldn't you be up already, getting things together if we're really going, I say.

—You're pretending to be asleep, I know it, I say.

I turn over, face up. There's the ceiling above me in a shadow that the rays of light coming in through the cracks in the blinds don't reach. I turn toward her. Her back is to me. Her shoulders rise and fall as she breathes.

—You're pretending to sleep, I say.

She shivers.

—Don't shiver, I say. Don't shiver because I know you're more awake than me and you're trying to piss me off.

I put my hand on her shoulder and start shaking her. Suddenly she sits up on the edge of the bed. She looks at me. Her hair is falling on her face and her eyes are narrowed.

—How are we going hunting if it's raining out? she says.

—Who says it's raining? I say.

—It's been raining all week, she says. Think it's going to stop today, just like that?

—It wasn't raining last night, I say.

She walks out and comes right back in, leaving the door to the courtyard open. A gray shimmer filters through.

—No. It's not raining, she says. What about instead of going hunting we stay home? she says. Are we really going to pack everything up and head out like a bunch of gypsies?

—I wasn't farting around when I asked for the truck, I say. I had to ask the foreman for it. When we have the truck for a day, we're not staying home.

She shrugs and walks out again. I'm lying face up. There's the ceiling, in the bedroom, which the gray light filtering in from the courtyard illuminates slightly more. The joists crisscross under the zinc sheets. The girl comes in.

—We're going hunting, I say. We're going to Colastiné, and we're bringing back a big pile of ducks.

—Are we going in the canoe? she says.

—Sure we are, I say.

The girl runs out. I sit up on the edge of the bed. Now the oval mirror reflects me back. I get up and dress. Then I go out to the courtyard. The light is gray. She comes out of the bathroom.

—Are you going to shave? she says.

—No, I say. It's the day of the worker. I decide if I shave or not.

—I'm not going out if you don't shave, she says.

—I just told you it's the day of the worker, I say.

She leaves. The courtyard is bare, there's no weeds. There's the black stumps of the trees I pulled out. I've smoothed out the ground where the trees had been. What's left in the courtyard is the bare ground, the solid brick wall, and the two mutilated trunks. I go to the bathroom and do my business and then I wash my face and comb my hair. I go back to the courtyard.

—Can I drink some *mate* before we leave?

There's the two black tree trunks I pulled out. The rain's been falling on them for a week. The ground has been smoothed out by the rain. There's not a single furrow. There's just the bare courtyard now.

—Can I or can't I? I say.

—I can't do a million things at once, says her voice from the kitchen.

—Do I have to make it myself, then? I say.

She looks out the kitchen door.

—I'm not your maid, she says. She's holding a package wrapped in newspaper. She's just finishing wrapping it up.

—I've told you before I don't like you wrapping food up in the paper, I say.

She throws the package at me. It hits my arm, and the paper breaks and four loaves of bread fall on the bricks and mud in the courtyard. She wants me to kill her. That's what she wants. She stares at me furiously from the kitchen. The fury is just in her eyes, because her mouth is contorted into a weird grimace, laughing. That's what she wants. I stoop and pick up the bread. The one that fell in the dirt is muddy, and it's left a mark on the ground. I throw the bread into the air, away from the house. The bread sails through the gray air, awkwardly, darkening as it moves off, and then it disappears behind the wall.

—Easy, Gringa, I say.

247

I gather up the paper, but it's ruined, useless. I go to the kitchen. She comes in after. Then the girl comes in. I wrap up the loaves and put them in a canvas bag. Then I go get the shotgun and the cartridges, which I set out the night before. The shotgun's base was removed. It's heavy. I throw it over my shoulder and pick up the cartridge belt and all the rounds. Back in the kitchen, she and the girl are making some bundles with dish cloths and packing them in the canvas bag. I see they've put the kettle on the flame and that the *mate* and the straw are on the stove. I leave the cartridge belt and the rounds on the table and fill the *mate* with yerba.

When the kettle starts to steam, I take it from the flame and carry it to the courtyard. I lean the shotgun against the wall and sit down in the low chair in the corridor. They go by with the things, packing the truck. She's in front, with the bag, and the girl follows with a package. Now the courtyard, where they were, is empty. And it's empty at the back end except for the black stumps I threw there, soaked from the week of rain. There's just enough space between them for a person to lay down, the crown of the head touching one and the base of the feet on the other. She reappears from the street.

—Are we going or not? she says.

We're going, I say. I put down the *mate*, inside the inverted lid to the kettle. I grab the shotgun from the wall and get up.

—Did you take the cartridges? I say.

—Yes, they're in there, she says.

There's the truck, in the street. The girl is waiting in the cab, looking straight ahead, through the windshield. There's the railroad bed, intersecting the street, blinding it. There's trees and ditches on both sides, and there's the houses clustered in between the trees and beyond them the open land.

She gets in the truck and the girl sits on her lap. I cross the little bridge and get in the cab from the other side. Reddish mud filters up through the rubble they've used to pave the street. It stains my shoes.

I start the engine and we leave. We make an awkward U-turn at the corner and drive in the opposite direction until the Avenida del Oeste. We take the avenue to the boulevard and turn toward the suspension bridge. There's no one out. At the mouth of the bridge there's a gray sentry box. The structure vibrates as we cross. There's an echo.

—It's going to start raining any minute, she says.

We leave the bridge and turn onto the smooth blue road. It's divided by a white line that shifts now to the left of the truck, now to the right, now between the front wheels.

—Hand me the gin, I say.

—I said hand me the gin, I say.

—I'm telling you to give me that bottle, I say.

Finally she unscrews the metal cap and gives me the bottle. I slow down and take a drink, straight from the mouth. She holds on to the cap. I hand back the bottle, not looking away from the road, and then I put both hands back on the wheel. We cross a bridge. Its iron and cement pillars slide backward quickly, flickering. She takes a drink from the mouth of the bottle too, then she caps it.

—You won't even see the ducks, from drinking, she says.

I don't say anything.

—Are we going in the canoe, Papá? says the girl.

—Sure we are, I say.

—Shut your mouth, she says.

—Let the girl talk, I say. She's not bothering anybody.

There's another bridge. Again the iron and cement pillars slide backward quickly, flickering, and the white line stops when the bridge starts and starts again when the bridge stops.

There's the marshes around us, with their inlets and their squat trees and the wild grasses that don't seem to move. The empty marshes, till the land touches the sky. The flat inlets that don't even glimmer. On both sides, until the eyes get tired of looking. I press my foot down on the pedal, until it touches the floor.

—Thirty years old, this truck, and it runs like a clock, I say. It's got some pickup in first. The ones they make today are tin cans.

—There's a flock of whistling ducks, she says.

She points, stretching her hand out until it touches the windshield. The girl leans out over her knees to look. Slowing down, I do something similar. To the north, a group of black dots moves slowly into the distance against the gray sky, flapping, forming an angle, with the leader at the vertex. I say *flapping* but I don't see any flapping. All I see is the angle of black dots, moving, and the empty sky.

—It's going to rain any minute, she says.

—It's not going to rain, I say.

I'm still leaning forward, and I look up at the flock again. High up, the angle of black dots, now slightly more open, with the leader at the front, moves to the north, in the vast empty sky.

We pass the checkpoint, where the road divides. The white line follows the curve of the road toward the water and separates from us. Now the truck is traveling along a straight strip of smooth, blue road, without a white line. We drive at least two kilometers past leafless trees and burnt fields. Then, at a squat motel building, we turn off. We leave the asphalt, and the truck jumps when it crosses the border that separates the asphalt from the wide, sandy plot in front of the motel. We pass alongside a cluster of bitterwoods with yellow leaves, onto a path of white sand packed down by the rain. At first there are houses on both sides of the path, obscured by the foliage, but soon there's only the path that narrows as it penetrates the countryside. Sometimes clusters of plants jump out in front of the truck and the path slips away with a sharp curve. Suddenly a gate stops us. I get out of the truck, unhook the gate, and open it. I cross the opening, stop again, get out again, close the gate, and get back in, continuing on. Ahead there's nothing but empty country, and at the end a large hill covered with eucalyptus. We drive along the path, with vast spaces of open country on both sides of us. The truck's progress is labored and lurching. Finally we stop at the base of the hill, on the near side as we approached. Beyond the hill is a broad meadow, beyond that the lake—which isn't visible—and beyond the lake, and higher up, the city. The columns of the suspension bridge are visible to the left, and to the right the towers of the Guadalupe cathedral. The gray sky is limpid, but tense. We get out.

She walks around briefly, close to the truck, and then takes some comic books from the cab. She sits down on the running board and starts flipping through them. I strap the cartridges to my belt and grab the shotgun from the truck.

—Papi, says the girl. When are we going in the canoe?

—Later, I say, and walk away.

I start moving across the meadow, where there's no path. The grasses snap under my shoes. Every so often I step in a puddle and sink into it. I stop and turn around, seeing the truck a short distance away. She's sitting on the running board, reading, and the girl has climbed onto the roof, looking in my direction; she makes a gesture with her hand. I turn around and keep walking.

I turn to the right, still moving toward the lake, and when I've walked a short distance more the truck disappears behind the hill of eucalyptus. I walk a little farther and then I stop, and am still.

I crouch. I prop the breech of the shotgun on the ground and rest the cold, blue metal barrel against my cheek. Through the

251

grasses that here and there obscure my view, like a fog, I look at the city. Two columns of black smoke rise to the left, where the smoke stacks of the train station are vaguely visible. The smoke looks motionless, fixed, the upper border of the columns wider and thinner than at the bottom. In the other direction are the towers of the Guadalupe cathedral, and a tiny cottage, that can be sensed more than seen, projects through the foliage at the water's edge. Then, for a moment, I don't see anything else. I look without seeing. I don't know how much time passes. I'm crouching, with the shotgun between my legs, my cheek resting on the cold barrel, looking without seeing. When I straighten up, my legs are cramped.

I load the shotgun and then start moving slowly, half-crouched, toward the lake. It's visible now, about three hundred meters ahead. Suddenly, at eye level, about ten meters away, something takes off from the meadow. It flaps and picks up altitude. I aim, slowly following the flight of the duck with the sight on the shotgun. I raise my gaze and it gains altitude. Then I shift the sight just ahead of the duck's body and pull the trigger. The blast, pregnant with the smell of gunpowder, makes a small cloud of smoke and presses the breech softly against my shoulder, but the duck keeps flying. I aim again, moving the sight just ahead of the duck's body, and pull the trigger. I miss again. A trail of smoke rises from the barrel of the shotgun, and when I touch the barrel it feels hot. The gunpowder smell lingers. I unload the empty rounds and stick them in the cartridge belt. The golden bases of the cartridges wrap around my waist, extending evenly, identically, from the loops. The two that I've put back into the empty loops, discharged, are covered with stains and the primer is flattened. I take out two intact rounds, leaving the loops empty, and load the shotgun. Then I latch the shotgun and start walking again toward the lake.

The duck has disappeared into the gray sky, away from the city and toward the hill of eucalyptus. I continue toward the lake. I listen to the snapping grasses that I crush with my muddy shoes. I straighten up and turn around. The hill of eucalyptus is smaller now, and all I see is the green mass of leaves—a strip of green foliage more transparent at the upper edge. I keep going toward the lake.

I walk more than an hour. More. Every so often I crouch, setting the breech of the shotgun on the ground and touching the barrel to my cheek, and I look without seeing. I stare at some bare spot on the ground, where the grass is thin, and I look at the yellow leaves of the grass without seeing them. Sometimes my eyes stop on one blade, whose edges are withered and discolored by the frostbite, more withered the more they are exposed to the destructive air. I've been approaching and moving away from the edge of the lake, without ever reaching it. Finally I arrive, to where the water almost touches my feet. From there the city is like an arm's length away, and the hill of eucalyptus is hidden. The water is smooth, gray.

I turn my head abruptly toward a duck that is taking off among the grasses, away from the lake. I take aim and follow it quickly with the sight, leading its body a shade, and pull the trigger. It shudders, convulses, flaps, and its flight stops suddenly, as though it collided with an invisible wall in the empty space. It falls straight to the ground, some fifteen meters from where I'm standing. When I get there, brushing aside the grasses, it's still twitching, and it flaps two or three more times. Then it stretches out a leg and is still. I've hit it in the nape, and blood is splattered across its blue neck feathers. I pick it up by the legs and take it away.

Now I walk with my back to the city and the lake, toward the hill of eucalyptus. I have to walk a long way and then turn gradually to the right before I see the truck. Finally it reappears, behind the hill. When I'm close, I see her sitting in the cab, and the girl is coming to meet me. She grabs the duck.

—Is it dead? she says.

—Completely, I say.

I sit down on the running board with the shotgun at my feet.

—Hand me the gin, I say.

I speak in a loud voice, with my back to the cab, looking out toward the city.

A moment later I feel the bottle hitting me softly on the head. From what's left in the bottle, I can tell she's been drinking.

—Don't make me carry you out of here later, I say.

—I'm hungry, says the girl.

She drops the duck into the truck bed, pushing it through the wooden stakes. Then she starts spelling out the words on the sign that is hanging from the stakes.

—*Mo-li-no ha-ri-ne-ro ese ah*, she says.

—Gringa, I say. This girl is hungry. And so am I. What did you bring us?

—Dogshit, she says.

—I know that, I say. But how'd you make it? Milanesa? Stewed? How?

—You're a crook, she says. Stealing from the union.

That's what she wants. It's obvious that's what she wants.

—Alright, Gringa, easy, I say. Tell us what kind of dogshit we have for lunch.

—Stealing from the union, she says.

—*Mo-li-no ha-ri-ne-ro ese ah*, says the girl.

I take a long drink from the gin. I close my eyes. I fill my mouth up with the gin and then let it fall into my stomach. It burns, going down. Meanwhile I screw on the lid. Then I put the gin on the ground, near the shotgun.

—Gringa, I say.

—What, she says.

—Don't mention the union again, or I'll get angry. Don't make me angry. Aren't we having a good time? We're spending a day in the country, the whole family, it's nice. Isn't it nice? Behave yourself and get down from the truck because it's time to eat.

—There's milanesas and cheese and a bunch of stuff, she says.

I hear her moving around inside the cab and then get out, on the other side. She passes in front of me and reaches over the planks of the rails. She takes out the canvas bag and sits down on the running board. The girl sits down on the ground, in front of us.

—Careful with the shotgun, I say.

I pick up the shotgun and prop it between my legs. She takes out two or three packages from the canvas bag and leaves them on the ground. Then she takes out a bottle of wine.

—I forgot the corkscrew, she says.

She spreads a cloth over the ground and starts opening the cloth bundle on it. There's cold milanesas, cheese, salami, and half a dozen hardboiled eggs. There's also the three loaves that I wrapped up in the kitchen.

I hit the bottom of the wine bottle against the ground until the cork pops out. A stream of wine follows it and splatters us. We all laugh.

—Good times, I say.

We eat, and drink the bottle of wine.

—Let's go back, she says.

—Now? I say. I want to try for another duck first.

—It's going to rain, she says.

—Stop with that rain, because it's not going to rain at all, I say.

—I want to go out in the canoe, Papi, says the girl.

—Shut your mouth, I say.

—Last night I dreamt that you were going to shoot that duck, says the girl. I dreamt that Mami and I were waiting here in the truck and that you walked to the lake and there were three shots and then you came back with the duck. I dreamt all of it.

I softly punch the door of the truck.

—Powerful machine, I say.

—If you're going to shoot that duck then get going, she says. I'll go crazy if I stay here another hour.

—You were crazy before we got here, I say. Before you were born.

—Alright, she says. Get going.

—Do you remember, Gringa, that time we went to Buenos Aires on May first? I say. There were a million workers there, at least.

—At least that many, she says.

I stand up. Maybe I'll get another duck, I say.

I pick up the shotgun and point the barrels at her.

—Should I pull the trigger? I say.

—Cut it out, don't be stupid, she says.

I point the barrels away.

—If you shut up and keep quiet, you can come with me, I say.

—Yeah, she says. And who's going to watch our things?

—No one comes out here, I say.

—Are we going out in the canoe, Papi? says the girl.

She shrugs. Fine, let's go, she says.

We start walking through the meadow, coming around, and after we've walked a couple of hundred meters, the truck has disappeared, blocked by the hill of eucalyptus.

I walk ahead. She and the girl follow. I can hear the grass snapping under our shoes. Sometimes it comes up no higher than my knees, and sometimes our feet sink into puddles that appear suddenly, hidden by the underbrush.

—This is bullshit, she says, behind me.

—The less you talk, the better, I say, not stopping or looking back.

—I'll talk as much as I like, she says.

When I stop and turn around, the barrels are pointing at her. I point them down, at the ground.

—I said that if you came with me you would have to be quiet, I say.

La Gringa makes a face, but doesn't say a thing.

We reach the edge of the lake, without flushing a single duck. She and the girl are staring at the city, their mouths open.

—That's the Guadalupe cathedral over there, she says.

—And the suspension bridge, says the girl.

We walk along the shore. They're going ahead now. Suddenly they stop, looking toward the city again. Their backs are to me, some five meters away. The barrels are pointing at them. I'm transfixed for a moment, staring at them. Nothing happens. There's the lake, glowing, and the city beyond, and closer to me their silhouettes, sharply contrasted against the vast open sky. I ask myself if there's anything that could erase them. But even if they were erased, they would still be there, always. There's nothing for it. They'll always be there. But I can't lower the barrels. They're standing there, apart, against the vast open sky. Their outlines glow, sharply. They're still.

I crouch, setting the breech on the ground and resting my cheek against the cold barrel. Then she turns around and looks at me.

—What are you staring at like an idiot? she says.

—Nothing, I say.

—There's no canoe out here, says the girl.

—Later, after this, I say, standing up.

They walk toward me, away from the lake. The girl stoops and picks up a snail from a strip of damp, reddish ground at the edge of the water, where our tracks appear.

Then she stoops and picks up another snail, then she runs a few meters away and picks up another. I see her running, sharply, leaving a trail of small impressions on the reddish strip and then bending toward the ground as though she's been hit by something, straightening up again and running again, moving farther off and then returning quickly toward us, growing in size, with the three snails in her hand. She hits the girl's hand and the snails fly out and fall back to the strip of reddish earth.

—Leave that mess alone and don't get yourself dirty, she says.

—She's not hurting anyone, picking up snails, I say.

—You're not the one who's going to be washing all her clothes, later, are you? she says.

I bend over and pick up the snails and give them back to the girl, who puts her hands together and receives them in the cup formed by her two palms.

—If you don't take me out in the canoe like you promised, I'm not letting them go and I'm getting everything dirty, she says.

—Why don't we just give her whatever wants? she says.

—If she picks up three snails nothing's going to happen and no one's going to die, I say.

She turns around and looks toward the city.

—Aren't those the warehouses at the train station? she says.

—Yes, I say. Those are the warehouses. And over there behind them are the grain elevators in the harbor.

—And isn't that the city offices? she says.

She points to a blurry, white mass rising above the cluster of buildings and foliage.

—I'm not sure, I say.

—Alright, she says. Are we going back or are we staying out here for the rest of the year?

—Let's stay, Papi, says the girl. For the rest of the year.

—Alright, I say. We'll stay out here for the rest of the year.

—That's great, I say. For the rest of the year.

—What do you think, Gringa, I say. Should we stay for the rest of the year?

—Huh? I say. Huh? The rest of the year? What do you think?

—Alright, I say. Don't make that face.

I walk up to her and touch her face with my palm. She throws her head back, grimacing, and then lunges out of reach.

—Don't get smart, she says.

—We'll just get one more duck and then we'll leave, I say.

—Can I keep the snails, Mami? says the girl.

—Fine, you can keep them, she says, but careful getting your clothes dirty because if you do you'll pay for it.

I turn around. In the distance there's the green strip of the hill of eucalyptus, and the expanse of the meadow before it. We move away from the water, to the left of the hill of eucalyptus. She and the girl follow behind. I feel the grass snapping under their shoes. Suddenly, some twelve meters away, a duck flaps and rises from the meadow. It flaps noisily, gaining altitude, but then rises in a straight line, like a bullet. I aim. The animal's black, compact body slides obliquely through the gray sky without leaving the sight by even a millimeter. I pull the trigger and feel the recoil of the blast against my shoulder. The duck continues sliding in an oblique line into the air. I put it in the sights again, at a greater distance, and pull the trigger a second time. For a moment it looks like it's been nailed to something in the sky, because it flaps briefly, desperately, without advancing or falling. Then it falls, in a corkscrew shape, flapping and thrusting its legs, and disappears in the pasture. The three of us move quickly, looking for it, snapping the grasses as we move. She's panting, and the girl moves ahead. We stop at the spot where we've seen it fall, and we start walking in circles, separating the grasses with our feet. The grasses bend and snap, and here and there we sink in up to our knees.

—Without dogs you're just farting around out here, I say.

—It'll show up, she says. It has to be here somewhere.

—I obviously hit it full on, I say.

—Are you sure it fell around here? she says.

—Absolutely sure, I say.

—I specifically saw it fall here. It was flying toward the lake and I shot it right around here, I say.

—It might have walked away, I say.

—I'm going to wring its neck when I find it, she says. So it learns not to get smart.

We keep walking in circles, making the grasses snap under our feet. Each of us forms our own circle in the middle of the open space, and every so often the circles intersect. They overlap each other and are confused.

—My legs are a mess, she says.

—Should we leave it? I say.

—Here it is! says the girl, crouching and half disappearing into the grass.

We struggle toward her, running, getting twisted up in the tallest grasses. When we reach her we stoop. I can hear her panting in my left ear. The duck is lying there, alive, under a cover of wild grass, looking at us with distrust.

—Trying to escape, huh? I say.

One of its wings is broken. I shot it right in the joint; its feathers are decimated and bloodstained near the root.

—Poor thing, she says.

When I reach out, the animal flaps. I grab it by the feet and pick it up. It twists desperately, flapping and snapping its beak furiously but weakly.

—I'll hold it Papi, says the girl, throwing away the snails and wiping her hands.

—Careful, I say.

I hand it to her. She grabs it by the legs and raises it to her face, to see it better.

—Did you see its eyes, Papi? she says.

—Alright, she says. We've got the second duck. Are we going now or not?

—No, I say. We're staying for the rest of the year.

—So funny, she says.

—We're going to drink us a gin, we've earned it, I say.

—Already onto the gin, she says, laughing.

—Papi, what happens if I carry it by the neck? says the girl.

—Nothing happens, I say. But careful not to let it get away cause if it gets away I'm likely to snap your head off.

—No, says the girl.

—They've probably stolen everything from the truck by now, she says.

—And there was so much for them to take, I say.

—There was the plates and the towels and your watch, which I put in the glove compartment, she says.

—You two go ahead, I'll be right there, I say.

She looks at me suspiciously.

—We'll be waiting there all night, won't we? she says.

—I said I'll be right there, I say.

—I'll be there in a minute, I say.

—Alright, but just a minute, she says. If more than a minute goes by, I'm taking the girl and we're walking out.

—Alright, Gringa, I say, laughing.

They start walking away, toward the hill of eucalyptus. They don't move in a straight line, but a curved one. They're walking from the left edge of the meadow to the right side of the hill of eucalyptus, behind which the truck is parked. I watch them move with difficulty across the vast open space, and she is swallowed up to her waist every so often by the grass, and the girl completely. Then I crouch, pull down my pants, and do my business. I clean myself with some grass. Afterward I remain crouched, staring at a fixed point in the grass, not seeing anything. The shotgun is lying on the ground, next to me. The wooden breech has been polished by wear. The weight of the shotgun flattens the grass. Then I stand up, button myself up, pick up the shotgun, and start moving toward the hill of eucalyptus, watching their tiny figures, her and the girl, in the distance, shaking the grass and sinking into it and then reemerging completely every so often in places where the grasses are thinner. Sometimes they seem to struggle in one spot, without advancing. They are the only things in motion in a motionless expanse. I don't even hear the grass snapping under my shoes. Once or twice I stop, the first time to load the shotgun, the second to look back at the lake and the city beyond. The light is fading in the sky. Its gray color has turned smokier, and a black lining has formed around the heavier clouds. About three hundred meters from the hill of eucalyptus, a black bird shoots up from the grass, flying toward me and then changing direction suddenly toward the hill when it sees me. I take aim and set its quick black body in the sight. I pull the trigger and it falls suddenly, in a straight line, without flapping its wings once, like a stone, although a stone would have exploded into sparks upon receiving the birdshot, for sure. I look toward where it has fallen and hesitate a second, but then I keep walking toward the hill. When I get back the girl is sitting in the cab, pretending to drive, and she's sitting on the ground, reading a comic book.

—It's dead, Papi, the girl says when she sees me.

I throw myself on the ground, next to her. She doesn't even look up from the magazine. The girl gets down from the truck and comes toward me with the dead duck. She holds it out, in front of my face. The duck hangs from the girl's hand, by the neck.

—It's dead, did you see? she says.

She holds it out in front of my face, by the neck. I slap it away and the dead duck flies off and falls to the ground with a dry, dirty sound.

—You'll stain my clothes, I say.

The girl picks up the duck and throws it in the truck bed, inserting it between the boards and letting it fall. She goes back and forth between the pages of her magazine, to check on what she's just read and line it up with what's happening on the page she's reading. Then she reads the entire page again and turns it and starts reading the next one.

—Hand me that gin, Gringa, I say.

—Yeah, she says, her voice distracted, not stopping her reading and not making any other movement than turning her head slowly, to follow the frames.

—Give it here, I say.

—Huh? she says, not looking up from the magazine.

She's right next to me, within reach, I'm lying on the ground, face up. There's the green bottle, next to her, between her and the truck. There's the girl, behind us, killing time around the truck bed.

—I said hand me the bottle, I say.

—I'm getting sick of telling you to give me that bottle of gin, Gringa, I say.

—Are you going to hand it to me or not? I say.

I slap the magazine away and it flies through the air, loudly, and lands on the running board and then on the ground. I turn around, quick, just before her hand can hit me in the face. Her hand hits the ground. I roll away from her.

She crawls toward me.

—Don't let me catch you, she says.

—It was a joke, Gringuita, I say, laughing.

I get up. She stands up too and starts chasing me. I turn away and lunge, laughing. When I look back at her, still running, I see her furious expression. I run to the back of the truck and hide behind the girl. She approaches, running. I lean on the girl's shoulders and push her softly. She gets tangled up in the girl, shoves her, slides away, and then chases me around the truck. Finally she sits down on the running board, panting, and picks up her magazine. I go up to her, panting too, smiling. I kneel down and pick up the green bottle.

—Alright, I say. I'll let you give me one knock on the head. But just the one, huh? Don't take advantage.

I close my eyes, waiting, but nothing happens. When I open them again, she's looking at me with her eyes wide open, remote. The rage is gone.

I pick up the bottle of gin and examine it in the fading gray light.

—You barely left a drop, I say.

I unscrew the cap and drink what's left in the bottle. Then I get up, take a few steps away from the truck, and throw the bottle as hard as I can into the meadow. The green bottle makes a stiff curve in the air, diminishing as it moves away, and then falls between the grasses and disappears.

She goes on reading. I sit down next to her, on the running board, and wrap my arm around her shoulder. She doesn't even seem to notice that there's an arm around her shoulders. I start to exert pressure, pulling her heavy body against mine.

—Come here, next to me, I say.

—Come on, Gringuita, I say.

—Stop, she says.

—I said stop it, she says.

—Are you going to stop or not? she says.

But then she relaxes and falls into my shoulder. There's the meadow ahead of us, extending toward the lake. It's empty. My arm slides from her shoulder to her smooth, white neck. Her open mouth presses against my hard jaw. I can feel the dampness of her soft lips against my jaw. Difficult to erase.

In a low voice she says, I'm going to keep you up late tonight.

—Yes, I say.

Her entire soft body covered in her cotton clothes is pressed to my side.

—Let's go, she says.

—Yes, I say.

—Now. Right now. Let's go, she says.

—Yes, I say.

She pulls herself away suddenly.

—I'm tired, she says.

I get up. The shotgun is on the ground. I pick it up. I take out the empty cartridge, slip it into the belt, and replace it with a fresh one. I look up at the sky.

—It'll be dark soon, I say.

—It's going to start raining any minute, she says.

—The ducks start coming down to the water about now, I say. Do you want to go see them?

I give her a very quick, knowing look. She looks me in the eyes. Then she looks quickly at the girl.

—It's getting dark, she says, half laughing.

—Come on, I say.

She turns toward the girl, who has climbed onto the back of the truck and is staring motionless into the horizon beyond the meadow.

—Your papá and mamá are going to the lake and will be back really soon, she says. Don't move from this spot, and behave, understand?

—I'm coming too, says the girl.

—No, she says. Your papá and mamá have to talk. Stay here in the truck and we'll be back really soon.

The girl climbs inside the cab, with the magazine in her hand.

We start walking back toward the lake. She goes ahead. She stands out sharply against the gray sky, which is turning the same color as the barrels of the shotgun. I can see her clearly, two meters ahead of me. There's nothing else, just the meadow surrounding us, and beyond that the lake, still invisible, and the city, somewhat higher up, now blurred in the foggy dusk. The shotgun is cradled under my left arm, pointing at the ground. The grasses snap under our shoes. I raise the barrels slowly until they're pointing at the center of her back. Her body is so sharply outlined against the gray dusk that sometimes I have to look away. She stops suddenly and turns around.

—Let's not go too far because it's getting late and the girl's alone, she says.

She glances at the barrels of the shotgun. I crouch and rest the breech of the gun on the ground and press my cheek against the blue metal of the barrels. She sits down on the ground, looking around her uncertainly. She's saying something now, but I'm not sure what. I'm staring at a fixed spot on the ground, not seeing it.

—Here's fine, she says.

She lays down face up and pulls her dress up to her waist. Her fat, white legs are crisscrossed with faint blue veins. Then she takes off her underwear, putting them on the ground next to her, and I can see her sex at the vertex of her half open legs.

—Here's fine, she says. Come on.

I put down the shotgun and climb on top of her.

—Now, yes, that's it, good, no, she says.

—Okay, stop, no, careful, now, she says.

—Slow, a little more, no, good, she says.

I stare at a clump of grass just above her head. The leaves are yellowed already from the first frosts, more withered the more they are exposed to the air. I hear her moaning and her voice in my ear. Then I get up. She stays where she is, her legs open, covering her eyes with the back of her hand. I stand up the rest of the way and button up. Then I pick up the shotgun. There's the lake in the distance, and beyond it there's the city, casting skyward two or three columns of smoke that are erased by the darkening sky. She cleans herself with her underwear and then puts them back on. Quickly, she straightens up her clothes and her hair. She's distracted, not looking at me.

—Gringa, I say.

—What? she says.

—Nothing, I say.

I turn around and start walking back toward the hill of eucalyptus. I can feel her steps behind me. She'll be looking at my back, outlined against the dark horizon of trees. She'll be seeing my silhouette glowing in the afternoon light. I walk, moving first my right leg, then my left, my right, my left, my right. I stop suddenly and turn around. She stops too.

—What is it? she says.

—Nothing, I say.

—It's something, she says.

—No, I say. I thought I heard flapping. But no.

—Enough with the ducks, she says. Let's get going. I'm spent.

She comes up next to me and we walk together for a stretch. Every so often we sink to our knees in the grass, and sometimes we splash through puddles. The light is falling quickly. Now we can only see clearly what's immediately surrounding us, a few meters around. Everything else is cloaked in the blue dusk. The eucalyptus are a black strip. When we get back to the truck, it's completely dark. The girl is waiting in the truck.

—We have to pack up, she says.

—Did you get another duck, Papá? says the girl.

—No, we didn't, I say.

I hear her opening the door to the truck.

—Where's my bag? she says.

—Here it is, she says.

—Just wait, I'm getting the flashlight, she says.

—I'm just standing here. I'm not doing anything, I say.

I hear the door close again, hard. Then I hear her steps on the grass, and suddenly the flashlight is shining in my face.

—Just standing there, huh? she says.

—You look like an animal with that beard, she says.

—Turn off that flashlight right now, I say.

My head is thrown back, my eyes closed, my jaw clenched. She has me pinned to the ground by the light.

—I said turn off that light, I say.

—Turn off the flashlight, Gringa, or I'm going to shoot you, I say.

She laughs. I cock back the hammer, ready to pull the trigger—the metallic sound is heard clearly over her laugher, which for its part is the only other sound in the total silence—and the light turns off. But the laughter continues. It turns into a cough. And then into her clear voice, which echoes in the darkness.

—Help me pick up all this dogshit, she says.

The beam of light projects over the ground. It shines on the wine bottle, the balled up towels, the magazine, on the thin grasses that cast a moving shadow which spreads and stretches out, away from the path of the beam of light. The beam of light then breaks against the mud flaps and travels across the lettering, white on a blue field, which is washed with reflections. She stoops and picks things up and throws them in the truck bed. Then I see the beam of light brush over the roof of the truck and then insert itself above us, into the foliage of the eucalyptus beyond. Several rays pierce the first row of eucalyptus and break up against the hill. Suddenly the light shuts off, and as I start to move through the darkness toward where I imagine the door of the truck is, the light hits my face again. That's what she wants. She wants me to. The light shuts off, and I hear her laughter in the darkness. I'm sure she wants that.

I grope through the darkness until I touch the surface of the door. I hear the girl's voice.

—I was carrying it by the neck and it died, she says.

I feel for the handle and open the door. I get in. The girl is sitting behind the wheel.

—Move it, I say, pushing her out.

—What's that shit in your hand? I say.

—The duckies, says the girl.

—Why are you carrying that shit around everywhere? I say.

I turn on the dashboard light and start the engine.

—Hey, wait for me, says the girl's voice from behind the truck.

I push the gas pedal without putting it into gear, to warm up the engine. My teeth are clenched. The engine roars. The accelerator touches the floor of the cabin. I stay there briefly, my teeth clenched and my eyes closed, and then I slowly let off the accelerator. I push it into gear and start forward, coming around.

—Watch out, I'm here, says the girl's voice from somewhere in the darkness.

—I know you're there, I say.

I come around. I drive slowly toward her, standing with the flashlight pointing at the ground. The beam of light shines on her feet, together, her shoes covered in mud. She tries to get in, thinking I'm going to stop.

—Where are you going? she says.

I pass alongside her. The headlights illuminate the sparse grass between the sandy tracks. The winding path disappears into open country.

—Where are you going? she says again.

I drive some thirty meters and stop. When I hear her steps coming close, I start up again. Thirty meters later, I stop again. The girl laughs. When I hear her steps again, I start up again but then stop right away, less then ten meters ahead. She's panting.

—You'll pay for that, she says.

She hits at me through the open window, landing her hand on my shoulder.

—Get in quick or I'm leaving you, I say.

She hits me again through the open window, and I rev up the engine with the stick in neutral. She passes quickly in front of the headlights, stumbling, and then disappears again into the darkness. She opens the passenger door and gets in. She's barely sat down before I start moving. The truck lurches over the path and winds its way out of the meadow.

—You'll pay for that, she says.

—One of these days you'll pay for that, she says.

—You'll see who you're dealing with, she says.

—As sure as God exists you'll pay for that, she says.

—That and everything else, she says.

The headlights illuminate the sandy path and suddenly hit the gate. I brake hard and we all lurch forward, reeling and bumping into each other.

I get out. The gate opens inward, and the front of the truck is too close, so I get back in, reverse, and then brake hard again. I get out again and open the gate all the way. Then I get back in the truck and cross the opening. I don't stop again.

—Aren't you going to close the gate? she says.

—You're drunk, she says.

—This guy thinks he's the king of the world, but all he's good for is stealing from a union, she says.

—Easy, Gringa, I say.

Because what she wants is that I. Now we pass a small hamlet alongside the path, and then in the black sky I see the green glow of the neon sign of the motel. I reach the road and turn toward the city. We pass the checkpoint and continue straight, the white line that splits the road shifts to the left, to the right, and now under the wheels of the truck.

—Slow down, she says.

—Slow down, she says. The girl's with us.

—Don't you see this little child with us? she says.

—Can't you at least take pity on the child? she says.

—Not even on the child? she says.

Then she shuts up. I turn onto the suspension bridge, and at the exit I have to brake suddenly so I don't smash into a car that passes me on the waterfront. We go straight up the boulevard to the Avenida del Oeste, turn on the avenue, then turn again, and then turn onto the street covered with rubble. I stop suddenly. The house is dark.

—Get out, I say. I have to take the truck back.

—Liar. Where are you going? she says.

—I said get out, I say.

—I'm not getting out, she says.

—I want to get out, says the girl.

—Shut your mouth, she says.

—I need to pee, says the girl.

—Let the girl out and take her inside, I say.

—I'm not getting out, she says.

—I'm peeing, Mami, says the girl.

I take the keys from my pants pocket and hand them to the girl.

—Here, I say. Go pee, and then go to bed.

The girl gets out.

—Get out right now, I say.

—I won't, she says.

I start the truck and take off full speed. At the first corner I turn and drive three blocks on the street paved with rubble. Suddenly I see a light coming through the door of Jozami's store. I slow down, cross the narrow bridge, and park the car in the courtyard. I feel around on the seat for the ducks and the shotgun. I grab the ducks and the shotgun—the barrels are cold—and get out. She gets out too.

—You could've said you were getting a drink, without making such as fuss, she says.

The light coming through the door is weak. I slip on the mud and then grope with my foot for the brick path that leads to the door. She's walking ahead. We go inside.

There's Jozami the Turk, don Gorosito, and two women. I touch la Gringa on the arm and whisper to her, Watch the way you behave and what you say.

—You're going to pay, she says.

We say hello. I order two rums. I leave the shotgun and the ducks on the counter, near the edge, and just stand there. I see everything clearly.

—Out hunting? says Jozami.

—Lots of ducks out this time of year, says don Gorosito. There was a time when me and the boys would go out duck hunting and come back with all our bags loaded up. We could eat duck till we were sick of it and there was still some left over to share around the neighborhood.

—What we got today isn't even enough for us, she says. My husband's a bad shot, is the thing.

—Where'd you go? says Jozami.

—Over by Colastiné, she says.

Jozami pours the two rums. He comes over and leaves mine next to the ducks and the breech of the shotgun.

—A roasted duck is really tasty, says don Gorosito.

—There aren't many tasty things left in your life, are there don Gorosito? says one of the women.

She has her back to me. The three others are standing in a semicircle opposite her, facing me. Jozami's hands are resting on the counter.

—But don't forget what don Gorosito was in his youth, says the other one.

—Ask around and they'll tell you who Pedro Gorosito was, says don Gorosito.

—Men these days, she says, aren't worth a thing.

—That's so true, says the woman who spoke first.

—It's like I'm always saying, says the other one. She's standing next to the counter, her shoulder almost grazing against don Gorosito's.

—Join us, Fiore my friend, says don Gorosito. Come enjoy this friendly circle with us.

—Watch out, she says. He's pissy.

—It's like I'm always saying, says the woman standing next to Gorosito. Men today aren't good for *anything*.

—All they're good for is chasing after *negras*, she says. Like this one here—every blessed day he spends chasing after *las negras*.

—Just ask and they'll tell you who Pedro Gorosito was, says don

273

Gorosito. Not bragging, but I was a slick dresser in those days, and remember I was a goalkeeper for Progreso in the forties.

—He spends all day chasing after *las negras*, as if I wasn't as female as anybody, she says. As *anybody*, and even more so.

I take a drink of rum and leave the glass on the counter. The other woman, the one standing next to the cans of food, is looking toward me, though she doesn't stop talking. That's what she wants. Even though her back is to me, I can tell, from her tone. She's got her back to me, next to the counter. If I turn my head toward the pile of cans and I close an eye, I can erase her. Now there's just her voice, because I've erased her. I open my eye and she reappears. I close my eye again, my head turned slightly toward the pile of cans, and I erase her again. Because she wants that, she's asking me for it. I don't understand what she is saying. I know she's talking about me. For me.

—You can't trust men these days, says the woman standing next to Gorosito. They've got a lot of *interests*, and all they're good at is lying about it.

—This one here goes crazy when he sees a *negra*, she says. He goes nuts. The filthiest *negra* could make him drop everything. Could make him steal or whatever else. Like if I wasn't as female as anybody or even more so.

I erase her again, turning my head slightly toward the pile of cans and closing my right eye. I open my eye slowly, and the cloudy image sharpens again, until she reappears, moving her shoulders and gesturing.

—I used to have a place right downtown, near the government offices. You can go down to the neighborhood and ask who Pedro Gorosito is, says don Gorosito.

While she talks her head moves. Her neck and her back follow the movement, and then her arms come up and then they fall alongside her body.

274

—One's never enough for them, says the woman standing next to Gorosito.

—Some parts of them are good, says the other woman, looking at me.

—Pour me another gin, Jozami, *che*, says don Gorosito.

—What good? she says. They're all dogshit, that's what they are.

—Let's see if you can shut your mouth right now, Gringa, I say.

—All they think about is drinking and chasing skirts, she says. And this one here is the worst of them.

—Shut up, Gringa, I say.

—Then they try to shut you up, just when you're starting to air out the laundry, she says.

—Gringa, I say.

—Easy now, I say.

She turns toward me, smiling. I smile.

—It's alright my love, she says.

She opens the bag and takes out the flashlight. Suddenly my eyes are filled with light. I close them and throw my head back. She switches the light on and off, on and off. It's obvious that's what she wants. It's obvious she's trying to make me understand it.

—Turn that light off, Gringa, or you'll get what's coming to you.

She turns it off. The scene reappears, covered with sparks of light and red blurs, until eventually everything is clear like before.

—That's how I've got him, she says. In the light. He makes life bad for me.

—You know what's coming to you, I say.

—He makes life so bad for me, she says.

—Let's go, I say.

—Kids these days have no memory, but the name Pedro Gorosito used to be on everyone's lips, years back, says don Gorosito.

I finish my rum in one swallow and leave a fifty-peso bill on the counter.

—Finish that rum and let's go, I say.

—I decide if I want to go or not, she says.

—No. Let's go, I say.

She drinks her rum slowly, deliberately, to piss me off. She's got the flashlight in her hand. Then she picks up the bag from the counter and gets ready to leave.

—Good night everyone, she says.

I wave. We leave. It's raining.

—Didn't I say it was going to rain? she says.

—Yes, you did, I say.

—When I say something it's because I know something, she says.

In the darkness I feel her stop in front of me, blocking me from the truck.

—Get going, I say.

—Didn't I say a thousand times that it was going to rain? she says.

—Yes, I say. Keep walking.

—When I say something is going to happen, it happens, she says.

I've got the shotgun under my right arm, the ducks in my left hand.

—I'm not going anywhere, she says.

She stands between me and the truck. I can feel her breathing in the darkness, and the clicking sounds of her bag against the flashlight. For a moment, I do nothing. Then I step forward and touch her, push her, and I feel her stumble back. She lets out a sound and then the light comes on—a beam of white light that flashes and searches for me until finally, after grazing my hand, my chest, and my neck, it covers my face. It's a blinding flash charged with burning sparks, issuing from a core of rigid whiteness. It pins me down in the darkness.

—Didn't I say it was going to rain? says her voice. Didn't I? Didn't you hear me say so?

Then I raise the barrels of the shotgun up into an oblique line. Then I just pull the triggers, one after the other, and when I do the blasts sound so close together that the second one is like a stutter of the first, the echo of the first, and it fills the damp air with an explosive sound that's pregnant with the smell of gunpowder. At the moment I pull the triggers my left hand lets go of the ducks and they fall to the ground. The flashlight falls too, and the beam of light casts off in a random direction and then is still. The light hits something and is interrupted and then continues, breaking up toward the dark street. I walk around the flashlight and get in the truck.

I turn around hard, cross the bridge, and turn the corner. The engine roars. When I reach the avenue I realize that I've driven the whole way with the door open, that it's been slamming crazily against the metal frame. On the avenue I find an open bar and stop the truck. I get out and drink two gins at the counter, one after the other. Then I go back to the house. I park the truck in the darkness and go inside with the shotgun. I turn on the light in the girl's bedroom. She's sleeping. I approach the bed and raise the shotgun to her head. I pull the trigger, but there's nothing but a metallic click. Then I go to my bedroom. There's the dresser and the oval mirror, which reflects me as I pass. I leave the shotgun on the bed, take off the cartridge belt, and set it next to the shotgun. Then I go to the courtyard, pick up the kettle and the *mate*, both cold, from where I left them that morning, and go to the kitchen. I dump out the old yerba, pour in some new stuff, and when the kettle starts to whistle I take it and the *mate* and the straw to the corridor. I sit down in the low chair.

The rain falls on the mutilated black trees lying in the courtyard. The corridor light illuminates them weakly. Still, they're blinding. The cracked bark fills with water, and parts of the bare courtyard are suddenly reflective. It's blinding. I close my eyes briefly, pressing hard. When I open them, the wet stumps and the bare courtyard are still there.

And I realize that I've only erased part of it, not everything, and there's still something left to erase so it's all erased forever.

NAM OPORTET HAERESES ESSE

Juan José Saer (1937–2005), born in Santa Fe, Argentina, was the leading Argentinian writer of the post-Borges generation. In 1968, he moved to Paris and taught literature at the University of Rennes. The author of numerous novels and short-story collections—including *The Sixty-Five Years of Washington* and *La Grande*, also available from Open Letter—Saer was awarded Spain's prestigious Nadal Prize in 1987 for *The Event*.

Steve Dolph is the founding editor of *Calque*, a journal of literature in translation. His translation of Juan José Saer's *The Sixty-Five Years of Washington* was published by Open Letter in 2010. He lives in Philadelphia.

Open Letter—the University of Rochester's nonprofit, literary translation press—is one of only a handful of publishing houses dedicated to increasing access to world literature for English readers. Publishing ten titles in translation each year, Open Letter searches for works that are extraordinary and influential, works that we hope will become the classics of tomorrow.

Making world literature available in English is crucial to opening our cultural borders, and its availability plays a vital role in maintaining a healthy and vibrant book culture. Open Letter strives to cultivate an audience for these works by helping readers discover imaginative, stunning works of fiction and by creating a constellation of international writing that is engaging, stimulating, and enduring.

Current and forthcoming titles from Open Letter include works from Bulgaria, France, Iceland, Peru, Poland, South Africa, and many other countries.

www.openletterbooks.org